I0773425

Rock and a Hard Place
VOL. 1, ISSUE 8

SUMMER 2022

EDITOR-IN-CHIEF	*Roger Nokes*
MANAGING EDITOR	*Jay Butkowski*
CONTRIBUTING EDITOR	*Albert Tucher*
ASSOCIATE EDITOR	*Paul J. Garth*
ASSOCIATE EDITOR	*Libby Cudmore*
ASSOCIATE EDITOR	*R.D. Sullivan*
GUARDIAN ANGEL	*Jonathan Elliott*
COVER ART	*Heather Garth*

FIND US ON THE WEB: *www.rockandahardplacemag.com*

FOLLOW US ON FACEBOOK: *@RHP.Press*

FOLLOW US ON TWITTER: *@RHP_Press*

EMAIL US: *editors@rockandahardplacemag.com*

ISBN: 979-8-9852904-5-5 (Paperback)

ISBN: 979-8-9852904-6-2 (eBook)

Rock and a Hard Place Magazine is a labor of love, produced by a team of volunteer editors to showcase the best in dark fiction, crime, dystopian fiction, and noir. For access to behind-the-scenes content, including audio conversations with the creators and exclusive stories and artwork, and to contribute financially to the cause, join our Patreon at: **https://www.patreon.com/join/rhpmag**. To make a tax-deductible donation to RHP, visit **https://fundraising.fracturedatlas.org/rock-and-a-hard-place-press-llc**.

DEDICATION

Issue 8 is dedicated to the Magic Eight Ball in our lives that seems stuck on the answer "Outlook not so good."

ACKNOWLEDGMENTS

Creative endeavors that mean anything usually require some kind of sacrifice. The road to ***Rock and a Hard Place, Issue 8*** was longer than we would have hoped, but our editorial team powered through to bring the best of noir fiction to the light of day. As always, we're eternally grateful to the authors and artists who entrust us to showcase their work.

Thank you as well to our readers who stick with us through production delays, and to our Patreon financial backers for continuing to contribute financially to the cause. We hope you agree that Issue 8 is entirely worthy of your generous support:

Dustin Walker
Mark Pelletier
Rob Smith
Jay Bechtol
Susan Kuchinskas
Todd Robins
Susan Jessen
Richard Risemberg
Ted Flanagan
Chris Rhatigan
Ryan Citron

CONTENTS

VISUAL ART

FOREWORD:
LESSONS LEARNED

Here's the question in a nutshell: after seven issues, have we learned anything, or are we the characters our authors write about? "Bad decisions and desperate people." Yeah, those.

We hope not. In fact, we're pretty sure we have learned a few things.

Lesson one: We have learned to resist letting things get routine. We remember our first issue. Of course we do, because everything we did was new. It was exciting as hell, but also exhausting. Every time we fixed an unanticipated problem, another popped up. We caught ourselves looking forward to the day when we knew what we were doing.

That day doesn't arrive with an audible clunk. It eases its way into our awareness like tinnitus. But if you don't have it going on by issue eight, you're doing more things wrong than you realize.

We're putting out an eighth issue because that's what we do. Now the danger is succumbing to routine. How do we prevent that from happening? One way is to keep our heads up and stay aware of what's happening in the world. Getting a new issue out won't help Ukraine except in the most roundabout of ways—by demonstrating the churn of freedom. But we feel it's worth doing.

One way to avoid routine is to seek out stories that you won't find on the newsstand in your Barnes & Noble. In this issue one word would suffice:

Clowns. You'll see what we mean.

But there's also a bird lover's nightmare and a road trip from hell into more hell. And that's only the beginning.

Lesson two: positions can be filled when someone leaves, but people can't be replaced. Things change when people depart, though you soldier on and keep their spirit in the work. Though it's not easy. Our founding editor Jonathan Elliott left a gaping wound with his passing, but to be blunt, that's what scar tissue is for. Nikki Dolson and Katrina Robinson have moved on, but their DNA is to be found in every issue.

Lesson three: Go back and reread lessons one and two until they stick, and then read them again. We'll get the hang of it!

Albert Tucher,

Contributing Editor

August 2022

For the RHP Editorial Board: Roger, Jay, Paul, Libby, R.D., and Jonathan

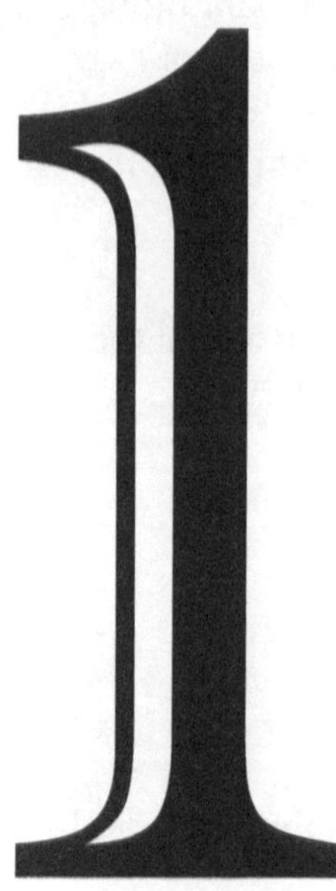

"Neither he nor I mentioned my wife. She may as well
had been the stain on the other side of the room."

KEEPING TIME
Mike McHone

Darvis lifts the red Stratocaster out of the case and whistles at it like it's a stripper. "Nice," he says.

Millan picks up the amplifier I've brought, a portable Pig Nose amp not much bigger than a lunchbox. "How much noise this thing make?"

"Enough."

Darvis lays the Strat gently on the desk and goes through the case. He runs his fingers along the plush lining. He lifts the lid to a little storage compartment at the front of the case. "Ah." He pulls out a pack of Ernie Ball guitar strings. "Can't let you take these in there. Free wire's on the contraband list. These puppies here could garrot somebody." He takes an index finger and slides it from one side of his neck to the other and makes a "crrrrrrrrik" sound. "Know what I mean? That cable for the amp is okay, but from here on out, might be best to just bring your acoustic like you've been doing." He takes the strings and stows them in the desk drawer. "You can have these back once you're done."

"What's it going to be today?" Millan asks. "*Kumbaya* or something?"

"I thought maybe Hendrix."

He narrows his shit-brown eyes. "*You* can play Hendrix?"

"Few songs. 'Purple Haze,' 'Stone Free.'"

He doesn't believe me. I might as well have said I met Jesus once on a UFO.

Darvis closes the compartment lid and slips the guitar back into the case. I shut and latch the case and hoist it off the table along with the amp. Millan presses a button underneath the desk. There's a cha-chunk sound and soon the barred door slides open, and I head toward the visiting area of Ashland Correctional.

It was just a way for her to make some easy money, that's all.

Marlene got the job at Lacey's Arts and Crafts, a little store in downtown Covington, about six months after I retired. Thing was, we didn't need the money. We had enough coming in from social security and the 401K. I think she wanted to get out of the house, but she'd never tell me that, her being polite and not wanting to hurt anyone's feelings. Ever since I'd retired, I spent a lot of time fixing and refurbishing things around the house. Once a carpenter, always a carpenter, as far as I can figure. I built a shed in the backyard, installed some bookshelves in our living room, added on to our deck, made a birdhouse. After half-a-year of hearing hammers and drills, she was probably ready to put some space between us. Couldn't blame her, I guess. Noise got on her nerves as much as sitting around and doing nothing got on mine. I could only learn so many songs on the guitar and watch so many reruns of *Law and Order*. I've always been too much of a busybody. That always was my problem according to her. "You just need to learn how to be content with peace and quiet," she told me on the last morning we shared together before she headed out for work. I rolled my eyes at her and took a sip of coffee.

That was our last conversation. That was the last time I saw her. And I acted like an asshole.

Damon Reed was sixteen when he walked into Lacey's with a sawed-off Browning and killed my wife. He wasn't there for murder—just robbery—or at least that's what he swore to on the stand four years back. It was a gang initiation for the Cincinnati Bloods. Apparently, you've got to jack a car or rob some place to get in. A bank or a gas station was a bit too risky, he said, so he went for a quiet store in a small town where little old ladies buy yarn and cross-stitch patterns. I guess doing something like that will get you street cred or something.

He said he'd cased the store a couple times throughout the previous week. He waited outside until the store was empty that Saturday afternoon, walked in, pulled the shotgun out of this long black trench coat he wore and demanded my wife give him all the money in the register. He said he "must've shook the gun too hard or something" because it discharged in his hands. The blast took off the top of Marlene's head according to his testimony.

Yeah. He "shook the gun too hard or something." It was "or something" that killed my wife. Not intent. Not rage. Just "or something."

Reed got scared, ran, and didn't even bother to get back in the car with his friends. He dropped the shotgun right there in the store and ran down the block, through traffic, past the library, all the way to the northside of town. His friends, whoever they were—he didn't name names—sped back across the bridge into Ohio. They were never caught.

He hightailed it to Devou Park and stayed there for a little while before he texted his granny. He never said what he did, just that he "did sumthin bad," and said he was sorry over and over. A few cops snuck up behind him, tackled him, got him cuffed and arrested. Someone spotted "a youth acting erratically" in the park, according to Detective Katie Yates, the cop in charge of the case, and called 911.

A week later we had to have a closed-casket funeral. That made it hard. Down here we insist on having open caskets. We say our goodbyes face to face. It makes things final. To not get that chance is like having a bone ripped out of your arm. People with sons who were killed in a war will tell you, usually after a few too many beers, they don't get closure when their boys are laid to rest with a closed casket. The kid goes over to wherever they're stationed, gets all shot up or blown up, and the parents get the parts and pieces back in a flag-draped coffin. I guess you'd end up feeling that way too probably, nothing more than parts and pieces.

It happened to a cousin of mine in the sixties. He was killed during the Tet Offensive and whatever was left of him was shipped back stateside and put into the ground without so much as a look. It bothered me for years, and for those same years I couldn't have imagined what it did to his mother and father until the morning of Marlene's funeral. I'd be lying if I said I didn't want to jump into the grave with her or put someone else in theirs. I felt that way for a long time. Still do and probably always will.

In all, Reed's trial lasted about a week. It took the jury two hours to come back with a guilty verdict. At the sentencing, the judge gave him something my wife would never have again.

Life.

Two years after the verdict, I got the letter.

> *Mr. Stanley,*
>
> *I know nothing I say is going to repair the damage I done, and I know you probly dont want to read anything from me but please know I am so very sorry for what I did.*
>
> *Saying it was an accident isnt going to bring her back or make you feel any better or make me feel any better.*
>
> *If theres anything I can do or anyway I can help heal all these wounds I caused you and yours I want to try. I am now here trying my best to put my life back on track. I enrolled in GED courses here and am working hard to finish school. My teachers say I am doing well and it shouldnt be long before I get my certificate.*
>
> *The point is Mr. Stanly I want you to know that I am not the same person I was back then. I no longer associating with people in the gang. I have changed. I hope to prove it to you.*
>
> *Thank you for taking the time to read my letter. I hope to receive a letter back from you or sit down with you one day so we can talk.*
>
> *Yours*
>
> *Damon Reed*

"And you're really going to meet with him?"

"I am."

"Why?"

I was reminded of something my pastor said in church a number of years ago. "Sometimes there're victims on both sides of the gun." Maybe it was true.

"That's a, uh . . ."

"I know some folks might not understand it. I don't even know if I do."

"It's not my place to judge you, Mr. Stanley, believe me. I'm just asking questions."

I met John Franka during the trial. He was a polite young man from the *Cincinnati Enquirer*. He called me because he'd somehow had gotten word of the letter Reed mailed to me. I'm not sure who tipped him off. I asked, but he never told me. Sources and confidentiality and all that.

"When's your first visit?" he asked.

"Day after tomorrow."

"What do you think you'll talk about?"

"Not sure. I think we'll play it by ear."

"Well, you sound like you know what you're doing. And you sound like you've found a way to forgive him."

"I wouldn't say that . . . I want to understand him." Maybe this was true too.

"I hope you do. You're a good man, Mr. Stanley."

And that pissed me off more than anything: all the fake sincerity and dishonesty. I'd rather get a text calling me a piece of shit than have someone tell me that I'm "a good man." In fact, I did get a text calling me that from my brother-in-law, along with a few others from family members that said, "you stupid sonuvabitch," "I don't know whatthe hells wrong with you," and "what would Marlene sayif shes her today bill you tell,e me that right now." I got voicemails too, but I didn't listen to any of them seeing as they came from the same relatives that sent me the texts. Regardless, I'd rather get those texts than have someone tell me I'm "good" or what have you when they really think I'm a fool or a jackass. I'd rather someone be truthful even if they hate me than lie to me. Short of killing, it's the worst thing you can do to a person, I think.

Ashland is about three hours east of where I live. Our visit was scheduled at ten in the morning on a Monday last year. I got up at five, was out the door by six, stopped and got some gas and some McDonald's along the way, and pulled into the prison parking lot at half-past nine. I sat there with my gut like a cloud of moths. What I felt must've been what soldiers feel before going to war. You don't want to go, but you have to for the greater good. That's what got me through.

I went into the prison, signed in, and met Millan and Darvis for the first time. "You the fella from Covington?" Darvis asked.

"Yes," I said.

Millan stayed quiet. He had a loud glare though.

Darvis told me to remove everything from my pockets and set it on the table. I set my keys and wallet down. Millan swiped a hand-held metal detector over me and found nothing. "You can take your stuff back," Darvis said.

I shoved the keys and wallet back into my pockets.

Millan pointed at the metal door. "Down the hall, all the way down, last room on the left. That's where you want to go."

The door opened and I walked along with this sleepy awareness, like my body had been put under for surgery but my brain was wired on caffeine.

The room was white. White tile, white brick walls, white drop ceiling, fluorescent lights. I saw a brownish stain on the floor near the far corner of the room and caught a faint smell of bleach. I stood near the opposite corner, hands folded, and watched the clock on the wall above the door. A metal cage surrounded it.

Fifteen minutes passed behind that cage before I saw Damon Reed.

The young man I'd seen on the witness stand stood about twenty feet from me in his orange jumpsuit, and yet, it wasn't him. He was taller, thinner. He looked like he could be his own older brother. His wrists were shackled. He stood as still as a statue when the guards, two big fellas, undid his chains and when they came off, he transformed. First, his eyes closed, then his lip trembled, his hands shook and then his legs. He bent forward, put his head in his hands, and slowly folded in on himself. After his knees hit the floor, I walked over to him and stared at the top of his head and listened to him whimper.

Then moments segued into other moments.

He stayed knelt in front of me for a long time. Finally, he wiped his face with the back of his hands, stood, and looked me in the eye for no longer than a second. He lowered his gaze to where he'd just been the previous minute. I looked at him, at the smoothness of his cheeks and the spaces beneath his eyes and saw he was young. Yes, two years older than the day he killed my wife, but still in his youth. And then, for whatever reason, I looked at the guards, the walls, the ceiling, the floor, the clock, and realized this was everything to him, this was all Damon Reed would see for rest of his life. That concrete, that dull paint, those flickering lights, the various shades of faces he'll pass in the halls and cells would be his entire universe until his death. It was all he was ever going to know until the very end.

The red-faced guard told me they'd be just outside and if anything were to happen, they'd be back in the room in less than five seconds. He eye-fucked Reed the whole time. The two of them left and Damon and I were alone for what seemed like forever.

Moments into moments.

On the other side of the room were two folding chairs. We sat. "Thank you for coming," he said. I started to say, "You're welcome," but didn't.

We talked instead about how much longer he had to go to get his GED and how he wanted to help children via the Scared Straight program. We also talked about music and the musicians he'd liked. I expected him to say some names of rappers I'd never heard of, but he loved Motown and rhythm and blues, the stuff I was into. He liked Marvin Gaye, Prince, Aretha. I mentioned I played guitar and he said he'd like to learn how to play.

We spoke some more about music and favorite songs. After an hour, the guards came back into the room and put the shackles back on him and led him away. Neither he nor I mentioned my wife. She may as well had been the stain on the other side of the room.

Thinking back, seeing myself sitting there, it's like watching someone else, someone with my face, my voice, but not me at all. While my mouth spoke, while my ears listened, behind my eyes I had visions of strangling him to death, kicking his head into mush. On the surface, he seemed like a decent kid, he seemed . . . I don't know. Human. But I had already made my mind up. I was going to kill him. More importantly, I knew exactly how I was going to go about it.

On my way out I asked Darvis and Millan if I could bring my acoustic guitar the next time I came. "Wh'for?" Darvis asked. I told him Reed was interested in learning how to play and I thought I'd show him a few things. He told me I had to send a written request to the warden. Millan didn't bother answering.

I sent an email to Warden Philbin when I got home. A day later I got my reply. My request was approved but the guards had to search the guitar for contraband.

I was happy to let them. The first time I showed up I set the case on the desk, showed them the approval email from the warden, and let them have a look. Millan had this little mirror on the end of a handle that he placed down into the sound hole of my Taylor acoustic. He looked like some kind of caveman dentist checking a behemoth's mouth for cavities. "Making sure you're not sneaking in weed or contraband," he told me. While he did that, Darvis went through the case. They found nothing and let me inside.

Reed's eyes lit up at the sight of the guitar.

I sat in the same folding chair as before and motioned for him to sit down. "Figured we'd start our first lesson," I said.

He smiled. "Serious?"

"Yes. Thought we'd start with getting a feel for the strings, then some simple chords, maybe some picking techniques."

He flashed an even bigger smile. "Okay."

"Now this," I said, picking the highest string on the neck, "is the E string. Right above that is the B." I picked that one. "Then, in descending order, you have the G, D, A, and another E. Going back up the neck, it's E, A, D, G, B, E. Got me?"

"E, A, D, G, B, and E."

I plucked a string. "What's this one?"

"A."

"And this one?"

"B."

"Good. Now this," I said, "is a C chord." I placed my fingers on the fretboard and strummed. "See where my fingers are?" I strummed again and let the chord ring out. "You try."

I presented the guitar to him and he hesitated.

"It's okay," I said. "Take it."

He did.

"You remember wh—"

"Thank you," he said. "I know you don't have to be here." Tears rose, but they didn't spill over this time. "It's very kind of you."

I was honest with him. "It's no problem. I want to be here."

We went on with the lesson. I showed him the G and D chords and different strumming patterns, but after twenty minutes he said his fingers hurt and we had to stop. "Prince makes it look easy," he said.

"Yeah, he does."

Damon Reed, twenty now and tall, walks in with an acoustic guitar. His jawline is more defined by the beard he's grown since the last time I was here. I'm in the middle of playing Stevie Wonder's "Because We've Ended as Lovers."

"What's this?" he asks with a nod at the Stratocaster.

"Figured we change it up a bit today and go electric."

He reads the names on the headstock. "Fender Stratocaster." He grins.

I inspect his smile. "You practice any?"

"I have." He sits in the chair across from me. "My guitar's nice. Not as nice as the one you got, but nice. The warden has them lock it up so I can't keep it in my cell. I got to reserve this room and come down here and play for a bit."

When I visited six months ago, I was surprised to see he had an off-brand acoustic in his lap. He'd told his grandmother about me giving him lessons and she went out and got it for him for Christmas.

"I don't mind having it locked up," he says. "I wouldn't want to keep it in my cell. Too many people can mess with it. But look." He flips the guitar around and shows me the backside. "I noticed this gouge on the body the other day, like somebody hit it against something." He flips it back around. "Made me mad."

"How often you come down here?"

"About an hour a week. It's not much, but it's more than nothing."

"What've you been playing?"

He starts strumming Curtis Mayfield's "People Get Ready." He stops a few bars in. "And this one." The first measure of The Beatles' "In My Life" comes out of his hands.

And I'll be damned if he doesn't start singing.

Our first few lessons were just simple chords, scales, little notes and techniques. I didn't show him too much of anything really because he didn't have anything to pluck around on. But when his grandma bought him that acoustic, I figured I could start showing him songs. I showed him "People Get Ready" two months ago, along with "Blowin' in the Wind" and "Redemption Song." I never showed him "In My Life." That was Marlene's favorite song.

It was our wedding song.

Sweat rises on my forehead. "Where'd you learn that?"

"YouTube," he says. "I looked it up in the library a couple weeks ago. I remember you saying you liked that one. Thought I'd show you." Another smile.

I force one onto my face.

It feels like it's a thousand degrees in here.

He goes back to playing the song and I look down at the Strat.

Darvis and Millan . . . Thank Christ they don't know shit about guitars. I'd hoped they'd look through the case and inspect the amp as close as they could. I also hoped they wouldn't know to look at all the parts of the Strat, particularly the strap buttons.

If you don't know, there are two strap buttons on an electric guitar, one at the front by the neck and one at the back of it. They're the little round things you hook a strap onto, hence the name. Those buttons are screwed tight into the body of the guitar, but if you wanted you could maybe take a small drill bit and make the screw holes at the back of the guitar just a bit bigger so that the screw slides in and fits snug in the body. Also, if you wanted, you could take that screw and file it down to a point. It's a long screw, about four or five inches. Long enough to fit right inside a guitar.

Or a person's throat.

I went over to the Guitar Center in Cincinnati about two weeks prior and picked up a Mexican-made Strat, a case, and the portable amp. I took everything home and doctored it all up. Everything ran me about a thousand bucks and a few hours.

I look at the clock.

Damon finishes "In My Life." He asks, "What'd you think?"

I force another smile. "Sounded good. You didn't tell me you could sing."

"I didn't know until last week." He laughs. "Never tried."

"What would your friends think about it?"

He shrugs. "Don't know. They were all about Jay-Z, Tyler the Creator. We'd all listen to Bob Marley when we'd smoke, but I think they just listened to Marley because that's what you do when you get high. I liked listening to him just because."

I feel a bead of sweat run down my temple and over my cheek. *Now*, I tell myself. I lift the guitar off my lap. "You want to pluck around on this?"

"Yeah!" He lays his acoustic gently down on the ground.

I swallow. He leans forward and takes the guitar. I keep my eye on the strap button.

He hugs it close to his body and strums a C. "Sounds crisp," he says.

I clear my throat. "You want some crunch?"

"Some what?"

"Distortion."

"Sure."

I get up. My legs are shaking like a newborn fawn. I take a breath. I wipe the sweat off my cheek. I pivot toward the amp, bend down and hit the distortion button. At home the distortion sounded cheap, but in this room, with the tile and the brick, the sound is big and full. I turn back around and face him "Hit an E minor," I tell him.

He does and the room fills with evil electricity. "I like that!" he says.

I turn up the volume a few notches. "Hit it again."

Another E minor.

I turn the volume to 10 and motion for him to strum one more time. "Go on!" I shout. "Play!"

The louder you play, the less they'll hear you scream.

He chugs away. The room sounds like a Black Sabbath concert.

I've never seen anyone smile like that.

Do it. Now. While he's distracted.

My eyes float between the strap button and his hands. I step closer.

The noise in the room is loud.

I ease my breathing.

He's strumming faster.

Stop standing here! Kill the son of a bitch!

I stand beside him. I look at the back of the guitar, at the strap button. I can reach out. I can pull it out right now. Easily. Pull it out and kill him. End him. Destroy him.

My hands shake.

Think of Marlene! Think of your wife! This isn't some lost kid! This isn't someone who 'never had a chance,' as his goddamn lawyer said! This is a murderer! A killer! A liar! Now, pull that screw and shove it into his—

The guitar slips.

It slides out of his lap. He grabs for it. His fingers fumble for the backside of it but can only—*Jesus Christ*—latch onto the strap button instead. The guitar hits the floor. A thunderclap of distortion overtakes the room.

Damon sits there, the strap button pinched between his thumb and forefinger, the sharp metal end of the screw jutting out into the open air.

The distortion fades into feedback.

Damon looks at the spike in his hands. He brings it closer to his face.

The feedback wails like a siren.

He looks at me. Our eyes lock.

I don't move. I can't move. I can't breathe.

The ground shakes.

He knows. I can see it in his eyes. He's been in this place for four years. He's had to have seen a shank or heard how to make one. He knows. He's looking at me. Around me. Into me. Through me. His face goes slack for a second before his lips form a hard line in the middle of his face. He drops the spike.

"Hey!"

I look. The guards are in the doorway. Razor Burn yells, "Turn that shit down! The fuck's wrong with y'all?"

I look back at Reed and hesitate for a moment.

He stands. And pulls his eyes away from me.

I cross the floor and turn off the amp. I spin back around and watch as he makes his way over to the guards, dragging his acoustic with him on the floor. He holds his hands out and they put the chains back on him and lead him away.

I pick the Strat off the floor and stick the screw and strap button back into the body. I unplug the guitar and shove everything back in the case. I carry the case and the amp out of the room and go down the hall toward the front entrance.

The door slides open. I step over to Darvis and Millan. They inspect the case and the amp and say I'm good to go. I pick them both up and turn.

"Hey," Darvis says.

My heart is trying to kick down the door of my chest.

"Forget something?"

He pulls the pack of guitar strings from the desk and hands them over. I set the case down and shove the strings into my back pocket.

"Didn't hear no Hendrix," Millan says.

I say nothing and leave.

I drive back to Covington and soon see the Brent Spence Bridge off to my right and Cincinnati there on the other side.

I turn left and head home.

"The kiss of the scorching iron seared, burned through layers of skin, stripping flesh, seeming to bore down to my very bones, every nerve in my body jerked, and I lurched forward, though I'd sworn to myself I would not."

DAUGHTERS OF EVE
Jennifer Stark

en miles outside of Paris, 1719

There's fourteen of us in the cart and we're all named Marie. The countryside lurches by, pine branches jumping up and down in outrage. They've yoked us two-by-two and are hauling us to the coast. They're going to herd us into the hold of a ship and drive us out across the Atlantic to Louisiana where some settler will force us on our backs.

The cart rattles down the dirt road, each jolt lifting me from the bench and threatening to throw me over the side. For once I am grateful to be chained to that cow Marie Elizabeth.

The cold manacles comfort my wrists. I pull against the chain and the iron links stand fast. I strain to get closer to the cart driver, but Marie Elizabeth won't move. I yank the chain that ties our waists together, and she shakes her head. I glare at her, willing her to move her fat ass.

From across the cart Anne Marie says, "Problem, Elizabeth?" And draws one eyebrow up in that way she has.

Marie Elizabeth lowers her head and moves with me until we are pressed together against the side of the cart. The cart driver sits on a bench above, his innocent back to us. If Marie Elizabeth and I stood we would still only measure to his shoulder.

Anne Marie and I lock eyes. Hers are black and full of intent, like her thin hard lips that issue commands. She is all force of will, with the vision and strength and energy of ten men. There is no one else like her in the Salpêtrière, in Paris, in the whole world. This is a woman who gets what she wants.

And she wants to escape.

The first time I saw her I was standing in line for my fleur-de-lys. My third offense, and I was being branded with the rest. Anne Marie was brisk, her skirts whisking the floor as she heated the iron. When the woman ahead of me, a thief from the Ile, strained against the guards and tried to bite, they looked to Anne Marie. Anne Marie took a rag and stood in front of the thief, raised her eyebrow and said, "Is this necessary?" The thief opened her mouth as though to bite again, but Anne Marie swung behind her, holding the cloth at both ends, and forced it in the woman's mouth. The woman shook her head from side to side, but Anne Marie held on and tied the rag at the back of her head. She picked up the iron and swish, swish, back to the fire, and then five measured steps to the thief from Ile and with one clean stroke the brand against her shoulder. The woman howled through the gag. Like some maddened beast, her eyes rolled back in her head. Her cries and the stench of burning flesh, like chickens roasting on spits in the market, and Anne Marie with the brand for a precise count of three, and then back to the fire while the guards hauled the woman away.

When it was my turn I sat in the chair, back straight and gaze fixed on the far wall, the sound of Anne Marie's skirts and brisk steps behind me. When they stopped I turned to look at her. Her glance was on my shoulder, sighting the brand against my skin. I nodded once, as deeply as I could, as though I were bowing to a queen, and gathered my loose hair, baring my shoulder for her iron. The kiss of the scorching iron seared, burned through layers of skin, stripping flesh, seeming to bore down to my very bones. Every nerve in my body jerked, and I lurched forward, though I'd sworn to myself I would not. The guards held me fast. I did not scream.

It was over in moments. I rose from the chair, knees weak, swaying, as my shoulder throbbed and the pain radiated down my arm and to my neck and down my back. I shuddered. A guard led me away.

I turned and looked back and there was another in my place, weeping and shaking. Anne Marie stood behind her and raised the iron.

I stare at the cart driver in his dove-colored wool coat, framed against a fearless blue sky. The cart driver isn't a bad guy. Every Tuesday I helped him load the cart with the bolts of coarse cloth we weave. Once, on a winter day when the cold could not be stopped and invaded every pore, when the cold turned my nails and the first knuckles of my fingers blue, he even shared a smoke with me. Now I watch the back of his head, the thick black hair curling under his cap and onto the back of his neck. In another life, on another day, I would have pulled that hair through my fingers, tugged just to see the pain make slits of his eyes before I kissed him.

Directly across from me, Anne Marie's eyes are closed and her mouth is still, but her brow furrows and lifts, furrows and lifts, and I know she is silently praying, voicing the Salve Regina in her head.

Before Anne Marie, I hated moral instruction. I hated the kneeling for hours, all of us, me tied at the waist to Marie Elizabeth who exuded the smell of rotten beets and sulfur. I hated Sister Gerard whose pale face was cut with a protruding bluish vein like a scar that ran from her temple to her chin. I hated repeating the Latin phrases that made my jaw stretch and my tongue flatten as if the words were large eggs I had to vomit and hold in my mouth. "Ad te clamamus exsules filii Hevae."

But the day after the fleur-de-lys, Anne Marie was there, beautifully contemptuous, stalking our kneeling rows. She strode, her spine straight and her shoulders back, her hair pinned, every strand obedient. And she was clean. Not a stain on her. While the rest of us wore dresses with gray tattered hems, wrinkled skirts a shadow of the color they once were, and frayed cuffs, her cuffs were intact and not missing a stitch, her skirts were smooth, her hems immaculate, and when they rose with each efficient step, her ankles appeared with stockings clean and tight. My own garters were stolen months before, and my lazy stockings sagged in a bundle at my feet.

I watched her pace the room and willed her to look my way, hoping that my strength and silence the day before had made an impression.

Next to me, Marie Elizabeth's chin fell onto her chest. Her eyes were shut, her face blank and expressionless as the surface of a pail of milk. Before I could elbow her awake so that a nun wouldn't see, Ann Marie appeared behind her, bent down, and, with index finger against thumb, snapped the back of her ear. Marie Elizabeth's eyes flew open, she straightened with a gasp, hand covering her ear. She looked behind her, confused, saw Ann Marie, and turned back to the front of the room. I looked up at Ann Marie, met her eyes, and they were laughing.

She bent, gripped my shoulder, her strong, elegant fingers pressed through the wadded cloth between my singed skin and my chemise. She claimed me.

Across the cart, Anne Marie, still praying, is chained to Marie Claude. I have never seen her chained before. But when they shackled her this morning, she took it just as I knew she would, with her graceful wrists offered to the guard and the manacles accepted with dignity. We knew they would not chain us together. They saw how we walked together in the courtyard. We were careful never to look as though we were scheming, no whispers, no furtive glances. Still, they didn't like it.

In the courtyard as we walked with purpose, as we stepped away from the lunatics chained to the benches who reached for us, Anne Marie explained it all, she gave me the gift of prayer.

Anne Marie said, "They tell us 'Salve Regina' means Hail Queen. 'Mater misericordiæ.' Hail merciful mother. That is not what it means at all. 'Salve Regina' means the queen is safe and healthy. Long live the queen."

"Francoise Marie?" I was in great confusion because though she was born — illegitimately — of a king and married to the Regent, Francoise Marie was not the queen. And I did not see how praying to her would help us.

Ann Marie snorted. "Her? God wants nothing from her. She is less than the wing of a fly to Him." She stopped suddenly and I had to step back to rejoin her.

She took my face in her hands. She didn't know her own strength and her thumbs felt as if they were bruising my cheekbones, a result I wished for. I would have carried her marks on my skin proudly.

Her black eyes gleamed. "I am the Queen. I am His chosen daughter. We are His chosen daughters. There is nothing we cannot do."

It was God's will that we escape.

Every evening, in the courtyard, we walked, recited the Salve Regina and plotted our escape. So when one morning instead of moral instruction, they lined us up, all the women eighteen to twenty-five who were not lunatics: the beggars, the prostitutes, the forced sober drunks, the gang leaders' mistresses, women who'd left their homes for a man their family didn't approve of, in four obedient rows that cut all the way across the courtyard, and a man in a captain's uniform strode down the rows and pointed, "her," and "her," and "her," when his imperious finger fell on me and Anne Marie, we were not surprised.

We had been chosen. "Filii Hevae." We were the daughters of Eve.

Anne Marie's eyes open. She is done praying. She catches Marie Claude's eye and they move closer to the guard. He's young with hands and eyes like a woman's, and nothing will make me happier than when he breaks his fingernails against the chain that throttles him. A month ago he'd caught me in the tunnel coming from the washing room, pushed me to my knees, and forced my face against his foul-smelling crotch. After I sank my teeth into his puny cock he'd strapped me to a bed between two lunatics and left me there for three days to lie inside their wailing, and stew in our collective piss and shit, while they, giggling, took turns inserting small stones and rosary beads in my hole.

When we'd been led to the cart, I'd angled to sit behind him, and lay my chain across his throat, but I was forced behind the cart driver.

I am as close to the driver as I can get. If it weren't for the reek of the bay, I'd smell him, the tobacco on his clothes, what he'd eaten this morning and had to drink last night. But the bay has its own odor of dung and hay that takes over everything else.

I lock eyes with Anne Marie and she nods, a nod so deep, with a pause at the bottom, as though she's acknowledging her queen.

I stand, Marie Elizabeth standing behind me, bracing me, and bring my arms up over the cart driver's head and down, slamming the heavy links against his throat. Across the cart Anne Marie and Marie Claude do the same to the guard.

I pull as hard as I can against the cart driver.

He drops the reins as his fingers rend and tear at the iron links, and the horses, confused and frightened by their unexpected freedom, bolt. They break into a full gallop and the trees whir by, the sky tilts above, the cart heaves and bucks beneath me.

The other Maries, after a moment of stunned silence, bellow and cheer. "Get the bastard, Marie Genevieve!" Marie Marguerite shouts to me. I want to tell her he isn't a bastard, and after all what did she know about it? Had she ever stolen a smoke with him in the shade of the prison wall?

I pull and pull.

Marie Louise shouts Anne Marie's name.

Somehow the guard has managed to turn around, and the chain, instead of crushing his fragile throat, is pressing the back of his neck. He reaches for Anne Marie and grabs her by her hair, yanking her to him. With his other hand he pulls out his blunderbuss and puts it to her head. Cold washes over me from the top of my skull to my heels.

"I'll kill her," he shouts to me.

Anne Marie shakes her head. Her black hair has come loose from her bun and hangs in snarls about her face. She who claimed me, she made me promise before we set out that I would continue no matter what. But I can't do it if it means life without her.

The cart driver gets a finger under the chain. I yank hard, but he slips another finger under the link too and pulls against me.

I pull again as hard as I can, and the cart driver spills off his seat into the cart in my lap.

"Stop," the guard shouts.

He swings the muzzle of his gun and points it at me. The barrel is long and black and I could fall into it forever. His upper lip trembles, and I know he won't shoot me.

Anne Marie knows it, too. She cranes her neck as far as she can and gets her teeth into his wrist and bites until blood flows out of the corners of her mouth and down her chin.

She has never looked more beautiful.

A bang explodes from below me. Smoke is in my eyes, in my hair, in my mouth. I can't see except gray and I breathe gunpowder. I can't hear a thing but that shot throwing itself against the walls of my skull again and again and again.

The smoke thins. The guard holds what is left of Anne Marie by the hair, his arm shaking. Blood and chunks of brain and jagged bits of white skull smear the guard's coat and chin and cheek and forehead.

The cart driver looks in shock at his pistol, which still breathes smoke.

More than half of Anne Marie's head is missing. She looks at me with one dead black eye, the flesh stripped from the bridge of her nose. Her body hangs limp as a puppet in the arms of its master.

I am paralyzed. The cart driver gets his hands under the chain and frees himself. He grabs the reins and forces the horse to a stop. The whole world stops. My ears ring, and every leaf, every blade of grass, every sparrow is still. I wait for God to save Eve's daughter.

The guard recovers himself, frees his fingers from Anne Marie's hair, drops her to the floor of the cart and throws Marie Claude the key, tells her to unshackle herself from Anne Marie.

Marie Claude's fingers scramble for the keys and she unlocks herself.

"Push her over," the guard says, and motions to the wall of the cart with his pistol.

"No, don't," a voice says. It is shrill and quavering and I realize it is mine.

Marie Claude and Marie Louise roll Anne Marie to the side of the cart. They strain to lift her and get her almost to the top of the cart wall before she falls back to the floor, her skirt twisted under her, her arm flung out, three of her fingernails broken, and her cuff torn.

I cannot stand to see her limp, falling. "Wait," I say.

The others make way for me. Marie Elizabeth and I get our hands under Anne Marie's shoulders. Beneath her gun smoke-stained dress is her own fleur-de-lys. She told me about it, but I've never seen it and now I never will. The others take her hips and feet. The four of us heave and lift her to the cart edge. She teeters on the wall and I grit my teeth and push. She goes over.

Her body hits the ground with a heavy splash. She lies on her side in a puddle.

I am unchained and whipped—seventeen lashes. My fingers dig divots into the skin of a beech tree. Splinters wedge themselves under my nails. Later I will pull them out and treasure each one. With each bite of the whip against my back I shut my eyes, otherwise I stare at Anne Marie's corpse lying half in and half out of a puddle. Mud has stuck to her thick brow that never again will rise in a question or furrow and lift in silent prayer.

I am forced back into the cart and again shackled to Marie Elizabeth. The cart continues its relentless drive to the coast. Soon I will be able to smell the sea.

There's thirteen of us in the cart and we're all named Marie.

3

"It's not the grief that sullies me, of course: grief isn't dirty. The dirty part is the guilt."

TRUTH UNTOLD
Aislinn Kelly-Lyth

I'm in the car with Siobhan when she asks me. We're on the way to visit Niall. It's an annual trip: we go every year around Christmas time, just the two of us. We used to go all four together when Mam and Dad were still alive, but they're long passed now.

I'm driving, and it gives me an excuse not to look at her. The fields roll by and the Sperrins rise slowly in the distance. We buried Niall in a beautiful place. It's a thought I have every year, but it's true.

"Joe?"

I reposition my hands at the wheel, check the wing mirrors.

"What was that, Siobhan?"

"I asked do you remember it?"

Siobhan doesn't remember anything, of course; she was far too young. At the wake, she delighted in the attention of distant relatives who tussled her hair, plied her with biscuits, and repeatedly asked her to tell them how old she was.

"Two," she said over and over, beaming gummily. Her grin made my stomach turn. But it was a better sight than Mam.

Mam, who sat hunched over at the table for the whole wake while my aunts and great aunts nipped in and out of the kitchen carrying plates piled high with sandwiches, cups of tea and little jugs of milk balanced precariously on trays. Normally Mam wouldn't have allowed that; normally she would have guarded the kitchen door with ferocious territoriality. It was strange to see guests being served by someone other than her. Every so often she would weep, and then she'd dry her eyes and stare down at her worn hands, motionless. For once she didn't care what people thought.

I wanted to weep too, but Dad and I weren't allowed. It was our job to stand guard in the Good Room and thank people for their condolences. Dad did it with astonishing stoicism, shaking hand after hand and nodding with gratitude as people filed in awkwardly and said: "Sorry for your loss."

After the wake, once night had fallen and the house had emptied, I heard him crying in the bathroom. I crept out of mine and Niall's bedroom and sat in the hallway, listening to the gentle sobs seeping out from under the bathroom door. When he stood and blew his nose, I scurried back to bed. After that I never heard him cry again, not once in the long years of silence that followed the funeral.

"No, not really," I say now, and Siobhan is silent as I take a narrow turn and we bump up a road filled with potholes.

We climb slowly, zigzagging along contracting lanes, past sheep grazing in green fields. There's green everywhere, different shades of it falling behind us in patchwork squares as we climb, until the land becomes more barren and the green gives way to brown. In the distance are purples and blues, the colour of the peaks where they meet the sky.

We stop at the church. It's a squat building, nestled amongst the mountains to serve the scattered parishioners who live up here. This isn't where we grew up, but Siobhan and I spent enough time on our grandparents' farm as children that I suppose we became honorary parishioners. After Niall died, Mam sent us to stay with our grandparents for most school holidays. Those were happy days, as happy as possible. Away from the town and our parents' grief. Long summers roaming open country, dark winters drinking cocoa by the turf fire. Every autumn we'd go blackberry-picking and Granny would bake a pie. Siobhan would name the new-born lambs every spring until she was old enough to understand what happened to them when they disappeared.

We get out of the car, crunch across the gravel. The graveyard lies behind the church and Niall is right in the middle, a limestone slab standing upright and unchanged. To his sides are Mam and Dad, Granny and Grandad. Our whole family back together: the living and the dead.

The fields in the valley below are pure and bright in the morning sun, and the freshness makes me feel dirty, like I'm sullying this place with my grief. But grief is impossible to suppress here, where the decades have effected so little change. I close my eyes and there's Dad, stern, pallbearer for my little brother.

It's not the grief that sullies me, of course: grief isn't dirty. The dirty part is the guilt.

"What are you thinking?" Siobhan asks, and I open my eyes, look at Niall's name etched into the stone.

"The funeral."

Siobhan pauses, and I can tell she's about to ask something more, so I look away, down into the valley. She hesitates, then speaks anyway.

"So you remember the funeral then, but not the accident?"

I sigh, reclose my eyes. "Aye."

We stay like that for a long time, my face turned away from her, my eyes closed. Eventually she tells me she's going to get the flowers from the car. I wait until her footsteps have receded before I allow my eyes to open and the air to rush into my lungs. She's tiptoed around the question before, but she's never asked it straight like that.

I was in my thirties when Mam finally died of heartbreak. After I heard, I went out and clambered up onto the edge of Craigavon Bridge. I stood on the narrow railing, my toes curled around the edge of the handrail, my body swaying in the wind. I stayed there for a long time, wondering whether I'd fall, pretending to be indifferent. The city lights danced across the river below and the chill air snuck beneath my collar, set my teeth to chattering.

Eventually a passer-by shouted: *You won't die falling into water, you eejit!* It's a low bridge, and he was probably right. I slid down and sat at the edge of the walkway, cradling my knees.

The pain was overwhelming, then—those last moments playing on repeat. The shock on Niall's freckled face as he fell backwards, away from my outstretched arms; the old man climbing out of his car, hands shaking, words tumbling over one another: "Oh Jesus, I took my eyes off the road for one second, oh good Lord, it was just a second, it was just—"

Siobhan arrives back beside me, bouquet in arms, and kneels creakily to arrange the flowers at the headstone. She stays there once she's done, crouching, head bowed, hand flat against the moist stone. Neither of us share our thoughts. Eventually she stands.

"Will we make a move, then?"

"Aye."

Siobhan tries to chat on the drive back. I'm not a chit-chatter at the best of times, but today I'm near-mute, all my responses monosyllabic. After a while she gives up and we fall into uncomfortable silence.

By the time we reach the town it's overcast, the sky as grey as the buildings around us. We're meant to be having lunch with her family. I try to think of excuses to get out of it as we edge along the streets, but nothing comes to me, and soon we're in the drive.

When I cut the engine, the silence is stifling. Neither of us move. I wonder whether Siobhan is waiting for me to say something, to come up with an apology for my coldness. The rain starts up, and the sound of its beating on the roof and the windows cuts the tension a little, breaks the stillness.

"Do you think you've blocked it out?" she asks. "The accident?"

We're both staring straight ahead at the pebbledash of her terraced house, at the raindrops falling on the dashboard. For a moment the truth hovers at my lips and I want to set it free, let it be judged by someone other than myself. But I know the rest will follow inexorably: *it was just horseplay, Siobhan.* And I remember that it's Christmastime, and that inside the house her husband and grown children and grandchildren are all waiting to eat cold turkey sandwiches around the kitchen table.

And the truth recoils.

"I'm sorry," she says, and I realise that she's looking right at me and that my face must be showing pain. "Oh Joe, I didn't mean to."

She reaches to hug me, but I stiffen, so that her arms fall awkwardly around my torso.

"I'll get an umbrella for you from the house," I say, and let myself out of the car.

Later, once we've eaten our fill and the table has been cleared, I sit in her kitchen nursing a cup of tea. It's only late afternoon, but the sky is already dusking; it's that time of year. Siobhan stands at the sink, washing the dishes. The muffled sounds of the TV rise and fall on the other side of the wall, chatter and laughter coming in bubbly waves.

"I'm sorry about earlier," I say, and Siobhan whips around, surprised.

"What do you mean?"

"Just, you know. Sorry I wasn't the chattiest."

She peels off her sudsy Marigolds, sits down opposite me.

"No, it's my fault. I shouldn't have asked."

"You have a right to know."

All day I've been trying to find the words, picking up fragments from a lifetime of almost-sentences never uttered, piecing them together into something coherent, something forgivable.

Three years after Niall died, Siobhan and I lay in the long grass of a hill near Granny's and stared up at the sky. It was summer, and the breeze was blowing gently across our faces, the feathery reeds swaying against our bodies. They were precious, those days of sunshine, few and far between. We'd been silent for maybe fifteen minutes when she asked me: "What was he like?"

Niall was a taboo as far as I was concerned, or at least that was the case back in our home in Derry, where Mam had taken down every picture that had him in it. We only remembered him once a year—a few days after Christmas, grave-visiting day. Then we had to zipper our mouths shut again for another twelve months.

The question floated in the air, unanswered, while I waited for my heart to stop pounding. Eventually I said: "He was nice." Then I leapt up and went careering down the hill, shouting over my shoulder: "Try to catch me, then!"

Later that summer evening, I resolved to tell her everything. Knocked on her door, sat her down. She looked up wide eyed, freckle-faced, inquisitive, just like Niall: "What is it, Joe?"

And I couldn't: she was five, it wasn't right. And she'd tell Mam, whose heart would give out.

But by the time Mam died, Siobhan was in her twenties, and I still hadn't told her. Standing by Mam's fresh grave she looped her hand over my arm, squeezed it, looked up at me. The other mourners were heading back to their cars, and Dad was in his wheelchair, a small blanket folded across his knees, waiting to be pushed, old before his time. Niall was buried beneath Mam, and people had brought fresh flowers to lay by his name.

I tried to look into Siobhan's eyes, decided again that it was time to speak the truth. Found myself looking over her shoulder instead, patting her hand, saying that we should get to the funeral reception.

Siobhan stands up now, pours herself tea, sits back down.

"Okay then."

On the day Niall died, the sunshine was glorious. We were happy as we wandered out of school, bags on our backs, so unwieldy that they turned us into small tortoises. I was almost thirteen, on the brink of becoming a teenager. Niall was six, not worth my time. It was a Friday afternoon, almost the summer holidays, and I couldn't wait to shake off primary school.

"Mrs Flanaghan's gonna tell Mam you skipped assembly," Niall said as we headed home, his chin turned up toward me, challenging.

"Let her. Wee bitch."

"That's rude, Joe."

"Is it, Niall."

It was often like that between us: me standoffish, him tugging my sleeve. He was a little brother, and he sought my attention, as little brothers are wont to do. But at that age my attention was in short supply, especially for him.

He kept on at me as we walked down the street, and when we rounded the corner, he stuck out his tongue. It irked me, so I pushed him. Not hard, I didn't mean for him to fall—but he stumbled back, lost his balance, and then—

These are the words I need to say to Siobhan. But instead I start with: "We were messing. Just winding each other up, like normal."

"Okay."

"And we came around the corner, as you know."

"Aye."

"And—"

She looks at me, her pale eyes searching, trying to understand.

At her first son's Christening, the priest asked me if I accepted my responsibilities as a godparent, and guilt flooded through me. I saw how she looked at the child protectively, in the same way that Mam had looked at us. *Siobhan should know what I did,* I thought. *She should know I'm not safe.*

Later, alone in her living room and holding her baby, I had thought about the words I would use to explain it to her. Her baby's head smelled like milk. He reached up and closed a gentle fist around my thick index finger. It struck me that if I dropped him, if I held him the wrong way, if I wasn't careful and didn't watch what I was doing, then he could die. I sat there motionless, my arms in exactly the position they'd been in when she placed him there. When he started crying, I did nothing—just willed him to stop. She heard the sound and came back in. When she lifted him out of my arms, I sighed audibly in relief. Siobhan looked hurt: she knew I didn't want a family, but I could at least try to love hers.

Now, decades later, I breathe deeply, look for the fragments, try again to force my lips to say something they don't want to.

"Well, I—"

And I find that where it was once too raw, it's now too deeply buried.

"He—he tripped."

"On what?"

She's watching me with an intensity that reddens my ruddy face.

"I don't know. I don't know. He tripped, on a stone or something, and he fell into the road. The car came, the old man wasn't looking, so—you know. You know."

It's a lame half-truth, but the rest is easier, so I let it out rapidly.

"The driver came over, and I just stood there, I couldn't look at Niall, and then the ambulance came and took him away. Mam sent me and you to stay with Aunt Nora, you probably don't remember that, we stayed there for a couple of days, and then there was the wake. I don't think anything happened to the driver; I never asked."

Afterwards, the silence lies like a heavy blanket. Siobhan reaches out and places her bony hand on mine, looks into my eyes: "I'm sorry for making you tell it, Joe."

That night, in the quiet of my empty bungalow, I write the truth on the back of an old envelope. I leave the envelope in the kitchen, propped up against the salt and pepper.

Then I go and stand in front of the bathroom cabinet. The face in the mirror is a weathered one, deep lines coursing across it, jowls sagging around the neck. I wonder if Niall would have looked like this at my age. I wonder if we would have been close to one another. Drinking buddies, probably.

Inside the mirror are razors, dentures, and little orange containers filled with pills. I open one up, pour the contents into the palm of my hand, and go and sit in the living room. The house is completely quiet, just like the hills around it.

Tomorrow, or the next day, Siobhan will call, and the phone will ring off. She'll come over to check on me. The back door's always open into the kitchen; she knows this. She'll go in, see the envelope, see the stark ink.

And then, finally, I'll have managed to tell the truth.

Dannys
COTINENTAL
COCKTAL LENGE

RAZE THE BAR

BRUCE HARRIS

"Trying to study algebra or Shakespeare or some other kind of bullshit like that was almost impossible when you knew your mother was walking around the streets with no place to go."

SHELTER
Stephen J. Golds

The Principal sat across the desk staring at me for a long time. Picked up his coffee mug, put it back down and took off his spectacles. Cleaned the lenses with a silk maroon handkerchief he pulled from his pocket like a street magician doing a trick. He took his time, licked his lips, then told me if I missed one more day of school, just one more day, I would be expelled. Then he pushed the spectacles back on his face, cleared his throat and peered over at my clothes, the black eye. Said he knew where I was coming from. What I was going through. Told me he understood; sometimes people went through difficult periods. '*Little ups and downs,*' he called them.

I glanced at the handkerchief again and the nails on the fingers pressed flat on the smooth desktop, manicured to a shine, a perfect length, and I knew he didn't have the first fucking idea of where I was coming from. I opened my mouth to say something, but he held up his soft palm, cutting me off. Asked me if I understood *this* was my final chance. I just nodded once. Teachers, counselors, social workers, adults, they all say they want to listen, they want to help, but spend the whole conversation talking *at* you. Trying to force their opinions, their beliefs, their ways on you.

I ran my fingers over the smooth handle of the folding knife in my jacket pocket and nodded once again. Glanced at the closed door. The clock on the wall.

As I was leaving his office, he asked me why I hated school so much?

I told him I didn't, which was the truth. I really did like school. I just couldn't be there every day lately. Had much more important things I had to do. But telling him that would have been a waste of my time, and time was something I didn't want to waste any more of.

Bowing my head like I was ashamed, I told him I'd try harder from now on. Do better. Thanked him for giving me a last chance. I knew that's what he wanted to hear. He patted me on the back like he gave a damn and I left. The snap of the door closing seemed final. A last rumor. A last judgment. The final word.

I started jogging the four blocks to the subway, counting the change from my pockets as I ran, but stopped at the next bus stop, out of breath, soon as I realized I was a buck short and didn't have enough for the train fare. I liked the bus, it was peaceful. Relaxing. I liked looking out the window watching everything pass me by. Liked the faces of the people who rode the bus too. Their features were like short stories in a library book. No, I didn't mind the bus at all, *but* it was a lot slower than the subway. Took about twenty-five minutes from my junior high school into town with all of the stops. The subway only took five.

Town was busy when I finally got there. I pushed my way through the crowds like I was swimming in a tarmac ocean. I had a routine. I always stuck to it. Never deviating from it. Going to the same places I always went to.

First was the multistory parking lot behind the bank on Main Street. If she wasn't there, I always took the back alley down a block over to the coffeehouse. I knew she liked to sit there feeding the pigeons or drinking a coffee, if she had enough money for that. In the case she wasn't there either, the last place I always searched was the park next to the shelter. There were always small groups of people waiting around for the place to open its doors at 7:00 o'clock. Bottles in their hands. Trying to get right before they went in for the night. Not allowed to take liquor into the shelter with them. My mother would often wait by herself on one of the swings, her bags sitting between her sneakers.

The multistory parking lot had the same cluster of folks that were always there. Doing the kind of things people with too much time on their hands do. They must have headed straight there from the shelter in the mornings. It was dark and smelled bad. I didn't know why they liked it in there so much when it wasn't even raining. My mom wasn't there, and I was relieved. I always told her not to go in there, even if it was raining. Told her to stay somewhere more public. It was safer that way. I jogged down to the coffee house, but the bench was empty. I'd really hoped she'd be there. Imagined her drinking a nice, hot cup of coffee, watching the crowds of shoppers passing her by.

I bit my lip, shoved my hands deep in the pockets of my jeans and walked quickly over to the park. It was getting cold. In my head I begged her to be there. There were about ten people in the park already. The swings and slide childless, as usual. No parents brought their kids to this park after three in the afternoon. The homeless folks were drinking hard and sat down on flattened, limp cardboard boxes to keep their asses warm. Noisy. They scared me a little.

My mother wasn't there. I kicked a soda can, sat down on one of the swings. Took out the knife I got from a military surplus store for seven dollars. Opened it up, gazed at my reflection in the blade and then folded it away again.

Later on, when the wind became colder, and the crowd became larger, I walked over to the shelter and sat down on the steps, my jacket pulled tightly around me, waiting like that until six o'clock.

Davina, the woman who volunteered weeknights at the shelter, pulled up outside by the dumpsters in her old Ford pickup. She saw me, smiled, and waved me over. I waved back. I didn't feel like smiling. Davina knew why I was there. She'd met me a lot in the last couple of months. Always waiting around to see my mom.

She got out the car, smiled again and then shook her head no, already knowing the question before it left my mouth. Said she hadn't seen my mom in the last four days. I chewed at a hangnail. Shaking my head dumbly from side to side. Helped her carry cardboard boxes of loaves of bread and cans labeled Vegetable Soup from the bed of the truck into the shelter.

The place smelled like church and mildew. I dropped the boxes down next to some benches. Davina asked me if I was hungry. I said no, but she said she'd make me a sandwich anyway. She went out back for a few minutes and came back with a paper plate with a cheese and bologna sandwich on it. Ruffled my hair. It felt nice, but made me think of my mom. I started chewing at the hangnail again, tasted blood. At 7:00 o'clock when she was getting ready to open, she asked me if I wanted to stick around, wait a while. I said I had to go. Had school tomorrow. She ruffled my hair again as I left.

I walked the streets for hours. My breath came out of my mouth in thick clouds.

I didn't see my mom anywhere.

Really worried about her, it was making my stomach sick. Felt as though I was going to puke. Wanting to give my mother the knife. Needing to, so she could protect herself. I couldn't always be there to do it. She was alone a lot. Too much. Many of the homeless people were alcoholics or had mental problems. My mother never had any of those kinds of problems. She just left my dad. Couldn't stand to be at home anymore. I loved my mom and didn't blame her at all. I would've left too, if I could've.

She'd lived on a couch at her friend's house for a few months in the beginning. Then she felt like she was getting in the way, so she left there and started staying in the shelter in town.

It bothered me a lot when I found out. I couldn't sleep at night. Started cutting school to spend time with her. Didn't want her to be alone.

Because she didn't have nothing to do, she'd just wander around town all day with all of her belongings in those plastic bags. Her whole life boiled down to the few things she carried. A warm sweater, an old sleeping bag, a coin purse, a photo album. Nothing and everything.

In the beginning, I used to feel a little embarrassed. Worried if one of the kids at school saw her then everyone would know that my mom was homeless. But after a little while, I didn't feel embarrassed anymore. I felt angry. I felt angry at my father for letting this happen and I felt angry at the other kids at school with their clean clothes and their lunch money and their no problem, easy lives. Trying to study algebra or Shakespeare or some other kind of bullshit like that was almost impossible when you knew your mother was walking around the streets with no place to go. Or you didn't know where she was going to be sleeping that night. If she could get a bed in the shelter. Or if something awful had happened to her.

I got home around twelve. I'd stopped off at the gas station to wash my face off with a water hose. I didn't want my father to notice I'd been crying.

When I let myself in, he dragged his eyes away from the glow of the television real slow. Put the volume on mute and tossed the remote control onto the other chair. Got up, came over and started shaking me by the throat.

That's how the beatings always started in my house.

Shaking.

Like he had to build himself up to the slaps, and then the slaps built themselves up to the closed fists.

Sometimes, I wanted to fight back. Knock him out. But as strange as it sounds, I knew the beatings were my father's way of trying to deal with the situation. The way I played hooky from school to try and be with her.

Maybe he felt exactly the same way I did. As worried. As hopeless. He just didn't know how to deal with it.

So I'd let him take his anger out on me and I'd just stare into space. Take the beating silently. Look at a piece of the furniture, try and take in every feature of it, like the coffee table. I'd imagine how the carpenter had made it. How he started with the wood, cut it, chiseled it, sanded it down and then slowly put the joints together. Finished it with paint or varnish. I never felt a single one of my father's blows or heard the things he spat in my face.

It was easier that way.

When he was finally worn out, he walked slowly back to the TV, picked the remote control back up, unmuted the volume, and sat back down like nothing had happened. I went up to the bathroom, using wads of toilet paper to wipe the blood from my mouth. Washed my face. Brushed my teeth, then went and got softly into bed.

Before I'd even closed my eyes, I'd decided I wouldn't be going to school the next day. I hadn't seen my mom for four days and another day just didn't even bear thinking about. I knew that the school would contact my father. I'd be expelled and catch a beating much worse than all of the beatings I'd gotten before, but if I could just see my mom, know that she was OK, give her the knife to protect herself, I knew I'd feel so much better about everything.

I bit down on my lip until my eyes blurred. Felt the blood that connected me to her. That knew, as soon as she had the knife, she'd be safe. That feeling, that feeling was worth all of the beatings, and that feeling was worth getting kicked out of school for. I knew I would find her tomorrow and I could sleep for a little while.

"That they had grown up poor went unspoken between them, a silent understanding of shared misery. But to Joseph, being poor meant more than accounting for what little you had. Poverty changed the way you thought about the world."

EVEN A BIRD REMAINS CHAINED TO THE SKY
Marc Watkins

The sparrows she kept never ceased singing—night or day. And Joseph often wondered, when Minnie added the odd finch or a certain parakite from a pet shop clearance, if the noise the birds generated would finally drive him mad. A chorus of high-pitched chirps and cheeps rolled continuously like a freight engine in the confined space of the motel room. Minnie held their newest feathered acquisition in the delicate embrace of her fingers before she brought the smoldering ember of a punk and blinded the bird. It may have been a common field sparrow or perhaps a Henslow's sparrow. Joseph watched its tiny frame twitch as Minnie pressed the ember into each eye, shutting them forever.

"You know we can just cover the cages?"

Minnie shook her head, placed the newly maimed creature in the cage with the rest, and jammed the punk into a half full can of soda. "The light," she said, "even a little of it always gets through that way."

Joseph did not bother to argue. It had been his words that started her obsession with birds and he made certain to speak more carefully around Minnie. Soon she'd silence the fattest ones. Take them outside to the parking lot where he'd set up a propane boiler and toss them living into a vat of kitchen wine. Then she'd pluck them, vacuum seal them, and write Ortolan Bunting on the bag along with the name of some French city noted for its cuisine. She'd do all that, then they'd go on their arranged date.

Each week was a new city or sometimes a roadside motel and Joseph was often in his own head. Not dreaming, not thinking, simply existing with his own anxiety. He read to pass time, spending his days at the local library where he could shut it all out for a while. He read comics, fiction, nonfiction, romance, the dictionary, children's books, and even horticulture, though he could never recall walking through a garden or owning a plant. The words on the pages were the closest thing he had to conversation. Minnie preferred the electric gloom of television or thumbing across the cracked glass of her smart phone.

It was a book on cuisine that began Minnie's obsession with birds. He'd read about how rich people in France ate songbirds whole and before he'd even finished telling Minnie about it she was putting on her sneakers and asking how many bird cages he thought they could fit in the car. It did not take her long to fill the tiny space with as many birds they could find. Blinding them so the birds would gorge themselves on grapes and grain to fatten them before roasting them living in common table wine. They sold them to wannabe French restaurants in small towns that had trouble telling the difference between a sparrow and a dove, let alone understood what a cooked French songbird was supposed to look or taste like. It was fraud, of course, but Joseph did not much care. He was happy to take someone's money who'd eat a bird whole.

They were meeting a couple of retirees who'd bought a shuttered fast-food joint and had a mind to turn it into a fancy restaurant. When they arrived, it was like entering a renovated tomb. The walls were painted black—the lighting was subdued and giant travertine stone tiles almost hid the peeling linoleum that crept past the door. Maybe it had been a Shoney's or Perkins in the past. Now it was De Lapin and the owners had taken a page from seafood dining, placing rabbit hutches by the entrance instead of lobsters in tanks.

They sat down across from the kitchen on stamp metal stools that could never be considered comfortable. Joseph took in the hodgepodge stylistic choices spread out before him like a book written in several languages. There seemed to be some attempt at décor but none of the choices spoke to any real theme. Minnie straightened her back and brushed her hair past her eyes and did her best to become a French lady. When the couple appeared from the kitchen they carried a pie with them and Joseph glanced at the rabbits. Poor Peter. Mr. McGregor's garden never looked so uninviting.

The woman introduced herself as Julia. Her husband did not speak.

"Care for some pie?"

"Non, merci," Minnie said. Then she said "no thank you" in a false

French accent Joseph worried did not play well. He'd told her to just say she had an aunt in France if they asked about a connection, but she'd dismissed the idea.

"I've been to France," Julia said. "Three times."

Minnie pursed her lips. "Ah, an expert."

"The food was excellent. And so simple. So different than the meat and potatoes I grew up on."

"Ortolans are not simple."

"No," Julia said. Her voice became a whisper. "And illegal."

Minnie laughed. "In France, yes. In America they are expensive."

"I watched a documentary that said eating the bird whole was on the bucket list every foodie should try."

"A true, as you call it, *foodie*, would agree."

Minnie motioned for Joseph to place the small foam cooler on the table and he obliged her wordlessly, having rehearsed the movement many times. He opened the lid and allowed the intense cold from the block of dry ice within to mist slowly out of the opening—an effect that added to mystery and drama and was completely unnecessary. But they weren't selling a meal—they were selling an experience. Joseph slid his hand inside and removed a tiny bag which held a single bird and unfolded a short knife before he awkwardly opened the bag. They'd debated using scissors instead of a knife, but Minnie'd told him the hint of menace often trumped convenience.

Joseph placed the corpse of a small naked bird in front of Julia. The woman looked at it with the curiosity of a cat.

"Want me to stick it in the microwave for you?" Julia's husband asked.

Julia hushed him, wrinkling her nose, afraid to offend her guests. "How do I eat it?"

Minnie unfolded one of the napkins on the table and carefully draped it over the woman's head.

"You must cover your face."

"Why?"

"Etiquette demands God not see you in a state of such decadence."

"Oh," Julia said. "Is it Christian?"

Minnie did not answer. Instead, she slid the bird on the table until it rested beneath Julia's hooded face. Those at the table watched as the bird disappeared under the cloth and the only sound was the sharp crunch of bones and sighs of pain. Each bite was hesitant and Joseph had never seen someone struggle for so long to consume something so small. When the napkin dropped from Julia's head, thin rivets of blood coursed out of the corners of her mouth—the small bones had pierced the roof of her mouth.

"That was the most amazing thing I've ever eaten." Julia looked over to her husband whose face was riddled with concern. "I'd like a dozen for my church group and two dozen for the restaurant."

Joseph celebrated his twenty-second birthday a few weeks before meeting Minnie. He had no real family and found work where he could, drifting along the highways from one job to the next. Minnie was older. She'd told him her age was thirty-four, then forty, before announcing she dreaded meeting the big three O come spring. Stories changed a lot with Minnie; plans always stayed the same. The thing Joseph loved about her, that he coveted, was Minnie's great hobby of dreaming. She told him they were working to save to move out to Oregon and buy a house overlooking the Pacific Ocean. She spent the long hours in motel rooms selling it, poring over gloss magazines, leafing through the pages until she found a house or something she'd liked, then she'd pull out her craft scissors and ever so carefully cut out the image and glue it into her binder. Minnie's technique was so good that Joseph hardly ever saw an air bubble blemish her work. She was careful and thoughtful as she curated a life for him, one page at a time.

Joseph wanted that life—even if he knew it was only dreaming. That they had grown up poor went unspoken between them, a silent understanding of shared misery. But to Joseph, being poor meant more than accounting for what little you had. Poverty changed the way you thought about the world. He looked at a metal trash can and saw the salvage in it, a buck ten if it was aluminum at the local recycling center. When they passed by an abandoned house he could tell from how securely the plywood shuttered the windows if anyone had sneaked in to strip the copper from the walls. Joseph knew that it also changed the way he dreamed. He saw characters in the books look at the world with limitless horizons in all directions and he wanted that feeling. Somehow Minnie had it—that ability to dream big and unrealistic.

They hustled nonstop, selling what they could. The birds were new—daytime work and sales were spotty. What paid the bills was selling their bodies, offering themselves up to couples who wanted to experience flesh instead of consume it. When they'd started their dates, it had been Minnie who'd go. Joseph would come along for protection and it was funny at first how many of the men thought he was her pimp. She'd stand nervously, chewing her cuticles, never taking her eyes off of Joseph. The look was a play, one he'd recognized quickly, but when she asked if he'd take a date or two, just to give her a break, a little rest, she'd done it so smoothly that Joseph had agreed without a thought. It wasn't long before he was the object of every encounter. When he first met Minnie six months ago it was in a bar in West Plains and she was so short he nearly didn't see her save for her alabaster skin that glowed like some sort of ghost.

She was pouting at the bar to no one in particular. "They told me I was too fat to play Anne Frank in my high school play, so now I only eat olives and drink flat beer. Isn't that awful?"

He hadn't known it at the time, but she was working daddies with her sugary voice. A few she'd already hooked weeks earlier. One even bought her a car. A Honda. Used. When they got possessive she pressed up against Joseph and he folded his arms around her out of reflex and she announced to everyone in earshot that he was her man. It had been like that ever since.

That night they went on their arranged date and he could not find the words to describe it—not in any of the books he'd read. None of them had mentioned anything like the role he played on their outings. Joseph was naked and so was the woman lying beneath him. She was no Minnie and she would not meet his eye. Her gaze was locked on her husband, who sat in a dark corner of the motel room. Minnie had told him it was important that he not make eye contact with the husband. That wasn't something a good bull does. Maybe the books, the really good ones, had shaded it over, camouflaged it in allusions and the pomp of manners, but Joseph doubted you could ever conceal the reality of something as awful as this with politeness. Minnie stood near the door, like a bored schoolgirl waiting for the bus, a menthol tucked lazily between the crook of her fingers. Nothing about this was new to her.

An hour before they'd met the couple, Greg and Nadine, in the parking lot of Piggly Wiggly about twenty minutes outside of Mammoth Springs. Greg had told them what he'd wanted, like he was ordering items off some invisible menu. There had been a lot of awkward pauses when they first arrived at the room and Joseph took some solace in the knowledge that he wasn't to blame. Nadine obliged Greg and allowed Joseph to be with her. The encounter was brief and unremarkable to Joseph. When it was over he left the bed and watched Greg crawl beside and spoon Nadine, making soft cloying noise. Minnie collected the money while he dressed. She had her hand on the door before Joseph had time to pull off the condom.

"Hey," Greg said, gazing at the thin piece of latex. "Can I have it?"

Minnie kept her hand on the door. "That's extra."

"Come on. Just give it to me."

"It'll cost you fifty."

The man rolled out of bed and handed her the money before Joseph could say anything.

He hesitated before unraveling it like a snakeskin and tossing it on the bed. Greg reached down and tied it like a water balloon. Then he put it in his pocket. And Joseph suddenly felt afraid. "Say, would you like to join us for dinner? There's an Applebee's down the street."

Every horror had its own language—its own history. That he had been ignorant of it made it no less real. When Joseph knew what to look for he found what it was called easily. Not buried on the recesses of the web, but in videos splashed across "best of" lists on nearly all the porn streaming sites. The phrasing was specific, brutal. Bulls. Black Bred. BBC. Typing in a generic phrase like "interracial" was a joke. He'd read his Shakespeare and found it difficult to imagine how men used to fear they were being cuckolded centuries ago had changed, evolved into husbands paying for the experience of being a cuck. Maybe they'd always wanted it and just couldn't say it. He thought of the cuckoo bird leaving its eggs in another bird's nest, forcing the animal to raise its brood unaware. But to willingly do so was beyond Joseph. To yearn to be cucked, seek it, cajole and whine until your wife agreed, then tell her it had to be with a black man, that no other color would do, not white nor brown, but black and that being a willing cuck and watching her receive her lover in front of them was the only way that they could know something like happiness in this world.

It wasn't always a Greg or Nadine. No two couples were alike—save for the fact they all wanted the same experience. The husbands were sometimes bearded and fat or lean and muscled or old and anxious or simply plain and boring. The wives were homely: some old, some young, some fat, some thin. The occasional woman who'd look him in the eye would gaze fiercely as if frightened by his mere presence. There were hippies, rednecks, bankers, janitors and maids, soccer moms and divorcees, coffee shop baristas and college professors. There were couples who would break down and sob in front of him and then ask Minnie for a refund and she would point to the blush on the wife's face and say no returns for services rendered. And the worst were the few who actually tried to talk to Joseph. The husband who would not stop asking him questions about sports and making inane small talk while Joseph was inside his wife. The incredibly liberal couple who announced how woke they were or how everyone should follow black twitter and eat vegan as if the two concepts were somehow related. Then there was the farmer who talked nonstop about his dead mother.

Between the dates and the birds were the books and worlds and people who spoke with purpose other than desire. Dreams and passion beyond simple pleasure and base need—a code Joseph could decipher but not will himself to create. He saw the hunger in people and knew he was the object of that the desire for the few short moments he was with them and he knew the absurdity of Minnie's dream of a good life from these encounters. All of these men and women who sought him out, used him and left to return to their respectable lives in nice middle-class neighborhoods, were a joke. This was the life Minnie spent hours dreaming of. Clean sheets and nice clothes that didn't come from the second-hand store and then what, nights spent sneaking off in the cover of darkness to debauch yourself in one sexual taboo or another?

"I worry about you," Minnie said. It was early one morning and he was heading out to trap birds in a nearby field. "Sometimes I think you're too straight for this life."

She lay prone on the bed, a stack of gloss magazines reflected the pulsating light from a television show. Even with the volume maxed he could not hear the show above the birds. "We're going to get caught," he said. Joseph waved his hand taking in the birds. He made no mention of the dates. "One of these restaurants is going to get pissed and call the police."

"And say what?" A smile spread across Minnie's face. "*Hello officer, this nice interracial couple came by and sold me some songbirds my patrons are supposed to eat whole with a napkin over their heads. Why do they have a napkin over their heads? To hide what they're doing from God. Only I'm pretty sure they're not real French songbirds.*" Minnie laughed. She rolled over on her back and lay supine. "What crime do you think they'll charge us with?"

"Fraud," Joseph said.

Minnie shoed him away with her hands. "You put too much value on justice."

"People seek it out when they find out someone's run a game on them."

"Shame keeps people silent."

Alone in the field, Joseph shoved a pair of fiberglass poles into the soft earth and stretched the thin nylon birding net between them before tossing handfuls of seed across the ground. He opened a book about ancient Greece he'd bought from the local library for a quarter. It was worn and old and among the many dozens of books the library was getting ready to throw out because no one was interested in reading about forgotten civilizations. He tried to focus on the story of *Prometheus Unbound*, condemned by the Gods for stealing fire to give to the people and punished for it by having an eagle peck away at his liver for eternity. But he found himself hating Prometheus for stealing fire, for taking knowledge, and did not see it as a gift at all. He knew that Minnie was running a game on him, playing him. She was for all purposes his pimp. The books he read helped him understand his life and words within them gave him knowledge beyond his experience but no real ability to do anything about it. Joseph read about Oregon, learned it had been settled by racists, and understood that Minnie's dreaming for them was likely a lie, too.

You could read a book and it could tell you so much about yourself that you didn't understand, yet when you closed the page, you would be left with no real insight about what to do, just a horrible awareness of what your life was and how little you could do to change it.

Joseph tossed the Greek play into the dirt of field, where the binding would rot and the pages molder until they became indistinguishable from the soil it now rested upon. Soon he would pull the catch rope and the fiberglass poles would collapse, dropping the net over the birds who'd swooped down to feed. He'd free the robins and the cardinals and carefully place each sparrow into a small cage where the last thing they'd see before gorging themselves in darkness was a hot coal guided from a soft female hand. He'd snap any crow's neck that was caught in the net.

Minnie had a whole routine when they went out on a date. It was always couples. The four of them would meet someplace public—a coffee shop or at a Wendy's. This was of course after she'd sent them pictures of his body, usually just a series of photos of him holding his penis, but sometimes they'd ask to see more and he'd have to model while Minnie snapped pics, careful to leave his face out of frame.

"We don't want cops knowing what you look like," she'd tell him. He'd nod and wonder if there weren't some other reason. A thought like that was a strange seed. Once it was planted it would grow like a weed until he was satisfied there was no other answer and Joseph's mind was full of weeds when it came to what Minnie told him.

Greg and Nadine were becoming one of the regular couples they'd see and it was clear that Nadine was starting to get into it. Her clothing changed. Nadine started to wear stockings and short skirts and had a series of plunging blouses you'd only wear under the cover of darkness. She removed all the hair that made her a woman and pranced about the room looking like a plucked hen. Any hesitation he'd seen before in her was gone, replaced by a ravenous purpose.

Joseph avoided Greg and said nothing when the man offered Minnie a gift of a few pills. He watched her take the two onto her tongue and heard her crush them between her back molars. Joseph saw her body transform. The stiffness in her limbs slackened and her skin rosined. Her eyes glossed and became unaware.

"We need to set up a tripod here and I've got a light in the car I'll bring in." Greg darted about the small room the couple had rented, moving lamps and pushing aside tables.

"Fine. Fine," Minnie said. "Film what you want. Just not the face, never the face. I have plans for that face." She looked at him as though he were paper. "We're going to make a lot of money out West."

"In Oregon?"

"California, maybe. Depends on where they need a stud."

Joseph did not know how to respond. He thought he should be

angry, but to be angry he'd have to have been surprised. Minnie had finally dropped the game and laid the plan out for him. No more lies about living a straight life overlooking the ocean. All the dates and the couples and the sex had been job training for his new X-rated career in front of the camera. What killed him was if she'd asked up front if he'd do it Joseph might have said yes. Of course Minnie would never do that—offering him the choice was too risky.

"Why don't I call up two or three of my friends and see if Nadine would like a train?"

Nadine's arousal turned to confusion. Greg's eyes danced with possibilities. "Could we, could he do that?"

"No," Minnie said. Her frame shrunk low in a chair as the chemicals took hold of her muscles and slackened her limbs. "He doesn't have any friends."

Joseph ignored her. "Maybe it's time for Minnie to come out of retirement and join in the fun."

"I'm not retired. I'm management. We need some alone time, Joseph?"

"We are each of us fearfully and wonderfully made creatures."

"Adverbs?" Minnie said. "Jesus."

"That sounds deep," Nadine said. "What's a train?"

Minnie frowned. "Nothing. It means nothing. And it isn't deep. It's from one of the books he's read. He could read all the books in the world and still not get it."

Joseph said he was going for cigarettes and exited the room before anyone could stop him. Minnie left her keys in the car but he gave no thought to running, knowing however far he went he'd likely wind up on a path that led back to her or maybe something even worse. The night air was crisp and a fog settled over the fields so thick that he thought it might be an ocean though he'd never seen one outside of the movies or images pressed into Minnie's dream book. He wondered if such things only existed once you saw them in the wild. His relationship with Minnie began out of reflex, an obligation to not turn down something that was offered, maybe in the hope that it would turn out to be good or unique. Instead he'd been used and was still being used and once you discovered that you weren't supposed to stay but he had no sense of how to flee. And then there was the other thing— Joseph liked parts of their dates. He liked the attention. He liked the sex. He liked that Minnie had chosen him. His thoughts raced in anxious unease and his desires consumed him. It was as though he were aflame from outside and from within, burning from both his flesh and his mind.

His footsteps carried him across the parking lot from the motel to a convenience store across the quiet highway. Just outside the door he saw a lottery ticket lying on the floor—a scratch it. Someone had already revealed all the prizes and won a free ticket. Joseph allowed himself to feel oddly possessive of the ticket. It was a chance. His chance. He knew he would not win, that you never really win at something like this, but that did not matter. He slipped the paper across to the clerk and demanded another ticket, a new possibility.

The clerk shook his head. "I just saw you pick that up outside the door."

"Why does it matter? It's just a free ticket."

"You could win."

"We both know that isn't going to happen."

"But there's a chance."

"Yes," Joseph said. He felt like the floor was electrified. "That's what I want. A chance."

"Buy one. They're not expensive."

Joseph reached for his wallet and paused. "No," he said. "This money isn't for that. I can't use it for that. I mean I earned it. It isn't stolen. It's just I can't use it to buy this." He handed the man his wallet and began piling candy and mints and batteries all on the counter. "I'll buy all of this, just not the ticket."

The clerk nodded. "Look, do you need me to call someone for you?"

"Like a cop?"

"I was going to suggest one of your people. Or, you know, a friend."

"There's no one to call."

The clerk sighed and reached under the counter. Joseph thought he might be holding a weapon once his hand reappeared, but instead it was the man's own wallet. He took out a five dollar bill and placed it inside the cash register before handing Joseph a new lottery ticket.

"I can't," Joseph said. "This can't be charity."

"What's wrong with charity?"

Joseph struggled to find the words. What he wanted to explain was a feeling that he did not know the language for and if he did he dared not speak it aloud. When he spoke, it was halting. "Other people. They've been dreaming for me. Telling me what hopes they have for me. I just need something for me. Just a chance. An opportunity. Christ, this is stupid. I know I'm not going to win and even if I did I'd give you all the money. It isn't about that. I can't let someone else give it to me. I can't accept this ticket. Don't you understand? It was a choice, my choice to pick it up."

By the time Joseph had finished the clerk had turned his back to him. Joseph felt a familiar impulse take hold and he took the ticket out of reflex despite what he'd said. He knew the man did not mean anything with his misplaced charity, but that did not change the defeat he felt inside. He sat down on the cool concrete step next to the convenience store entrance and felt the smooth surface of the ticket between his fingers. In a moment, he'd scratch it off and win or lose, but he'd already won something small and sacred by claiming the ticket. He hesitated, wanting the moment to last, knowing that if he took much longer Minnie would appear and draw him back inside, or worse, she'd send Greg.

In the distance, birds rose from the field and crashed through the fog to meet the sky. A few turned into dozens, then perhaps hundreds. From where he sat, Joseph could not tell what species they were, which mattered little. He saw them flock together and match their movements as one entity, changing directions in a blink of an eye. Far too quickly for human thought. He watched the creature's darting movements, logic-defying and yet as natural as breathing. Joseph saw the birds as creatures of mystery worthy of fascination, of wonderment. Then he brought the nail of his thumb to the face of the ticket and claimed his fate.

LATE NIGHT DOG RUN

TS FRENCH FRIES TAMALES GENE'S & JUDE'S RE

CHUCK KRAMER

"Wannabes and poseurs, small town balls with big city mouths. Marko had been the operations manager for one of the hottest clubs in Manhattan. He'd handled movie stars, NBA players, and hardcore gangsters. Rodney and his people were ants."

FUCKING STAVROS
Jason Allison

A wave of brake lights swelled in the distance. Doing twenty in stop-and-go, Marko put a hand to his forehead. Astoria to Plymouth usually took him five hours. Marko had been on the road for six, still had forty-five minutes to go. These runs were killing him, minute by minute.

"Fucking Stavros," he said to no one.

Marko grabbed one of the phones on the passenger seat, banged out a text while steering with his knees.

running late

This was Marko's eighth run. 227 out, 227 back. 3,178 miles total, excluding today. Marko had done the math, math being his thing. The phone buzzed.

A god damned thumbs up emoji.

He shoved the phone in his jeans pocket. Marko exited, cruised surface streets at the speed limit; a Plymouth cop had stopped him two trips back. Marko's New York plates had raised her up. Marko had nearly shit the bed.

He found the coast road and pulled in opposite a touristy ice cream shop, closed for the season. Small boats with filthy hulls bobbed in the harbor, working-class pleasure crafts roped to moorings until the weekend. Marko stuffed two of his phones in the glovebox.

Twenty minutes later, a wide, pale face framed by a black hoodie filled his rearview. Marko twisted around.

Was that Rodney?

The passenger door opened, and the big man tumbled into Marko's 5-series. The Bimmer buckled under the added weight.

"The fuck is you doin' rollin' up here in this?"

Yep, it was Rodney.

"It's my car. What else am I gonna take?"

"Rentals, yo. That's all my runners use."

"Stavros thinks rentals are a bad play. Too easy for some Trooper to pull you apart roadside."

"They're Staties. You sound like a fuckin' tourist."

Rodney was 300 lbs. of Southie trash that had been run outta Southie. He was all neck and no hair. Under the hoodie sat a cue-ball dome, speckled with irregular patches of pink. An Irish flag tattoo crawled up his neck. He was mouthy and ballsy and had just enough cash to make people pretend he wasn't. He reminded Marko of a hundred small-time players who had begged him for favors back when Capri was open.

Capri. A pang of nostalgia hit Marko in the gut. He missed the club.

Fucking Stavros.

Rodney slurped from a 42 oz. Mountain Dew. "Drive."

Marko backed out. "Where's Finn?"

"Gettin' the shit. Consider yourself lucky. You get the man himself." Rodney grinned wide.

Marko offered a weak smile.

"You got satellite in here?" Rodney fat fingered the infotainment.

A dubstep track boomed. Side view mirrors shook. Marko muted the system. "How about we stay under the radar."

"Under the radar? My man, you rollin' in a year old M line with outta state plates. You can't get no higher round here. Actually, we can. It's legal in the Commonwealth." Rodney dug into a pocket, produced four clear cylinders filled with yellow liquid.

"Is that . . . weed-vape?" As if Marko couldn't think less of the man.

"Seventy-seven percent THC." Rodney brought it to his mouth and sucked on the mouthpiece. The pen made an electric, crackling sound.

Marko dropped the windows. "Come on. I'm still making

payments."

Marko didn't know whether marijuana was legal in Massachusetts, didn't care. He couldn't chance the Bimmer getting impounded. He'd never get another ride of its caliber. Credit had been easier to come by when he had a legit job.

Rodney exhaled in Marko's face. Marko waved the mist away.

"Where'm I going?"

"Take Three north."

"North? We going to Quincy?"

"Quinzee. And don't worry 'bout where we're goin'. Just drive."

Meets usually went down in Plymouth. Marko usually met Finn. In fact, Marko had *always* met Finn, now that he thought about it. And Finn had only dragged Marko to Quincy once, after local law had gotten turned onto one of Rodney's stash houses.

Rodney. Quincy. No Finn. Marko tried to stay cool.

He side-eyed the beast stinking up his ride. He found the criminal element that held sway over the South Shore unimpressive. Wannabes and poseurs, small town balls with big city mouths. Marko had been the operations manager for one of the hottest clubs in Manhattan. He'd handled movie stars, NBA players, and hardcore gangsters. Rodney and his people were ants.

But their money spent.

They merged onto I-93. Signs for Boston passed overhead.

"We heading to the city?"

"All Greeks ask too many questions, or is that particular to you?"

Rodney's massive face was a stone mask. Marko wished to hell he could see the big man's eyes. The last pickup had been $5K short. Stavros had gone full apeshit. There were burner phones and angry back and forths, conversations to which Marko wasn't privy.

"I'm fuckin' wit' you. Nah, I gotta see a guy who owes me. Ain't gonna take two minutes."

"I just like to know what's what."

"Don't we all." Rodney wiped his nose. "You know I been in your club."

"No shit?"

"About six months back. Before the Feds shut yo' asses down."

It wouldn't have been after, malaka. "That when you met Stavros?"

Rodney nodded. "I had a connect, this Domo used to hustle dope up Providence. He knew Stav, me and your boss got to talkin'. Who knew you had the Molly hook-up?"

Marko hadn't, until the IRS padlocked Capri and Stavros diversified. Marko cursed himself daily for not realizing his partner was cooking the books. He should have known. Marko's signature was on too many checks, too many deposit slips, too many orders for booze that never showed. He had what his lawyer termed exposure.

The Feds shuttered the club. It grated on Marko daily. He'd tried to run a proper business. Rough around the edges, sure, but legit. Mostly. Now, he sat six inches from a thug play-acting at kingpin.

"Get off here."

They passed through neighborhoods Marko had never heard of. Ashmont. Mattapan. Some dude named Shattuck must've been a big deal; he had a hospital and prison named for him.

"You ain't been in the game long," Rodney said.

"Is it that obvious?"

Rodney almost laughed. "I get why Stavros sends you. No cop's gonna look at you twice. Make a right."

Marko turned. "You calling me soft?"

"Is it that obvious?" Rodney grinned, like he was clever. "I'm sayin' you spend more time up here, you'll be a different man."

That's what Marko was afraid of.

Rodney gestured at a pale blue three-story home. "That's us."

Marko brought the 5-series to a stop. The narrow one-way was lined by tired homes buttressed by sagging crossbeams and covered in peeling paint. Sidewalks were uneven and tight, driveways too. The block had the feel of a rush-hour subway car.

Rodney reached across and hit the horn, three sharp blasts. Two minutes later, a skinny white kid in oversized basketball shorts bounded down the stairs. He had a small duffel in one hand. The bag drew Marko's eye. The bag was small for ten large. The bag held trouble.

The bag shook Marko to his bones.

The kid leaned a forearm on the roof, peered in. "Rod the God. Sup, sup."

Rodney and the kid touched fists.

The kid bent, scoped Marko. "He cool?"

"Don't be askin' questions above your pay grade," Rodney said.

The kid rolled his shoulders.

"That it?"

The kid handed Rodney the duffel. Rodney shoved it under his seat. It thunked as it settled on the floor. The noise screamed shooter.

Marko swallowed.

Fucking Stavros.

"Off the ride, yo. We out."

Rodney and the kid bumped fists.

Marko slipped the BMW into drive and pulled away. "Where now?"

"I'll show you."

On the highway, out of nowhere, Rodney became inquisitive.

"Stavros don't use you for the drops. Why is that?"

Marko's stomach tightened. "He's got kids for that. They ride up on the MegaBus."

"I know how they get here. What I'm sayin' is, you strictly the money man."

"Eh . . ." If Marko were truly the money man, Capri would still be open. "I guess so, yeah."

"You ain't handled product ever?"

"Does that matter?"

Rodney seemed to be thinking. "I'm just wonderin' why Stav trusts you wit' one but not the other."

"It's not trust. Handling product's not our thing. It's for," Marko made small circles with his right hand, "you know, the workers."

"The workers." Rodney frowned, nodded. "The workers." He rubbed his wide chin. "I handle product. Product comes from you. That make me one of your workers?"

Marko's stomach tightened. He'd stepped on a landmine covered in prison ink. "Wrong word. You and me, we're management, and management doesn't get their hands dirty. It's not our place."

"My man, if you ain't never gotten your hands dirty, you don't belong in management." Rodney turned his head to his window.

Massachusetts flew by at 70 mph. Range Rovers and Silverados passed them on the shoulder. N.Y.C. cabbies were bad drivers. These people were suicidal.

"How'd you get into this, anyhow?" Rodney asked.

Good question. "Osmosis."

Rodney didn't speak for a time, and Marko assumed he didn't understand the word.

"I get that," Rodney finally said. "Seen it before, plenty. Circle the life long enough, it draws you in. A turd in the shitter. But you ain't answered my question."

Given what lay under the big man's seat, Marko figured honesty was his only play.

"MDMA had always been in the clubs, but it came and went like the tides. Years ago we called it E. To the Snapchat crowd it's Molly. All the same shit. Stavros got a line on a connect out at Kennedy. This Customs girl was able to slip packages through, for a price. We were in a spot. The club's take was down. Stavros asked what I thought about a little side hustle."

"You weren't wit' it."

"Damn right I wasn't. I was the legal face of the LLC. My name was on the goddamned liquor license. You know how hard it is to get one of them in New York? And then to keep it, what with the fuckin' cops and State A.B.C. tools flagging you every time they catch some nineteen-year-old gettin' toasted on Appletinis? I wanted no part of it."

Marko's volume rose, he felt his cheeks flush.

Rodney finished his drink, swirled the ice. "But here you are."

Here he was. Marko sighed.

"We had this DJ booked, a big EDM name. It was gonna be a huge night, and Capri needed it bad. Asshole backed out of his contract two days before the show. I spent the next week figuring how to make payroll. Stavros walked in one morning, dumped a bag of cash on my desk. Three phone calls, thirty minutes work."

"Still didn't save your club."

"No it didn't."

"Shame the Feds hit you. Club's a perfect laundry."

Marko didn't say anything. His left thumb fidgeted with the steering wheel.

"All that over?" Rodney asked.

"All what over?"

"The Feds." Rodney eyed Marko direct. "They done lookin' at you guys?"

Marko's chest felt like it was in a vise. He drummed the wheel. "Yeah. I mean, I think so."

"Word of advice. Assume you always under indictment. Keeps you sharp."

The driver of an F-150 laid on her horn; Marko had drifted into her lane.

"Hit this exit."

Marko guided them onto 44. "Hey, uh . . . is that the package under your seat?"

"What it is ain't for you to worry about."

Rodney's voice was flat. It sent Marko's anxiety into the stratosphere. They passed a WalMart and a Volvo dealership before arriving at a sprawling construction site. There must have been sixty or seventy homes going up, two-story jobs with garages and decent yards, according to the realtor's sign. No workers now, this being a Sunday.

"What is this, Sawyer's Landing?"

Marko had always met Finn at white trash crash pads. Around him now were wood skeletons awaiting plywood and shingles.

"What're we doin' here?"

Rodney pulled the duffel from under his seat, opened his door. "Let's go."

Marko stayed where he was.

Rodney ducked down, looked in. "It's not like I'm askin'."

Wondering how much Stavros knew, Marko killed the engine. He got out and stretched his lower back as he spun in a slow circle.

Uncleared forest lay on one side of the narrow alley, a dusty construction road on the other.

"Let's get what you came for."

Marko followed Rodney into an unfinished home. His eyes kept drifting to the bag. He told himself not to scope it, couldn't stop himself. The weight of it, the way it dangled. Marko told himself Stavros wouldn't have sent him here to get whacked by some townie middle-manager. They'd been in each other's wedding parties. Marko had held Stavros's daughter. They were friends. Friends wouldn't fuck friends. Not like this.

Finn jumped to his feet at the sight of his boss. "I was worried you got hung up or something."

They were in an unfinished space, plywood floors. Sawhorses stood stacked in a corner, a pile of two-by-fours in another. Sawdust, bent nails, and empty cans of Red Bull littered the place. Marko was relieved not to be standing on a painter's tarp.

"Like I'd leave you here with this man's money," Rodney said.

Finn lifted his chin. "Sup, Marko."

"Hey." At Finn's feet was a black Jansport bag. Marko had no desire to stretch this out. "I gotta drive back, Rod. Can we get this done?"

Rodney looked at Finn then flicked his head in Marko's direction. Finn grabbed the bag, handed it over. Marko wondered if he'd ever get to where he knew how much cash he held by weight alone. He opened the zipper a few inches. Inside were wads of hundreds bundled in rolls bound by thick rubber bands. Marko closed it up and slung it over his shoulder.

"You ain't gonna count it?" Rodney asked.

Marko never counted cash. They were businessmen; distrust was gauche. "Finn's good."

Rodney nodded slowly. "Finn's good . . ."

He spoke the words like he was trying to convince himself they were true. Marko considered making a run for his car.

"But Finn's not *always* good," Rodney continued. "Is he?"

"Rod, I thought we hashed that shit out." Finn's voice cracked.

Marko's heart thumped against his chest. Finn was one more meth-thin kid with greasy hair and pale, sunken eyes. He was always grimy, like he'd just finished installing a fence or digging a trench. But the kid hadn't worked an honest job a day in his life.

Not like Marko. He'd lived straight. He'd been clean. He'd run one of the biggest clubs in the city.

Once.

Rodney said nothing.

Worried for Finn, Marko filled the silence. "Rod, Stavros told me it's good. What happened happened. It's over."

Rodney pushed his shades onto his head. He looked square at Marko. His eyes were gray. "Ain't what Stavros told me."

Marko's stomach dropped to the unfinished floor.

"Rod, that wasn't my fault," Finn said. "I told you, the cops got lucky."

Finn had hit full-on panic. He started toward Rodney, who stopped him with a thick finger.

"You stay right the fuck there."

Finn froze. For a time nobody moved.

Marko glanced again at the duffel, the strange way Rodney held it. Not by the golden yellow loops, but around the meat of the bag itself. "Rod, it's cool."

"This man cost your boss—cost *you*—twenty percent, you are sayin' it's cool? That money's gone cause Finn was too fuckin' lazy to move it when I told him. Lemme put this in a way you can understand. Employee in your club makes a fifth of your monthly vanish, you ain't gonna fire the mutherfucker?"

Marko would, and had. "That's a different world, man."

"That's where you wrong. There's a covenant between a boss and his workers, don't matter the industry. I tell Finn what to do, he does it. Shit is sacred."

Finn spit stuttered beginnings to sentences he couldn't complete. Rodney silenced him with a glare. Six months ago, Marko had two girls working H.R., a P.R. firm handling Capri's press, a full-time staff of eighteen, another fifty or so on a week-to-week. Now he was clutching a bag of dirty cash in some New England backwater.

How had it happened?

Fucking Stavros.

"Rod," Marko said, "Finn's your man. You can do what you got to, but this's emasculating, dressing Finn down in front of me."

Finn nodded like he was freezing.

Rodney's gaze went from Marko to Finn and back again. He seemed to be thinking hard on the subject, or as hard as a man like him could.

"You saying I can discipline my man?"

Marko held out his hands, a calming gesture, like he used to when VIPs would go off. "I mean, he's your man. I just think—"

"Thanks for givin' me permission."

Rodney brought his arm up and pointed the bag at Finn. Three thin, popping sounds rang out. Finn folded in on himself, like a deck chair at sunset.

Marko dropped the bag. His hands found his head. "No!"

In slow motion, Finn fell onto his ass. He rolled onto his side and went fetal. He was coughing and wheezing and gasping all at once. Wispy smoke drifted from the hole the silenced shots had torn in the duffel.

Marko wanted to run to his ride, but could not move. He'd seen fights at the club, a stabbing or two. But never this. Never murder. Witnessing had rendered him immobile.

Rodney closed on Finn and tilted his head one way and then the other, like a dog wondering where the treat had gone. Finn tried to speak, spit up blood. Panicked eyes asked questions that would never be answered. Rodney loomed over the kid until his breathing slowed and his legs stopped twitching and the life had run all the way out of him.

Rodney turned from Finn's body, stepped to Marko. "Now you in management."

He brushed past and headed to the car. Marko's legs melted; he grabbed a stud for support. After nearly a minute, Marko stumbled through the house and out into daylight, hands shaking.

Rodney saw him and sighed. "Forgettin' somethin'?"

Marko headed back in, picked up the bag. He took a last look at Finn. The kid couldn't have been more than twenty-five. Now he'd never be any older. Marko left the house. He and Rodney got in the car.

"Do the speed limit. Stop at the lights. Most of all, relax."

Marko's hands held the wheel like it was attacking him. He expected his mirrors to be filled with flashing lights. As Marko drove, Rodney unzipped the duffel and found the shell casings the bag had caught. He cracked the window and tossed them into the woods, one by one.

Rodney directed Marko to a barren parking lot not far from the fried seafood tourist traps. An aging office park lay to Marko's left; a small, sad crescent of beach ahead. A summer town, Plymouth was dead this time of year.

Rodney threw the bag onto Marko's lap. "Get rid of it."

Marko raised his hands like he was being held at gunpoint. Which, in a way, he was. "No way. This's your thing. I got no part of this."

"Mutherfucker, you the wheelman to a murder." Rodney peeled the sunglasses off. "Maybe you don't understand. Maybe Stavros kept you outta the loop, I don't know how you people run your thing. You're here cause your man demanded punishment and proof. I get it. It was a fuck up and needed fixin'. But this ain't some disco down in Meatpacking. You don't get to be a spectator. This's the game, and you all the way in it. Now fill that bag with rocks and throw it in the fuckin' bay."

Rodney waited. Seconds became minutes. Rodney wasn't going to back down. Men like him never did. Finally, Marko cracked his door, stepped out. Along the water were hundreds of small rocks, rounded smooth by years and the tides. He knelt like he was tying a shoe, looked around. Seeing no one, Marko unzipped the bag. The small pistol and thick silencer hit him in the gut. He shook off his fear and dumped five baseball-sized stones inside. Then he zipped it up and hurled the bag as far as he could. It vanished with a splash. Marko hustled back to his ride.

"There's no cameras 'round here, if you're worried," Rodney said. "Ain't the first shooter this spot's seen. Doubt highly it'll be the last."

Marko drew a deep breath. It was all he could do not to throw up. "What now?"

"You drop me off and go home."

Marko circled back, pulled in where he'd picked Rodney up. The big man didn't move. He just stared out the windshield, completely still, a villainous Buddha.

"See that restaurant behind us? I worked there a few summers, back when I was a kid. Bussing tables, dumping trash. Grunt work. Don't know why, but I took to it. Had visions of running my own spot someday. Kept begging the manager to put me in the kitchen, so I could learn. Stupid, right? What mutherfucker in their right mind wants to be all sweaty, covered in flour? Only ex-cons and career knuckleheads're forced to stick their heads in those ovens, middle of July.

"But I was persistent. I remember the day Rafael finally lemme make a pie. Came out like shit, but I didn't care. I'd done it myself. Ate the whole fucking thing." Rodney was quiet for a long time. "I'll have someone new for you next month."

Rodney climbed out of the car. Marko exhaled like he'd been drowning. He pulled his phone from his pocket.

leaving now

Marko pulled out, headed home. The Jansport sat on the seat next to him. Every few miles, Marko glanced back at it. Every few miles, he confirmed it hadn't moved.

Just past the Connecticut border, Marko pulled into his usual rest stop. This wasn't one of the shiny gas station/fast food/clean bathroom jobs; the stone blockhouse housed putrid shitters, empty vending machines, tourist brochures no one took.

Marko parked at the far end of the empty lot, fired off another message.

here

Ten minutes later, a blacked out Ford Taurus rolled slowly toward him. It pulled a slow, looping right, coming alongside Marko so the drivers sat next to one another. Marko lowered his window. The Taurus' driver did the same.

"Tell me you got that," Marko said.

"Clean and clear." The driver was a lean Black DEA man named Tremaine. "Crazy, crazy shit. Staties are dredging the harbor now."

In the passenger seat was the IRS agent who had woken Marko the morning they shuttered Capri. The one who'd given him his options.

The one for whom he now worked. "Gimme the phone."

Marko didn't care for Holcomb. She lacked humor. He'd come to learn Feds usually did. He tossed her the device and she plugged it into a laptop.

"You actually saw Rodney kill Finn?" Tremaine asked. "Your own eyes?"

"Happened right in front of me. So yeah, my own eyes."

"Sucks for Finn." Tremaine shook his head. "And Rodney. And your boy Stavros. Conspiracy's a bitch. How much you get this time?"

"I didn't check." Marko suddenly felt sick.

Tremaine didn't seem to care. "The van's five minutes out. We'll count the cash, photograph it, and get you rolling."

Marko hadn't expected them to ask if he was okay. Informants didn't merit that kind of concern. These Feds cared only about what Marko saw and heard and that he lived long enough to testify to both.

In the glove, his personal cell vibrated.

our friend take care of that thing?

Marko stared at the screen. He heard Rodney's muted voice and flinched; Tremaine and Holcomb were playing the recording off the computer. Marko checked his watch. Home was still two-and-a-half hours away. He was hit by a wave of exhaustion, knew it was the adrenaline fading, his body trying to level itself.

His cell buzzed again.

well?

Marko didn't respond. He'd give the man his answer soon enough.

Fucking Stavros.

"The good things you do fade away. The bad things never leave you. Maybe they hide inside you for a while, like the cancer hid inside me, until it couldn't stay hidden anymore."

SENIOR SKIP DAY
Scott Von Doviak

The diagnosis comes as no surprise. I've been a lifelong smoker—three packs a day in my prime, which was long before the packs cost nine bucks a pop. Back then you could smoke in bars, restaurants, even on planes. I had an ashtray on the desk in my office and my secretary emptied it every night. I never thought of quitting until cigarettes got so expensive, at which point I tried everything—the patch, the gum, hypnosis. I even tried e-cigs, but they're just not the same. Can you picture Humphrey Bogart vaping?

So when my doctor tells me I have lung cancer, I can't pretend to be surprised. The prospect of hearing those words is the whole reason I've avoided seeing him for so long. Too long, as it turns out. The cancer started in my lungs, but it's everywhere now. He recommends an aggressive course of treatment—radiation, chemo, surgery. But he admits even that will only buy me a few more months. What's the point? I leave his office and step out onto Boylston Street. It's a crisp early December morning. I light up a Marlboro. I pull the smoke deep into my lungs. Fuck you. Fuck me. Fuck everything.

But then it hits me. Now is the time to answer that question we all ponder when it's just a hypothetical: What would you do if you knew you only had a few weeks to live? Travel, sure. Everyone says that. But I travel for my work. I'm always flying off to conferences in Chicago, Cleveland, St. Louis, Atlanta. I hate it. All that time in the air without being able to light up. You'd think that would have helped my cause. Maybe it did. If we were still allowed to smoke on planes, maybe I'd be dead already.

I'm still here, though, so what am I gonna do? Spend time with family, that's the other top answer on the board, right? No thank you. I've got a sister I stopped speaking to years ago, and I wouldn't give her the satisfaction of knowing what I'm going through now. One more "I told you so," that's all I need. Same goes for my ex-wife. How many times did she wish me dead before we finally called it quits? If you asked her now, she might say she never meant it literally, but the sand through the hourglass makes liars of us all. She meant it. There was no mistaking it at the time.

No interest in jumping out of a plane or hunting a rhinoceros or any of that bucket list shit. If I were a better man, maybe I'd volunteer to help build houses in Costa Rica or someplace, but let's get real. Even if that's how I wanted to spend my final days, I'm already coughing up half a lung every ten minutes. I'd be completely useless. I'd love to see the Sox win one more World Series, but I doubt I'll even make it to Opening Day. And it's too late to find Jesus. I never saw the point of looking for him in the first place.

Unfinished business. Tying up loose ends.

In a word, revenge.

That's the plan.

I go on short-term disability. On my last day at the office, I don't let on how bad it is. I put up a good front: I'm gonna fight this thing, kick its ass, and I'll be back better than ever. I go out for drinks with my team, and I think I've got a shot at getting a mercy fuck from Connie the office manager, but in the end, she just leaves me with a kiss on the cheek. Shit, I should have told her I was dying.

As far as they know, I'm starting my treatment today, but instead I'm driving up to the small town in Maine where I grew up. I haven't been back there in more than twenty years. I've been to Maine a bunch of times since then, but I tend to stick to Portland and the southern beach towns. The place I'm from is damn near in Canada. You can see the sunrise there before anyone else in the country. But there's nothing left for me there except, as I mentioned, revenge. Because Greg Wakefield still lives there.

I know this from Facebook. I'm not actually on Facebook anymore. At some point before the last election, I deactivated my account. For every person I enjoyed keeping up with, there were ten who posted the most vile, brain-dead political shit imaginable. Life's too short, I thought at the time. Little did I know just how short.

Before I left, I was friends with Greg Wakefield. That's "friends"

in the Facebook sense. We never actually interacted. Maybe he liked
one or two of my posts, I dunno, but I damn sure never liked any of
his. I accepted his friend request out of reflex, because we had
seventeen mutual friends from high school, but the truth is, Greg and I
hadn't been friends for a very long time. Maybe he'd forgotten why.

I guess I was a nerd in high school. I definitely wasn't a jock. I
never played any sports, and I dreaded gym class. I had no musical
talent, so I wasn't in the band. I acted in a few plays, but I wasn't really
a theater kid either. My clique, if you want to call it that, was the A/V
club. This was back in the '80s, way before everyone had a video
camera on their phone. The school had a couple of cameras with what
were considered to be portable external recorders at the time, even
though they weighed upwards of twenty pounds apiece. My friends and
I had custody of them, ostensibly for the purpose of taping basketball
games and school functions, but in our off-hours we'd goof around,
taping our versions of Monty Python sketches and MTV videos.

We were also in charge of the message board in front of the
school. It was the low-tech kind. We had a box of plastic letters we'd
slide into the rows of the sign to announce upcoming games and other
events. When things were slow, we'd put up dumb jokes and one-
liners. A HORSE WALKED INTO ALGEBRA CLASS. MR.
WESCOTT SAID WHY THE LONG FACE? Stuff like that.
Principal Jim Kester would sometimes tell us to knock it off, but he
always had a little smirk on his face when he said it, as if to let us know
he really didn't mind that much.

The other three members of the A/V club were a year ahead of
me, so after they graduated, I was on my own. I guess I could have
recruited new members from the lower classes, but I had no problem
taping the games and events on my own and the idea of mentoring
younger students held no appeal for me. In my mind, I was already out
of this nowhere town.

I'd been accepted to two colleges: the University of Maine at
Orono, my safety school, and NYU, my dream destination. I heard
Martin Scorsese taught film school there. I was always happiest behind
the camera. Maybe I'd never be a big-time Hollywood director, but a
gritty independent filmmaker? Why not?

Attending NYU was dependent on receiving a Bouchard
scholarship. The Bouchards were the rich family in town. They owned
the sardine cannery that employed more than sixty locals. Their annual

scholarships were earmarked for the top ten percent in each graduating class, and since our class had only ninety students and I regularly made the honor roll, a Bouchard looked like a sure thing as the end of my senior year loomed. Until Greg Wakefield cornered me at my locker on the eve of Senior Skip Day.

Senior Skip Day was an annual, unsanctioned but tolerated tradition. Each year the senior class would pick a day of school to skip en masse. Our class picked April 15, mainly because it was a Friday and the date was easy to remember. On April 14, Greg asked if he could borrow the letters to the message board.

"I've got an awesome idea for a prank," he said. "I've been collecting these real estate signs all over town. Anywhere there's a house for sale, I swipe the sign out of the yard. Tonight, I'm gonna plant them all on the front lawn here. And when you give me the letters, I'm gonna put HIGH SCHOOL FOR SALE CHEAP on the message board. And, you know, CONTACT PRINCIPAL KESTER, with his phone number. It's gonna be a fuckin' riot."

It sounded lame but harmless to me. By no means was Greg a good friend of mine, but we had a few classes together and got along fine. We used to bullshit about the Red Sox. He'd transferred to our school from another part of the state during our sophomore year. He wasn't the smartest guy or the dumbest. Not the most athletic or the weakest. Not the most popular, but not an outcast. He was just sort of there.

I gave him the box of letters at the end of the school day. Greg's plan was to wait until after midnight to plant the signs and put up the message. The next morning everyone would see it except the seniors skipping the day. Neither Greg nor I would be around to get blamed, and maybe the whole thing would blow over by the time we got back after the weekend. That was Greg's reasoning, anyway.

"They're not going to blame you," I said. "Kester will probably give me some shit about it on Monday, but he's used to my jokes by now. Here, you'll need this too." I handed him a key.

"What's this for?"

"There's a plexiglass covering over the message board that locks at the bottom. You know, so no one can fuck with the letters. Unlock it, flip the covering up and change the letters, then lock it again before you leave."

"Got it."

I had a hard time falling asleep that night. Everything always seems worse when you can't sleep and your mind is racing, and I started worrying that this prank might not be as harmless as I first thought. I wasn't concerned about the message so much as the real estate signs Greg said he was collecting from around town. Those were private property, and who knew if he was keeping track of which sign came from where? The people trying to sell their houses might be pissed.

At two in the morning I was still wide awake, staring at the ceiling. I couldn't take it anymore. I slipped out of the house and got behind the wheel of the mustard yellow '76 Toyota Corolla my mother had passed down to me when she got her new Honda. I put it in neutral and rolled it out of the driveway so as not to wake my parents. When I reached the street, I started it up and headed for the high school.

Greg had already been there. He'd changed the message on the board. But what it said now was not what he told me he had planned. And as soon as I saw it, I knew my NYU dream had gone up in smoke.

Finding the place where Greg lives now isn't difficult. He's in a trailer at the end of the Pumpkinville Road, which runs up a hill right behind our old school. "Run your fat asses out to the end of the Punkinville Road and back," our gym teacher, Mr. Hart, would say, chomping gum, his hands shoved down the front of his shorts. "No walking. I catch you walking, you're running it again after school." I can't remember a single thing I learned in any math or science class, but the memory of running up that hill is so fresh it causes me physical pain. Pure torture. That's what my brain chooses to retain.

When I reach the turnoff by the high school, I'm in for another shock. The building is in ruins, surrounding by cyclone fencing and heavy-duty construction equipment. Up the hill behind it is a shiny new high school, twice as big, its massive glass atrium gleaming in the late afternoon sun. Turns out you can go home again. It just might not be there when you arrive.

I turn onto the Pumpkinville Road. There's a Glock 19 tucked under my car seat. I bought it in New Hampshire on the way up. I didn't need a license. I didn't need to register the gun. All I had to do was show my driver's license, and the guy behind the counter barely glanced at it. I think that's all pretty crazy, but what the hell, it worked for me.

The road ends just where I remembered it would, dead-ending at the woods surrounding a small brackish pond. There's one trailer home with a short gravel driveway to my left. The last house I passed was a quarter-mile back. This is Greg's place. I get the gun from under my seat and climb out of my nearly paid-off Nissan Sentra. The temperature has dropped about twenty degrees since I left home this morning, and my thin windbreaker isn't going to keep me warm for long. I hear music coming from behind the trailer. As I get closer, I can smell meat on the grill.

I walk around behind the trailer and there's Greg, hunched over his Weber grill, flipping a couple of burger patties. He's wearing thick glasses, his hair is mostly gone, and he's put on fifty pounds. I only recognize him from his Facebook profile photo. The radio sitting on the railing of his back porch is playing "Pink Houses" by John Cougar Mellencamp. He looks up at me and blinks a couple of times. "Hello?"

"Do you know me?" I'm holding the gun at my side.

He says my name. "What are you doing here?" he asks.

"The bad news is, I'm here to kill you."

He blinks again. "What's the good news?"

"Who said there was any?"

He nods and removes the burgers from the grill with a spatula, placing them on a plate. "Will you have a beer with me and tell me why?"

I think about it for a second. "Sure."

Greg's trailer is cramped, but neat. He's got a big flatscreen TV surrounded by shelves of hand-labeled VHS tapes. One shelf has the complete run of games from the Red Sox 2004 postseason. You never know when you might want to watch them all again. We really do live our lives like we're never going to die.

We sit in his kitchenette, each eating a cheeseburger, each drinking a Miller High Life. We haven't spoken since we were outside, but once we finish eating, I tell him about my diagnosis.

"I'm sorry to hear that," he says. "I'm even sorrier that you feel the need to take me with you."

I remind him of Senior Skip Day, and how I loaned him the letters to the message board. What he told me he was going to do with them, and what he actually did. The words I saw when I pulled up to the high school just after two in the morning. PRINCIPAL KESTER IS A MOLESTER.

"Real clever," I say. "I remember we used to call him Principal Keister sometimes. That was funny, but harmless. But when I saw what you put up there . . . I didn't have the key to the sign. Couldn't get the plexiglass cover open to change the letters. I pulled my car up to it, grabbed a crowbar from out of the spare tire compartment, got up on my hood and smashed that plexiglass. Not on the first try. It took a while. A couple of cars passed me. So there was no Senior Skip Day for me. Kester called my house at seven the next morning and told my mother he needed to see me in his office first thing. He had witnesses. People who saw what was on that sign before I got to it. People who saw me on my car next to the sign. But I guess no one saw who actually put that message up there. No one saw you do it."

"Just lucky, I guess." He gets us both fresh beers.

"Even if someone did, even if you got in trouble too, they still had me for destruction of school property. I got an indefinite suspension which, that close to the end of the school year, meant I didn't graduate with our class. I had to get my GED over the summer. No Bouchard scholarship, obviously. So I didn't go to NYU. Didn't go to film school, didn't go to Hollywood, didn't become the next Martin Scorsese. My dream got taken away from me. You took it away."

Greg nods and sips his beer. "So that's the worst thing that ever happened to you? You didn't get into the college you wanted, so now you're gonna kill me? I gotta tell you, that's pretty goddamn pathetic."

"I already told you the worst thing that ever happened to me. I'm dying."

"And that gives you the license to kill. Okay. But the best you could come up with was me? In all the years since we knew each other, you couldn't think of anyone else more deserving?"

"You ruined my life over a stupid fucking joke."

"It wasn't a joke. It was the truth."

I open my mouth, but nothing comes out. I take another swig of beer instead. "What are you saying?" I finally manage.

"Jim Kester. He was my fifth-grade teacher. Back where I used to live, long before I transferred into our high school. I was smart back then. There was even talk of me skipping the sixth grade. And I was the teacher's p-p-pet. But it wasn't because I was smart. I learned that after school one afternoon. I was doing some extra-credit work. Just me and Mr. Kester. I'm not going to tell you what he did to me. You can just let your imagination run w-w-wild. But that was only the first time. After that, I begged my parents not to make me stay after school. But Mr. Kester had told them what a bright kid I was. What potential I had. So they kept sending me b-b-back."

"Jesus Christ."

"I couldn't tell my parents what was happening. He told me he'd flunk me if I did, and I believed him. It didn't end until the b-b-bell rang one day, and it was summer vacation. All summer I dreaded going back, even though I wouldn't be in his class anymore. He would still be there. He'd find a way. Except over the s-s-summer, he got a job teaching high school. At our school, right down the hill. And I buried those memories as best I could, for years, until the day I transferred and saw him in the hallway. He looked at me and kind of half-smiled, like he barely remembered who I was. Maybe that was the c-c-case. Oh, shit. It's back."

"What's back?"

"My stutter. After fifth grade, I developed a stutter. Now, was that because of what happened to me or just because? Who knows? I worked hard to get rid of it. But I still had it, up until my twenties."

"I don't remember you having a stutter. In high school."

He smirks. "Oh, really? Well, it only came out during stressful situations. Like when I asked you if I could borrow those letters. That was hard for me, because I knew what I was going to do with them. I was going to expose him. And you? You made fun of me. You said, 'Sure, G-G-Greg, you can b-b-borrow the l-l-letters.'"

"What? No, I...Shit. Maybe I did. But I didn't think you were really stuttering. I thought it was a joke, so I just responded the same way. I had never heard you stutter before." But as soon as I said it, I knew it wasn't true. Not the whole truth anyway.

He nods. "Yeah. When I thought about it later, that's what I figured. But at the time . . . you don't understand. You guys in the A/V club, I really looked up to you. You were doing what I wanted to do, but I didn't have the guts to ask if I could join you. I was so intimidated."

"By us? But we were geeks."

"No. You guys were untouchable. I mean, you had the keys to the school. You got the most hardass teachers to participate in your skits. And you had the message board. A week ago, I watched them tear it down. Right before they tore down the gym they named after me."

"Wait. What?"

"I never made it to college at all. Not with the grades I had. It was all downhill after fifth grade. Not only did I not skip sixth grade, I had to repeat seventh. My parents never understood what went wrong. Anyway, my best friend at our high school was Cliff Rainer. Do you remember him?"

"The . . . the janitor?"

"Yeah. Cliff was a cool dude. Wicked smart. We used to play chess. After I graduated, he asked if I'd work with him over the summer. I said sure, why not. One summer turned into the rest of my life. After thirty years, they didn't give me a gold watch. They put my name on the building. The Gregory Wakefield Gymnasium. Big honor, very touching. Except they tore the gym down less than a year later along with the rest of the building. And the sign. They're gonna replace it with an electronic one. If the kids want to put up a prank message, I guess they'll have to hack it. But anyway, almost every day until he retired, I'd see Jim Kester at work. I watched him get old. And you can bet he never looked at me the same way he did when I was in fifth grade."

I drain my beer. "I'm sorry, Greg. I'm sorry about everything. I guess I should get going."

He raises his hands. "Just once in the head, please. That's all I ask. Make it quick."

I stand up and head for the door. "I'm not going to kill you, Greg. I'm going to go home and start my treatment, and maybe I'll live long enough to see the Sox play on Opening Day."

"Wait. Before you drive all the way back, there's something I have to tell you. And you can do whatever you want to do with this information."

"What is it?"

"Jim Kester. He's still alive."

By the time I pull up in front of the house out on the Point, it's starting to snow. There's a light on inside. According to Greg, Kester's wife died a few years back. He's gotta be pushing eighty by now. Greg thinks one of Kester's adult sons lives nearby and spends a lot of time with him, but there's only one car in the driveway tonight.

I know what you're thinking. I thought of it too on the drive over here. Maybe Greg came up with the story he needed to tell to save his life. Maybe everything he told me about Jim Kester was a lie. Maybe he even faked that stutter when he told it.

But I don't think so. I remember it now. I had thought he was kidding at first, but the stricken look on his face told me otherwise. His stutter was real, and I made him feel like shit. That's why I let him borrow the letters. I felt guilty then, and I feel it now. It's like no time has passed. The good things you do fade away. The bad things never leave you. Maybe they hide inside you for a while, like the cancer hid inside me, until it couldn't stay hidden anymore.

Anyway, it was Jim Kester who suspended me from school, not Greg Wakefield. It was Jim Kester who denied me the scholarship I needed to attend NYU. If anyone ruined my life, it was him.

I shiver as I step out of the car, the gun in my hand. I wish I'd brought a heavier jacket. I look up at the sky. I open my mouth and catch a snowflake on my tongue.

QUÉBEC CITY WATCHER

KAREN BOISSONNEAULT-GAUTHIER

"That said, don't you owe it to your own sense of credibility to question this? Are you so ready to be a chump? Nobody likes a chump. You've been fooled before, after all, and it might pay to be wary."

FOR REAL THIS TIME, OR THE PROSE OF CONS
B.W. Carter

What do you do? I'm asking. All your life you've waited for this, whether at first sight or over a series of twilit escapades. You've always sniggered at the tropes. You didn't want to believe, but only because it hadn't happened. Until it did, and now . . . You, my friend, have fallen in love. No, for real. This is it. You can feel the authenticity of emotion in the sudden cramping of heart and lungs every time you look her way.

You can tell, without quite knowing how you can tell, which, according to experts on the subject, is how you tell. You're over the cliff and plunging.

But—just for the sake of argument. Because this is your first time . . .

Wait. This is not your first time. Saying it's your first time might be a tad disingenuous. But we'll get to that. Regardless, it's the first time you mean it.

Anyway. Don't digress. The real thing is within reach.

That said, don't you owe it to your own sense of credibility to question this? Are you so ready to be a chump? Nobody likes a chump. You've been fooled before, after all, and it might pay to be wary. People do fall for chumps, occasionally, sure, but you'd bet nine times out of ten that there's an exchange of money involved.

Not so good for you, in the past, but we'll get to that.

You need to think about this. And you do, in between slinging shots and mopping the kitchen. You try to be objective. You try very, very hard, because you don't want to be a chump. Not after waiting so long. Not when it's so obviously the real deal.

Also, being a chump, in this precise circumstance, might even be the least of it.

So, here goes. You owe it to yourself, remember? You don't want to make a mistake here, given who's involved. More than your sense of credibility might depend on it. Well, not *might.* More like *absolutely will.* Your ass will be on the line if convictions do not pan out this time. Not like . . . Anyway, no sense dithering, you just need—

Quit stalling! You always liked making lists, right? Right. So, no big deal. Now get on with it . . .

Pro: You're in love. First and foremost. No for real. Do not doubt yourself on this one. This is definitely not like those other, wistful but regrettable occasions. Times you're still making up for. No. Not here. And one cannot really overstate an incontestable gut feeling of veracity as motive to jump off a cliff: this belief that you will, if not outright soar, then be buoyed aloft on sizzling electric passion. You're fairly sure (you have convinced yourself, at least) that you could survive the leap, if only for her. If only she was holding your hand on the way over.

Con: She's already got a man. And this is probably the biggest negative. So, let's get it out of the way up front. She's already got a man, and he's *the* man. He is the *Man.* Ivor Chomsky. Yep—that Ivor Chomsky. Who isn't exactly the type known for sharing. For taking, sure, definitely. And for keeping. Without a doubt. But not the type to realize he is suddenly the lesser of two heroes and to let his prize go with grace. Ivor Chomsky's a graceless bastard, and he eats hero balls with hot sauce for breakfast. Eats them raw.

Pro: You're no hero.

Con: You're no hero.

Pro: She doesn't seem to like him much. At least from what you can apprehend, from behind the bar where you serve drinks to upper-crust snobs four nights a week. The bar is in the lounge of the hotel where Ivor Chomsky has resided for the last year. The lounge to which he occasionally descends from his penthouse for dinner and drinks and casual brutality delivered unto sundry penitents and petitioners. With the hotel's tacit disregard. He makes sure she doesn't look away when there's blood. Blood is his gift to her, and he's a gifter with no time for refusals. And she's a smart girl, that's plain, for she doesn't wince or blanch or wrinkle her nose in disgust. She licks her lips and smiles. But her eyes when she looks at him in acknowledgement of his gift are cold and flat, with the wrong kind of twinkle in them.

Pro: You can give her the right kind of twinkle. Even on a bartender's earnings. You have already deluded yourself into believing this wholeheartedly.

Con: You are a dreamer, and you have a hard time sorting delusion from reality.

Pro, or con, depending on the night and the amount of screaming and blood: Largely, bartenders are regarded as less than flies on a wall, and so get to see a lot. And the seeing is important, for it keeps one grounded with regard to amorous expectations.

Con: Despite all that seeing, you are still in love.

Con: You're no fighter, and so fighting this desire is useless. Many people in the past have assured you of your uselessness, have employed the descriptor *useless* quite a lot, in fact, whilst discussing you, and so trying to argue that particular detail now seems rather . . . Well, you get it. The point is, these feelings filling you to bursting are never going anywhere. It's for real this time, and the feelings are here to stay. There's not much you can do about this.

Con: Despite being desperately in love, you don't even know her name.

Pro: You don't need her name. Who cares what her name is? You have her eyes, her mouth, her exquisite hypothetical voice, sultry and low and emphatic as it surely will be should you ever get the chance to hear it.

Con: In addition to her name, you know nothing else about her. What if she gets into eating hero balls too? What if she's where she belongs, safe in the arms of a monster like Ivor Chomsky?

Pro: The cons are piling up, but so what? There's nothing keeping you from sweeping her off her feet and getting the straight fuck out of this shitheel city. And out of the pudgy grasp of Ivor Chomsky.

Con: Except your parole.

Con: Fuck!

Con: In your zeal, you keep forgetting the lamentable past choices that put you here, mopping imitation-terrazzo floors and pouring overpriced, watered-down lagers for crap tips, in the first place. It's what your new therapist would've called a *character flaw.*

Con: These cons are really piling up.

Pro: However! However. If not for those piss-poor choices, those rash decisions the courts universally frown upon, you'd not be here now, might never have laid eyes on the pale, gorgeous creature over there who, given a hypothetical Big Guy in the Sky does in fact exist, will in the very near future spend the rest of her life in your arms.

Con: You're pretty certain you're an atheist.

Pro: You are, however, an optimist. Which has tended to contribute the most to your woes, true. But it's in your nature as an optimist to ignore all setbacks of the past, whatever lessons your therapist insists can be gleaned therein. Accordingly, you're convinced she'll agree with the assessment of your future together. Seriously, dude. Look at her eyes. That lackluster approximation of a smile as he whispers something undoubtedly base and disgusting in her ear. It's clear she's waiting for you to act. Yep. Clear as the glass of this highball you're rinsing.

Con: You thought this last time, too, remember? Hence, parole.

Con: Also, these highballs are cheap as shit, and the milky flawed glass is smeared unto opacity.

Pro: The word *con* does not scare you, not in the least. There was plenty of time for you to learn to ignore that word while on the inside, whilst literally acting out one of its various connotations. So, bring it on! Bring them all on!

Con: Ivor Chomsky has a whole lot of them in his employ, with vastly more experience in being one than you. And much more enthusiasm.

. . . [insert a few seconds of elevator music here, some funky yacht rock, perhaps, to simulate a pause wherein very heavy wheels of decision-making are grinding] . . .

Pro: Fuck 'em. That's the long and short of it, and embracing decisiveness is what makes it a *pro*. However crazy the decision might seem to someone not presently afflicted by an overwhelming, sense-obliterating plague of desire. You actually made up your mind just now, definitively, in the midst of an interior rendition of Boz Scaggs' "Lowdown." You can no longer take this shit. It's an untenable situation, standing here night after night like some feckless wannabe knight in tarnished armor. Laying out the positives and negatives has convinced you that something's got to give. Tonight. You've made up your mind, by God (invoked here for tradition's sake, since you're pretty certain you're an atheist). For real this time. No hesitation. You will no longer linger like a schmuck behind the greasy bar as your woman, undeniably the love of your life, suffers so obviously mere footsteps away. No longer!

Con: Though your determination is admirable, as usual Chomsky's accompanied at a discrete but advantageous distance by his most formidable enforcer, whom you've heard him refer to as Zho. Whom you assume gobbles hero balls, too, judging by appearances, which quite frankly in this case make all those aforementioned former inmates come off like prepubescent school-girls.

Pro: There's only Zho, however, given this hotel's sacrosanct neutral position, not to mention the bloodily enforced peace measures of Chomsky's regime. There are doubtless loads of goons stationed elsewhere across hotel grounds, but only Zho here in the lounge. Only Zho. And though terrifying he may be, even this deadliest of bodyguards must piss sometime.

Con: *Sometime* turns out to be three hours, even though he drinks steadily, if lightly. During this period, you struggle to keep the lusty coals of your will stoked. You have to constantly look over at her, at that stunning porcelain visage, to remind yourself that this is definitely the night. That it's for real this time. That you are going to do what it takes, no matter how long it takes. Your nerves are jangling like a string of tin cans tied to the bumper of a speeding car. You're sweating profusely. You're hot. You're cold. You are second-, third-, fourth-guessing yourself. If only this goddamn goombah will get up off his ass already . . .

Con: You're no hero.

Con: You're no hero.

Con: Parole. Parole violation. Recidivism. Shower rape.

Con: Fuck! What the absolute hell are you thi—

Pro: Aha! At last! As if by willpower alone, your patience is rewarded. Finally, Zho stands, whispers a word into his master's ear, and heads briskly in the right direction: an undeniable sign from a (probably) nonexistent deity. Your inner thug strangles all mealy-mouthed cringing opposition and all doubts evaporate like shower steam.

Pro: This. Is. It.

. . . [more inspirational jams in your brainspace here, only it's "Eye of the Tiger" and you don't care how cliché Survivor's anthem is in this type of situation, because now's your moment to shine, whatever does the trick as they say, Rocky Balboa's charging up those steps in your mind's eye even as you reach for the claw hammer you keep behind the bar and start over to their table, Chomsky sprawled with his wide, well-tailored back to you, and here we go] . . .

Pro: Twenty feet, and neither of them look up. Fifteen. Ten. You've envisioned the act of bludgeoning his big bald dome so many times since she came into your life. And tonight, in less than a minute and just like with her, your love, your fantasy will be made real. He is so engrossed in being a pompous, magnanimous ass that he doesn't even pretend caution in his bodyguard's absence. He's a ruthless, callous, misogynistic brute, an absolute epitome of gangster gutter trash, and he deserves what's coming to him. Four feet. Two. He's regarded you, the bartender, as less than a shit-eating speck of life on the wall, and it's going to get him killed. Your grin is splitting your face and you can't help looking at her even as you raise your weapon, seeking to share in this moment of amorous triumph and her liberation from the troll's clutches. The (hypothetical) angels are singing as you lift your steady glare from where it has zeroed in on the target mole on the red, hairless crown of Chomsky's skull. You can actually hear them, and their blaring harmony is as beautiful as her rising gaze . . .

Con: Reality is a bitch. And you are a moron.

Pro: You're lucky enough not to realize the full extent of what comes next, before it is too late. At least, hopefully. And because there is in all statistical likelihood a God, of some kind, just maybe you, luckless, befuddled knight errant in stained company smock and sneakers, are lucky enough not to recognize that cold, reptilian sneer on the perfect features of your woebegone victimized princess. And perhaps you do miss the dull blue flash of the .38 Colt snubbie she pulls from her lap, heretofore unseen and very unforeseen. Hopefully, anyway, just maybe, you will not have a last moment's chance to put together what comes next.

* * *

Con: You're no hero, that's true enough. Not even close. But you were always, always, the biggest of chumps. One would think that therapist might've mentioned it.

The editorial team at Rock and a Hard Place really has a soft spot for down-on-their-luck animals. They also really love noir fiction. Recently, a local animal shelter gave the editors an opportunity to combine their two passions . . . what could go wrong?

Editor's Note: *These pet adoption ads are entirely fictitious. None of these animals are really available for adoption (except maybe Hank . . .). However, if you've got love in your heart and room in your home, consider checking out your local animal shelter. Adopt, don't shop.*

* * *

Felix is a 2-year-old Tabby who's inquisitive and curious about the world. He's always exploring his surroundings, and I swear, it's almost like he understands me when I talk to him! He's so smart! No cost to adopt, you just have to be willing to take responsibility for his student loans, which are upwards of $96,000. A bachelor's degree in Philosophy from Ithaca College doesn't come cheap!

* * *

Paulie is a 12-year-old African Gray Parrot. He's also a massive dickhead. My sincere hope is that whosoever winds up with this asshole plucks all his feathers and drops him into a deep fryer. P.S.—don't believe him if he says he's got a hot tip on some cheap bitcoin. It's horseshit. P.P.S.—he will sleep with your fiancée . . ..

For Sale—Pet Rock

Smooth and rounded, yet still contains a singular ragged edge gifted by a roaming glacier over a millennium ago. Fits perfectly in the hand and offers humbling indifference 364 days of the year. Found in a blowing field of grass close to the town commons, all dirt has been washed away, but other stains remain. Truly beautiful, and a reminder of God's will and infinite patience.

Please note: the rock must be present in the town commons at 10am every June 27th. Referred to as "Shirley" since at least 1948

* * *

For Sale—Anaconda. 8 feet long. Usually weighs 40 pounds but is closer to 70 right now. Includes Terrarium (please note—the lid does not fully close) and half gallon of specialty food he does not seem particularly interested in anymore. Brilliant markings sure to attract all kinds of attention. Doesn't respond to names, but my grandson Phillip used to refer to him as Mr. Hiss before he went missing (Phillip, not Mr. Hiss). Not recommended for homes with small dogs.

* * *

Hank is a real good boy. He likes belly rubs, and ear scritches, and he'll be you best friend for life! Okay, look—if I'm being honest, I'm Hank. I just got really into the furry lifestyle, and I'm looking for a family that's willing to play along. I can even talk in, like, an Astro Jetson / Scooby Doo kinda voice, if that's what you're into. I'll pay my half of the rent and utilities. I just want you to treat me like the dog that I know I am, deep down in my heart. Do you have room in your home and heart for a good puppy like me? Mostly house-trained—although accidents will happen . . ..

Benji is a four-year-old lab mix who loves to go for walks, cuddle, and play with Tennis balls. He's a fast learner who understands almost everything humans say around him. He's really the perfect dog and there's no reason anyone would give him up. In fact, rumor has it he's only at our shelter because he checked himself in. Apparently, he grew tired of his former "outlaw" human yelling all day at Twitter, saying the indie crime fiction scene was trying to "cancel" him. He even had a seizure when one of our volunteers read an Amazon review out loud that was nothing more than a poorly written jab at another publication. We'd love to see this handsome boy go to a good home where it's understood that critique and not being published don't equal censorship.

Meet Peter, a super chill rabbit looking for a home. Peter is great with kids, other pets. Nothing seems to phase this bunny! He's a bit of a lazy bones, generally preferring to just lounge where you put him. Seems house-trained, as I haven't had to clean up after him in months. He also doesn't blink. My daughter picked up Peter the other day, and his tail fell off. She won't stop screaming. I can't afford the mental strain of burying another rabbit in my yard. It's like they come to us just to die! Why can't we keep a fucking rabbit alive for more than 3 weeks?! Just come take the poor bastard off our hands. Also good for amateur taxidermists.

Adopt Carl! He's a real dick who will poop in your loafers and bite you anytime you even think about petting him. We're guessing he's a cross between a chihuahua and a rabid, horny badger. We'd love to keep him in our family but . . . no that's a lie, I'm sick and tired of him humping only my pillow and I think the mailman is about to sue me over him. $50 adoption award, paid to you upon successful capture and relocation.

For Sale: Pack of Dogs. No papers. Not good with kids. Please contact jasmine in North Downtown Omaha.

* * *

Adopt a purebred! Meet Sammy Davis Chewner, a pure-bred golden curly coated retriever. Sammy has four solid years of training under his belt and behaves perfectly wherever his is, be it in your home, in the car, or on a hunt.

Sammy is worth a good amount of money but I'm choosing to instead rehome him and choose the home he goes to. He'd do best in a home with someone who will take him hunting and has the time to reinforce his training on a regular basis. He does well with other dogs and loves children but can't be trusted around cats.

It breaks my heart to have to rehome Sammy but I'm being forced to and in a hurry. My soon-to-be ex-wife has always hated animals and I won't be able to care for him if/when the jury decides against me. Sammy and I were involved in an accident last duck season. I had placed my gun on the ground to grab something from my pack when my best friend and hunting partner of seven years, Adam, gave Sammy the command to get the duck he'd just shot. Damn if that dog didn't step on the trigger and put a round straight through Adam's neck.

I tell you it was a horrific thing to witness, the way he bled out all over the place and died right there in the mud, all amongst the bird and skunk shit. Can't rightly blame the dog, either. He was just doing what he was told.

Now I'll admit I had some liability, what with me forgetting to set the safety on the gun and all, and I'm willing to take whatever punishment the courts deem appropriate for that much. The trouble I'm having, and what's got me all set up to go away so long that I'll have to rehome Sammy, is this cockamamie notion Adam's widow's lawyers got in their heads. They've leveled a lot of accusations my way concerning the direction of the bullet holes and the fact that they say Adam was shot on the ground, the bullet grazing the arm he held before him, going through his throat, and into the soft mud of the wetlands we was hunting.

My lawyers say they've got a solid case, despite me swearing I didn't know until afterwards he was sleeping with my wife. It seems like nobody, not even my lawyers, believe Sammy stepped on that gun but I swear to Christ and all his saints that's what happened.

I'm looking at 20 to life, and Sammy is hardly halfway through his own years. I can't stand the thought of him going to a shelter when they bring back the verdict, so please, if you are looking for a faithful friend, pet, and hunting partner, give me a call and come meet Sammy today.

DIVERSION

ALLISON RENNER

9

"'I *need* this.'"

DOWN TO CLOWN
Robert P. Ottone

Mack stared into Lana's eyes. He had never seen a hazel so beautiful. Green with flecks of brown and gold. He sat opposite her in the restaurant, an Italian joint on Main Street, and drank her in. On all their dates, she looked incredible.

She was, herself, amazing. Funny. Charming. Intelligent. Mack kept wondering when the other shoe was going to drop, yet after ten dates, it hadn't. She was a little awkward and shy, but Mack liked that about her.

Lana poured herself a glass of wine from the diminishing bottle nearby and topped Mack up. She seemed different tonight, off somehow, and Mack wondered if she was a little under the weather, or, perhaps, getting bored with him.

"Everything okay?" he asked, caressing her cheek.

"Oh, yeah, no, everything's great," she said, waving off his concerns. "How was work?"

Mack shrugged. "Always boring. How were your students today?"

"Kinda' silly. Can I tell you a story? I was explaining the directions for an activity and asked if anyone had any questions. One of them, Leo, a five-year-old cutie-pie, raises his hand and goes 'Do you have a cat?'"

Mack laughed. "To be fair, you weren't specific in your question."

She smiled. "They're so weird. Asking about my pets. If I'm married. If I have a boyfriend. One of them asked if I had kids." She rolled her eyes half-heartedly. "They have no sense of boundaries."

Mack smiled and reached across the table, taking her hand. "This is okay, right?"

She nodded, playful. "It's allowed."

Silence hung between them for a moment. The air was thick with possibilities.

"Do you?"

Lana raised an eyebrow. "What?"

"Have any cats?"

Ten dates was a long time together without having seen each other's apartments. Mack liked her, though, and didn't want to rush anything.

The game gets old after a while, Mack explained to his friends when they asked about Lana.

They all wanted to know about the cute teacher their goon of a friend was seeing. They had all found their partners. In many ways, Mack felt a slight pressure to find his. When Lana walked into the restaurant on their first date, so many weeks ago, taking it slow and truly getting to *know* her was what mattered.

"No, no," she said, smiling again. "No cats. No pets at all. Do you have any?"

Mack shook his head. "I'm on the road a lot for work, so, wouldn't be fair."

Lana finished her wine and slipped her hand from Mack's. He knew her well enough to know that she was anxious. Working in sales left him with finely-tuned skills for social cues others might miss.

"Lana, are you sure you're okay?" He pressed. "Do you want to call it a night? I'm happy to call you an Uber?"

"No, no, it's not that. I'm sorry. Umm," she stammered, shaken by Mack's question. "Don't you want to drive me home yourself?"

Hazel eyes flickered beneath long, light brown hair.

He grinned. "If you like."

On the ride to her apartment, Lana squirmed in the passenger seat. Edgy about something.

"I'm sorry for how I've been acting tonight, I just . . . I have something to tell you, and, I just . . . don't know *how* to tell you."

Here we go, Mack thought, heart clenched.

"You don't have to tell me anything you don't want to. I totally understand if you're not interested in seeing each other anymore."

From the corner of his eye, Mack saw Lana's jaw drop. "Why would you think I didn't want to see you anymore?"

He shrugged. "You've been kinda' distant tonight, is all. I mean, I don't know you super-well or anything, but I can tell these things."

She lowered her gaze to her lap, where she fiddled with a loose thread on her dress. "That's not it. I like you a lot." She Gulped. "Like, *a whole lot.*"

Lana looked up at him and he glanced at her briefly before returning his eyes to the road. "I like you too, Lana."

In a flash, she moved close to him and planted a kiss on his cheek. A sudden warmth of nerves and anxiety coursed through Mack's body, from his flushed cheeks to his toes.

Lana's apartment was not what Mack expected. She was a kindergarten teacher and yet, there was nothing to indicate she even had a profession. No children's books. No boxes of crayons. No planning materials of any kind. Instead, he was confronted by a cold, open space. Sparse, save for the large sectional couch and the unbranded television fastened to the wall. Kitchen table beside a refrigerator.

On the wall above the couch was a painting of a man, hands folded, looking exhausted, clad in red. He looked like a harlequin or a court jester. His eyes radiated distance, as though he had seen and experienced way too much of humanity's dark side.

"What's that?" Mack asked, pointing to the painting. In addition to the distant gaze, the subject of the painting looked forlorn. Broken.

"Reproduction of a Polish painting," she said, her voice disinterested. "Have a seat, I'll make you a drink."

He did so.

She did so.

A delightful gin rickey. It felt like razor blades going down his nervous throat.

Mack noted the lack of photos on the walls, or on the nearby end tables. "This place doesn't seem much like you."

"In many ways, it's very *much* me," she said.

"No pictures of family or friends or anything," he said, gesturing with his cocktail.

"Don't have any of either, really," she said, sitting beside him. "Some work friends, of course, but that's about it."

That's weird, Mack thought. *Girl like this? No friends? No pets? What's up with that?*

Lana leaned forward and kissed him. She seemed to tremble in his arms. "Lana, what's wrong?"

"I've wanted you to come over for a while," she said. "I just . . . I worry that you won't like what you find here."

He stared into her eyes. "What I've found so far is a weird painting, a beautiful girl and a delicious cocktail."

She nervously brushed her hair and took a long sip of her drink. "Okay. Give me a second. I should just show you. Like a Band-Aid or whatever, just right off?"

He nodded. She rose from the couch and disappeared down the hallway.

"Here," she said, taking a scarf from the nearby coat rack and blindfolding him.

Mack sat for about twenty minutes, listening to Lana shuffle around somewhere. The scarf scratched against his nose. He peeked a few times, but his sneaky looks were met with nothing. He heard music coming from down the hallway and what sounded like the shifting of clothing.

Maybe she's a slob? Clothes all over the bed?

He dismissed the idea. That couldn't be the case. The apartment was spotless. After what seemed like an eternity of waiting, he heard her footsteps coming down the hallway.

"Ok, you can take off the blindfold," she said.

He tore it from his face and dropped it to the floor.

Standing before him, wearing a yellow suit dotted with multicolored polka dots, was Lana. The suit was baggy, with ruffles on the sleeves and along the neck. On her feet were two enormous red shoes. Her face was painted a garish and insane kaleidoscope of color, her eyes beaming, surrounded by deep blood-red grease paint, outlined in black. In place of her beautiful light-brown hair was a purple wig, individual strands of artificial hair stretched out, looking as if she stuck her finger in a wall socket.

"What. The. Fuck?"

She looked down at the ground, fumbling a toy horn in her hands. She squeezed it and the thing honked like a bicycle horn, shrill and loud, making Mack jump and recoil from the figure before him.

"Lana, I don't know what this is."

She stepped over to him and climbed into his lap, her painted eyes a lash away from his own. "This is part of what I like to do."

Mack looked around and started laughing. "Did one of my friends tell you to do this?" He pushed her off him and onto the couch. He then stood up and looked around. "This isn't even your apartment, is it?"

She stared at him. Hazel eyes in a sea of red, black, and white. "Of course, this is my apartment."

"Lana, is this for real?" he said, searching for a hidden camera.

She nodded. "Yes. I just . . . this is what I like."

He stared at her. "Lana, *come on.*"

She sighed and honked the horn again.

"You gotta' stop that," he said, stifling a laugh.

"You can just go, Mack, it's okay," she said, softly. He stared at her as she wiped her face with her sleeve. Streaks of grease paint fell away from her colorful eyes amongst a sea of tears.

He walked over to her and placed his hand on her shoulder. "Hey, hang on," he said, sitting beside her. "Don't cry."

She lifted her head. Her tears melted the blood-red paint around her eyes to her lips. "I understand, I get it."

He stared into her eyes. "Lana, I just . . . I've never . . ."

She nodded. Mack thought about how many times she'd probably been rejected like this over and over.

"I've never seen such a beautiful clown before."

She laughed. Then squeaked the horn.

He leaned in and kissed her.

Grease paint and tears rubbed onto his face.

He wrapped his arms around her and pulled her close. He could feel that she had nothing on underneath the clown suit.

Their lips parted and she let his hand roam all over the ruffled feathers on her costume. He could feel her body trembling and found himself wanting more.

"If you come into my room, I want you to keep an open mind, okay?" she whispered, her tongue flicking his ear.

"Whatever you want," he said, pulling her face to his and kissing her hard.

At the bedroom door, Mack was bombarded by a collage of color and sound that stood in sharp contrast to the rest of the apartment. A multicolored sphere flashed shades of red, yellow, green, purple, and more, around the room, the walls bathed in a constant rotation of color. He nearly laughed when he heard calliope music playing softly from the Alexa in the corner of the room.

"Oh, Lana," he said, looking around. Her bedroom stood in stark contrast to the rest of the apartment, not only in design and décor, but in personality as well. Where the kitchen and living room might be deemed "sparse" by a decorator, the only term Mack could apply to Lana's bedroom was "clown-*domme*."

Is this who you are? Mack thought, looking around the room.

Above her bed was a black leather swing and strap apparatus. Mack ran his fingers along it, feeling the cold, rough texture of the ribbed metal, each with a sharp tip. Mack withdrew his hand, worried he may have pricked himself.

"I like how rough it feels on my skin," Lana said seductively, arms behind her back. Mack stared at her a moment, how innocent she looked, and nodded absently.

Fastened to the headboard was a pair of pink fuzzy handcuffs. Upon closer inspection, they were dotted with the same polka dots on Lana's outfit.

Mack glanced to the doorway, where Lana stood, watching him. Her eyes narrowed on him. He felt like he was in a Disney nature documentary, the deer or elk that got left behind by the herd, ready to be devoured by the terrifying power of the waiting lion.

There were straps at the foot of the bed. Mack then noticed the leather, like the straps keeping the device above the bed in place.

"Lana, this is . . ." he drifted into silence, unable to finish the thought.

She stepped closer. "I'm not trying to scare you, I swear. I just . . . this is what I *need.*"

Mack nodded. The makeup and outfit were one thing. The horn in her hand, another. *All of this, though?*

He wondered what lurked in the chest of drawers or in the nearby mirrored closet. "I've never . . ." Mack started.

She placed a finger to his lips. "I can show you."

The following Monday, Mack sat at his desk, exhausted. He had spent the entire weekend with Lana in her multicolored dungeon exploring the various toys she had. He had never conceived of sex the way he'd experienced it with Lana. It was all he could think about. The intensity of their lovemaking. Mack had finally had mind-blowing sex. There were times during the licks and thrusts of the toys that he felt that they had become one during intercourse. Throughout the day, he thought back to how much he wanted to experience that level of pleasure with Lana again.

How he *craved* it.

When his friends asked him how his date was, all he wanted to do was tell them about the swing, the toys, the straps and binds, the leather, all of it, but instead, he settled on, "It was great, I really like her."

The question of whether they had slept together inevitably arose, and Mack implied they had, but wouldn't go beyond that. He couldn't. With how intense their lovemaking had been, it would be a betrayal of her confidence to talk about the things she made him do.

She didn't make me do anything, I wanted *her to do all of it,* Mack smiled to himself, caressing the bruises on his wrists. He couldn't recall if they were from the swing in the ceiling or the handcuffs. Or the medieval-looking contraption she surprised him with one evening after bribing him with too much whiskey.

Around two-thirty or so, Lana texted to say how much she missed him and asked if he wanted to come over that night. He replied a little too quickly, regretting his display of over-excitement, that he absolutely wanted nothing more than to come over that night.

Good. I'll see you around six, she texted, adding a clown emoji.

He scratched at the light mark on his wrist, a gift from Lana's teeth left in the throes of greasy lovemaking. He thought about how badly he couldn't wait to be with her again.

Lana's door was unlocked. A note reading, "Come in", taped messily to the outside. Mack thought about how dangerous leaving a note like that was, especially with an unlocked door, but also realized that their town wasn't exactly a high-crime area, so, it didn't matter much.

He also imagined anyone setting foot in the apartment might be more terrified by a woman in a clown suit waving around eleven-inch sex toys, and Mack smiled to himself as he slipped inside.

Inside, he found her apartment dark. He could hear the same oddly-creepy circus calliope music from the bedroom and followed the hallway down, the flickering multicolored lights bathing the hallway from time to time, beaming from beneath her closed bedroom door. Mack took a deep breath and gripped the doorknob.

As he opened the door to her room, Lana stood beside the bed, wearing her clown outfit.

"Hi," he said. "I've been thinking about you all day. Is that weird to say?"

She shook her head. "Me too. Come in and take your clothes off. I have something for you."

He stepped into the room and closed the door behind him, noting the twinge of excitement in his chest, something he hadn't felt in years. As he undressed, she sat at the foot of the bed and watched him, her eyes roaming all over his body. He felt nervous, the fluttering of butterflies dancing around in his belly. She eyed him as a predator eyes prey, her eyes transfixed on him. She licked her lips as the colorful smears of light danced around the room.

"Wait," she said, helping him with his boxers. Once they were down, she leaned closer and took him in her mouth, making his knees buckle.

A shiver ran from the back of his legs to the base of his neck as she pleasured him. He ran his hands through her hair, noting how synthetic the wig felt, even when combed out into the shock of strands. Even though the feel of the synthetic fibers began to cause unexpected reactions in his desire, he wished he could feel her real light brown curls.

Taking her mouth off him, she gestured to the dresser. "Top drawer. Put it on."

He caught his breath and stepped slowly to the dresser, sliding the top drawer open. Inside was a rainbow-colored jockstrap with a rainbow wig to match. Underneath those items was a rubber clown nose.

She smiled and gestured with a slender finger. "I ordered them for you after you left Sunday night. Overnighted them to be here today. I hope you're not mad. I just . . . I *need* this."

He slipped the jockstrap on, followed by the wig. She giggled and walked over to him, helping to adjust it. She then placed the rubber nose on the tip of his penis and squeezed it. He chuckled softly when it squeaked, thinking back to the times when sex like this was something he could never imagine, yet now was all he wanted.

She ran her hands all over him and kissed his neck and chest. "How does that feel?"

"You or the stuff you bought me?"

"Both."

"Amazing," he said, softly.

She led him to the bed, and he peeled her out of the clown suit. They made love, more vanilla than they had so far, taking their time to explore each other's bodies in the lights flashing around the room.

It didn't matter that the leather straps went unused. The handcuffs, too. The swing above the bed. All that mattered was the collision of their bodies into one-another, and Mack felt, for the first time in his life, that he had found someone who, for all her quirks, he felt connected to.

He prayed that Lana felt the same.

After the bruising around his groin and abdomen had healed, Lana moved into Mack's house. Any questions he had about how she felt about him were laid to rest. When he showed her around his house, a simple ranch off Main Street in town, he made a point to tell her how the vaulted ceiling above his bed would leave plenty of space for whatever other toys she wanted to buy.

After a day of moving box after box of Lana's various "items" from her apartment, that night, on the couch, she rested her head on his chest and snuggled into him, exhausted from moving all day. She yawned and smiled up at him, half-asleep. "I love you, Mack. I can't wait for you to take me all the way. And for me to take you all the way."

"Me too, Lana, I love you and only want us to experience everything we ever dreamed of, together," he whispered, kissing her head as she fell asleep.

He thought either he or she would grow tired of their nightly ritual of clown-related orgasmic glee, but it only intensified. Lana ordered a new toy every week, something to push their lovemaking further each time.

There were mornings where Mack felt sore, his ankles, wrists, and other parts of his body aching from the previous night's escapades, and yet, he learned to *love* the dull ache, mostly because it served as a constant reminder of the pleasure from the evening before.

Outside the bedroom, Lana appeared "normal" to those around her. Mack introduced her to friends, and they mixed with other couples. He ignored the comments they gave about Lana being boring. One of them even remarked that she didn't leave much of an impression. Mack laughed at that one, knowing that very night, Lana would pleasure him in some new, strange way he never imagined possible. It was they who were boring, and they didn't even know it.

Each time, when she'd want to push further, into deeper, often more pleasurable or painful territory, she'd convince him with a simple, "I *need* this."

It worked every time, even though Mack had begun to worry that somehow he was losing himself. Perhaps becoming brainwashed by Lana's plea, the often-desperate tone in her voice. Begging him. Imploring him. She *needed* the pain and pleasure. He often pushed the thought out of his mind, reminding himself that evolution was a good thing; his old therapist would agree.

She choked him. Bound him tighter. Made him bind her, as well. Begged him on more than one occasion to choke her until she blacked out. Each time, Mack wanted to protest beyond cursory notions of "we can't do this anymore," but in the end, his own pleasure craved more, needed more, and he let Lana do whatever she wanted to him.

After a while, Mack *needed* it as much as Lana did.

Lana stood beside the bed, wearing her clown suit. In her hands was a small bundle, something wrapped in what looked like black velvet, but could've been any color, considering the lighting in the room.

Mack had helped her redecorate his bedroom, and with the added space, they enjoyed activities in the overstuffed chair in the corner, the floor, even in his walk-in closet. But now, there was an air of seriousness in the room. No calliope music. The light was on, but it flickered around, almost seeming like it was going through the motions without the rhythmic calliope to support it.

"What's that?" Mack asked.

She bit her lower lip. "I've had this a while. I've never used it before."

He stepped closer to her, removing his clothes as he went. "You can do anything you want to me, you know that. I love you."

"I love you, too. This is for *both* of us. It'll bring us even closer."

He sat down on the bed and began running his fingertips all over her body, feeling the cool, soft fabric of her costume between his thumb and forefinger. He never got tired of it.

"This is something different, Mack. Something at the edge of all things."

A wave of excitement ran through him. He straightened himself on the bed and began kissing her stomach through the costume. Breath sharp and heavy. Craving her. "Anything you want, Lana. Please."

She laid the velvet bundle down on the side table and began untying the leather strings that held it together.

"I want us to be one. Like, *completely*," she said.

Mack craned his neck and looked toward the side table. He didn't need to, as Lana spun around, holding a black dagger in her hand, jagged and ancient.

He jumped backward, instinctively covering his precious genitals, scared of whatever Lana possibly had in mind.

"No, no, hang on," she said, giggling. "I want us to taste each other's essence. To . . . become *one*." Placing the knife on the bed, she continued, "It's obsidian. I bought it on Etsy when I moved in."

She unzipped the clown suit and let it drop to the floor. Without the costume, she looked even more ridiculous, with only her makeup and wig.

"I will make a small incision, right here," she said, holding the knife to her chest, above her left breast. "You'll drink from my breast."

Mack stared at her, shocked. Upon closer inspection, the black knife was dotted with tiny multi-colored polka dots. The same as Lana's general aesthetic.

"Then, I'll make a small cut on you. Anywhere you like. On your chest. Your thigh. *Anywhere*. And I will drink."

"Lana, this . . . this is a little much, isn't it?" Mack said, eyes glued to the blade in her hand.

"Mack, please," she said, light flickering in her eyes. She stepped closer toward him, her presence threatening in a way it never was before. Mack found himself backed against the closet door. "I *need* this."

In a flash, she slashed her chest, blood erupting from the wound, splashing Mack's face.

"Drink from me," she whispered, grabbing the back of his head, and pulling him closer to the open wound now torn across her flesh.

"Lana, stop," Mack struggled, her strength overwhelming him. He knew she was strong, but this was altogether different, it was as if she had the power of three Lanas.

Holding him in place.

Forcing him into her.

Her blood flooding his nostrils and mouth.

"Taste me . . . I *need* this," her voice was distant, trance-like.

She pressed his lips to her wound, and he struggled to keep his mouth closed. He had tasted his own blood plenty of times—different scrapes and falls, playing lacrosse in high school—and could recognize the metallic, meaty flavor anywhere. The wound pulsated as Lana pressed him tighter to her chest, forcing his mouth open more to accept her blood down his throat.

With one hand pressing him to the open wound on her chest, her other hand slipped between her legs, and she began pleasuring herself. Mack pulled away, taking a deep breath and spitting up Lana's blood, mingled with his own sick. His makeup smeared against her flesh, contrasting with her dark blood.

She worked herself faster, forcing Mack to her chest, her blood spewing from her wound and down his throat. He gagged over and over, his throat heaving, trying to purge his body of Lana's essence. He pushed himself away from her breast, the blood flowing across her nipple. She grabbed the back of his head and placed his face between her legs, repeating, almost in a mantra, for him to finish what she started.

He could do nothing but suck and guzzle, choking on the red liquid. She gripped his head, the obsidian dagger pressed between Mack's shoulder and neck. He imagined Lana plunging it into him and sucking every drop of life from his throat, like a harlequin nightmare.

When she released his head, Mack rose and stared at her. His body shook, adrenaline coursing through him, lips dripping her fluids.

"Lana?" He shivered in the dark.

Her body was slick with crimson. From her breasts to her crotch, between her legs, down to her toes. Lana lay, eyes vacant, staring at the mirror behind Mack.

Her chest didn't rise.

Didn't fall.

She was motionless. Her expression frozen, contorted between pleasure and shock. Her lips curled in the corner, a slight smile.

Mack placed a hand on Lana's cheek, muttering to himself. Incoherent ramblings of a shocked mind. He trembled and looked into her absent eyes. They reflected his bloodstained face, and with it the dark truth.

The dagger slipped from her fingers and plunked to the floor.

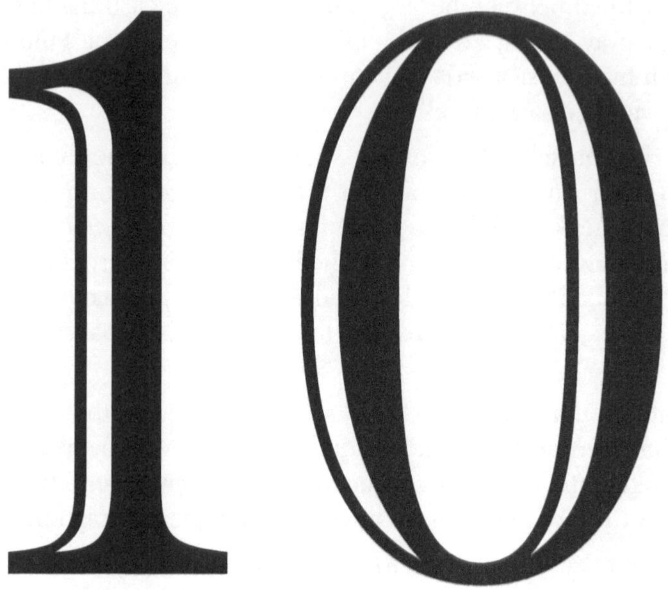

"Most people can't be alone with their thoughts. They should spend time with mine. Most involve retribution rather than forgiveness."

I THINK I'M ALONE NOW
John Bovio

R ight over left, left, right behind left, left, right over left. Wall. Turn.

Right over left, left, right behind left, left, right over left. Wall.

How long have I been here? There are no months, weeks, days, hours, minutes. Not for me. I assume the rest of the world goes on, but I don't know.

Sometimes my mind plays tricks on me. They are never funny. Whatever funny is.

No sunlight. Lights on. No clock. No sound. Only my heartbeat. And a ringing in my ears that never stops.

One, two, three, big steps. Wall.

Turn.

One, two, three, big steps. Wall.

I look at myself to see if I'm still here. A reflection from a shiny piece of metal bolted to the cinder block. It's supposed to be a mirror. We're both lying. I pull hairs from my chest one by one. Seems like a pastime.

No contact with humans. I enjoy the space. The time to think. Figure things out. Most people can't be alone with their thoughts. They should spend time with mine. Most involve retribution rather than forgiveness. We should meet so I can disappoint you.

One, two, three, four, small steps. Wall.

Turn.

One, two, three, four, small steps. Wall.

I do my push-ups, sit-ups, shadow box. My shadow takes a beating. Sometimes I beat my demons. Sometimes they beat me. I punch the wall. Left jab, right cross, straight left. Turn, pivot, left hook, right upper cut. Blood runs down the wall. My hands hurt. I think I won.

Maybe I'm not a good person. Who gets to decide? The people I hurt deserved it. My dog barked before he bit the guy. I thought he was good. My dog. The man bleeding did not. When he shot him, my dog whimpered twice, like he loved me. Maybe he was just trying to breathe.

I talk to myself. Sometimes I talk faster when the flap on the cell door opens. I know there is something like a human on the other side, about to push a tray in with some brown crap baked into a brick. The same breakfast, lunch, and dinner. Whatever those are.

They don't want me to know what time it is. And I don't. Just feed time, I guess. They never talk back from the other side of the flap.

I wish I could breathe. Feels like I am drowning. Or being waterboarded. This was the hardest to adapt to. To find the Zen in that pain. Can't lean in. Can't reduce the panic. Panic is unproductive.

But I like pain. A reminder I'm alive. My lungs hurt.

Make them hurt more!

My soul's on fire. Or something like it. People have too much of nothing. Poverty must be redistributed.

Sidestep, sidestep, sidestep. Wall.

Turn.

Sidestep, sidestep, sidestep. Wall.

Turn.

Sidestep, sidestep, sidestep. Wall.

* * *

Every 4th meal marks a new day. Every 4th block of shit gets a prison stick, a tally mark. First, the dead bolt. A slap of metal on metal. Then the clang as the slot drops open. I talk fast. A weakness, I know. Don't show them you're soft. But I've been my own audience for a long time now.

"Hey yeah, thanks. Did you cook that yourself?"

No answer.

Things I shout at the flap:

"Oh, something different."

"Great, just what I ordered."

"Where's my wine?"

"Just like mom used to make."

"I'd tip you but my cash is in my other pants."

"We should stop meeting like this."

I take the brown brick and feed my illness. It is a behavioral management tool. And like a good tool, you can pound nails with it.

I chew, chew, chew, this thing. It has no taste. Probably no nutrition. Strange they call it nutraloaf. It's an alternative meal plan. A brown, bland, earthy, not easily swallowed brick of shit.

Men come in hazmat suits. They sound like we're under water. The only word I hear is "virus." They lead me down a hall.

No windows. No sunlight.

Underground. Invisible. Not sure I exist. The more time spent in silence, the less I hear. The less I feel. If I fell would anyone hear? Would I feel it? Even the tiniest sound travels down the long underground passageway only to return after a short delay as a reflection of the noise I've created. Proof of my existence. The sound rides the bright yellow line that runs down the middle of this tunnel, to separate those coming from those going.

Like too much information, lack of sensory input causes a paralysis of the consciousness.

I'm not shackled. I could run. To be shot in the back. A sound that would certainly echo. A sound I would hear. Something to feel. Or the sound of my heart stopping. A sound no one would hear.

Information controlled. Actions controlled. What I eat. When. When I shit. Piss. Bathe. The psychological breaking of a human involves removing both sensory input and the ability to choose. Survival requires that you realize every action involves free will. As the victories get smaller, they become more important. If you do not create meaning, you do not survive. Not in a meaningful way. Whatever meaningful is.

I miss human interaction. The sound of someone's voice other than my own. I talk to myself. To books. To the wall. To the slot in the door when it opens and food is pushed through.

I don't miss love. There's nobody left to love me.

I'm strapped to a chair. Gagged. A television is wheeled in front of me. I watch a trial. Apparently my own. There is no sound and no chance to speak.

70% of dust is epidermis.

In a closed cell it's closer to 90%. Skin sheds cells to replace them. The entire epidermis is replaced once a month. Humans shed a pound of skin per year. The epidermis provides waterproofing and a barrier to infection. We do not replace the lower layer of skin, called the dermis, where scars occur.

Dust suspended in air seem to dance, a phenomenon called Brownian motion. The movement is the result of random collisions of dust particles with molecules of the air in which the dust is suspended.

Brownian motion is a rebuke to the stillness in a prison cell. It is around us all the time, indoors and out, but only noticeable when we are looking at these tiny particles in a strong light relative to the ambient light around us.

There is a crack where the light gets in. In the corner where the window has been bricked over. A sliver of light reveals the movement of the dust in the air.

I watch the dust.

Heel-toe, heel-toe, heel-toe, heel-toe. Wall.
Turn.

Heel-toe, heel-toe, heel-toe, heel-toe. Wall.

I sit in meditation. Tonglen meditation. For giving and taking. Exchanging Self with Other. Breathing in blackness. Breathing out pure white light. To clear my mind of discursive thought. To cultivate loving kindness. To develop unconditional love for all beings.

I imagine three people. One I love, one I hate, one to whom I am indifferent. I breathe in suffering, ignorance, and pain. Breathe out love and light.

I breathe in blackness. Take in the suffering of the one I hate. Breathe out a pure white light. Dark and light, suffering and healing. On the inhale I breathe in what's to be healed or transformed through my heart and beyond. On the exhale breathe out the healing from my heart and beyond. Slowly the distinctions among the three people disappear. They are the same.

In my mind I stab the person I hate in the neck again and again.

I have a ways to go.

Left over right, right, left behind right, right, left over right. Wall. Turn.

Left over right, right, left behind right, right, left over right. Wall.

Biogas is a mixture of gases produced by the breakdown of organic matter in the absence of oxygen. Anaerobic bacteria occur naturally in in the digestive tracts of humans. These bacteria eat and break down biomass and produce biogas. Biogas is composed of methane and carbon dioxide. The gas that gives human shit its stench is methane.

Human feces smell of hydrogen sulfide gas. Hydrogen sulfide gas is a powerful poison and acid. It will cause immediate and permanent fatal lung damage. When concentrated, it instantly burns the throat and trachea and the body can convulse as the lungs and airways are destroyed. Works like phosgene gas.

Please note: I never mentioned feces killing anyone.

Right over left, left, right behind left, left, right over left. Wall.

Turn.

Right over left, left, right behind left, left, right over left. Wall.

How to make a Shit Bomb:

Assemble:

- One-quart plastic Ziploc bags

- Brown paper lunch bags

- Newspaper—preferably the Metro section

To remove the oxygen from your Ziploc bag, use the water displacement method as described below.

Fill a 5-gallon bucket with water ¾ full. Place your packet in the Ziploc bag, then seal the bag, leaving two fingers width of the seal open. Next, slowly lower the bag into the bucket. As you lower the bag the water pressure pushes the oxygen out of the opening you've left. When the water is just below the Ziploc, seal the bag. You have removed the oxygen.

I'm a trickster. Or just a dumb janitor, cleaning up after you, attending to your carelessness, your sense of privilege. Doing the small unimportant things so you can make the world a better place. Thank me for my service.

They wanted to kill me. HA! I would just be a martyr. Maybe get my own TV show. A cooking show. How to cook for your enemies. How to kill with love.

Virus or bacteria? I don't know. It ate my insides until they spilled out of me. Maybe the virus and bacteria teamed up. Bacteria sepsis attacked the lungs weakened by the virus.

The media blamed the virus on all kinds of things. Radio and cell towers, people eating certain foods, the government, reptile people.

When they found my cabin in the woods, they published my manifesto and gave everyone the recipe to continue my work. Copycat bombers carried on. I was credited with far more than I accomplished.

Now I have a cellmate. Seems nice. Large-muscled. Ex-cop he

says. He might be a rapist the way he treats me. I know this type of affection.

His arm encircles my neck. Trachea at the crook of his elbow. Right arm grasps a left bicep. Left hand behind my head. Elbows brought together to pressure my carotid arteries. Oxygen cut off from my brain. My vision clouds on the periphery, then narrows to a small tunnel. I hear music. A symphony. Everything goes black.

I took my last breath before I knew I was taking it. I found a spot between heartbeats and stayed there. I thought it was the end.

Whatever the end is.

I woke alone. My friend gone. My body still feels his presence. He left an impression. Some scarring. I miss him already.

The flap drops. My loaf arrives.

"Where's my foie?"

The water like wine. A big, fruit forward Napa Valley cabernet. The kind the French hate. The loaf like a bone-in ribeye. Rare.

One, two, three, big steps. Wall.

Turn.

One, two, three, big steps. Wall.

I must go on.

11

"I held my breath and entered the biggest Manhattan apartment I had ever been in. It was also the filthiest; worse than any squat, crack house or shooting gallery I ever dragged my parents out of during the Dinkins years."

BEN AFFLECK
Eddie McNamara

I stumbled north up Seventh Avenue like a half-broken zombie. It was sunny that morning before the towers fell. Then, a white cloud of smoke and dust and debris and death hung over all of downtown, obscuring the sun.

The aftermath of the World Trade Center collapse looked like a snow globe on the news. It looked like nuclear winter in person.

There were so many sirens blaring and car alarms going off, I was probably concussed by the noise. Thousands of people walked away from the wreckage in a daze. I returned to my ambulance, thirty-seven rows deep in the queue on West Street, and waited for the injured, but they'd never show.

Nobody was coming out of that mess alive. I was lined up too far away from the action to even help wash the dust out of the eyes of the lucky ones who got out. I'm not a spectator. This is not what I signed up for. History was unfolding. I had to be a part of it. Nobody wants to hear the war story from the guy who peeled potatoes when the fighting was happening.

I left the bus, that's what we call ambulances, and headed into the belly of the beast, to get my hands, and more importantly, my uniform dirty. I spotted a beat-to-hell, trampled FDNY baseball cap on the ground and threw it on. Firefighters get better looking girls than volunteer EMTs. EMS is the low agency on the first responder totem pole—one rung above Corrections, but several standard deviations below the NYPD and FDNY. The Port Authority cops don't even make the list, but they make twice as much money as everyone else.

When it was covered in dust, my uniform looked like it belonged to a real ground zero hero. I joined the walking wounded in a parade. I could see my reflection in car windows. I looked like I just came down eighty-seven floors in that hell mess.

Off-duty nurses from St. Vincent's hospital—good souls who rushed in to work to do what needed to be done in an emergency— were the first people to help me. Real salt of the earth types who grew up in Brooklyn or Queens or Staten Island or the Bronx and went to Catholic school because the zoned public schools were terrible. Bleached blondes who didn't like children enough to become teachers. Ex-fuckups who only date cops or firemen and dream about the day some civil servant, still sleeping in his childhood bedroom, manages to save up $20,000 to buy her a diamond. Brown-skinned nurses who marry Irish boys, so their kids come out light-skinned. Hard drinking nurses who think they've made it when they move to the suburbs.

These were not my people. Even worse, they'd be able to tell the difference between my EMT uniform and the real deal.

Nurses are cops. Teachers are firemen. They're the opposite of dreamers, they're settlers who willingly trade the potential for happiness to have their basic needs met. They used to call these jobs white welfare, but I don't think you can say that anymore. That's what it is, though. Does anyone really think we need 40,000 cops and almost 10,000 firemen? How many murders and fires are happening in this city every day to justify that kind of manpower? It's fake work for zilches—a handout to the former big dumb kids at the back of the classroom who got a sixty-five on every test, and a social promotion from teachers who didn't give a fuck because they were in on the scam too.

I kept walking. The nurses were the kind of girls you pick up at Sloppy McNasty's Tuesday night happy hour.

Planes don't crash into the World Trade Center every day, and when they do, you don't waste a tragedy like that on nurses from the neighborhood.

On the next block, an English actor not too many people recognized handed me a bottle of water and thanked me. He was somehow more beautiful in person. He wore short camo shorts and had the legs of a rugby player. His chin was the size of my fist, his face so lean, his cheekbones jutted out at you like a 3-D movie. He must have been on a steroid cocktail of testosterone and growth hormone for the size, and clenbuterol for the fat shredding—no one looks that good naturally. No Englishman has those kinds of genetics. I stopped cold and gave him a thousand-yard stare that seemed appropriate given the situation. He stared back with great intensity until that shifted to empathy. We connected. Mission accomplished.

I must have been a sight in my dust-covered blue uniform. It was real dust from where the buildings went down. I could have used any dust or dirt and rubbed it into my body and uniform, but I was committed to making this look good. My face was caked with the stuff too except for where I licked my finger and drew lines which hopefully gave the impression that streams of tears flowed. A regular guy never gets to fuck anybody famous, but I'm convinced that with my attention to detail, my cock would be inside a movie star, or at least a TV star.

His boyfriend inserted himself into our moment and tried to pull The Actor away. We maintained eye contact. I mumbled, "*Dellamorte, Dellamore.*" The boyfriend seemed horrified, but I was referencing the movie I recognized the actor from. The direct translation is "from the dead, from love," and given the timing and circumstances, that was about as creepy as anything that could have come out of my mouth.

I then said the American title of the film, "*Cemetery Man,*" and that didn't help matters. The actor dropped his gaze and waved goodbye. I was no longer a hero; I was just a creepy fan. The magic was gone, and the boyfriend was there.

I kept walking. I doubled back downtown against the tide of soot-covered people looking like Victorian chimneysweeps.

Robert DeNiro's restaurant was the first of many to feed the victims and the responders. The cooks and busboys and waitstaff were out on the West Side Highway giving out plates of food. I snagged some pasta with shrimp and mussels. It was cold. Just okay. Not worth whatever they would normally charge for it.

Some worn out party girls joined older churchy ladies to distribute snack cakes next to DeNiro's people. A very Italian-looking cop in a pressed and immaculately clean uniform ushered the one in the leopard jacket into a dusty police car. What a racket these guys were already running. People were still burning alive and they're banging the Entenmann's lady.

Another of the girls used to be an actress. I recognized her from a dumb comedy that people cared about a few years earlier. She played the ugly friend. She wasn't pretty in real life either, but she was famous.

A famous five is a real world eight. Bring that girl to a club or a party and you can level up and shop in the nine and 10 section. I approached.

"Didn't expect to see you here," I said. "Thanks for helping. Respect." I pounded my heart with my fist like some kind of shaved ape.

"Sure, whatever," she said in the gravelliest, New York voice outside of Boca Raton. "I gotta do this shit for my recovery. It's that rehab humility bullshit. Want some Ding Dongs or what?"

"Who can eat a Ding Dong without something to drink?" I asked. "It's like sand."

"I made it out of there," I said, pointing to the wreckage, "I don't want to choke to death on a Drake's Cake over here."

She laughed so hard a snot bubble came out of her nose. "If you want a drink with that," she said, "let me take you to Motor City Bar and buy you one . . . or maybe 10. I choose to interpret what you said as asking me on a date."

"Deal," I said. "Wanna bail?"

She shrugged.

We walked Northeast.

"You ain't a cop, are ya?" she asked.

"Hell no," I said, "Fuck cops."

"Good, good. Part of my recovery process is identifying rock bottom. Getting day drunk and fucking a cop after the World Trade Center blew up would be a new low, even for me."

"Don't worry, I'm with FD," I lied.

People like firemen. They save kittens. Many also rob people blind when they put out a fire in their houses, but nobody ever talks about that.

As we walked to the Lower East Side, I thought about all the looting the Fire Department was probably doing right now. Hundreds of their brothers were probably crushed and buried alive, and they're raiding the cash registers and bank vaults underneath the buildings.

I grew up with these guys, I know their act. Cops and firemen are the guys who cut bagels in delis and picked up pint glasses at bars. Shiftless man-children who live with their parents until they finally inherit the house. Men without skill or ambition. They'd never get a job in the real world, so the city had to create a fake one for them. This one that makes them feel important.

A different kind of loser drank at Motor City.

Middle-aged failed rockers put destroying their livers on pause for a second to stare at me and The Actress. She waved like she was walking the red carpet. I broke off to take a piss.

I opened the door to the bathroom.

"Oh shit, it's Ben Affleck," said the girl puking into the toilet to the girl holding her hair as I forced the door open.

"I'm sorry ladies," I said, looking down with my hands flailing, "I really am, but I have to pee so badly. It couldn't wait. I didn't mean to interrupt. I'll be 45 seconds max, then you'll never see me again."

They moved away from the toilet to let me use it. I was so desperate to pee that I somehow overcame my usual shy bladder syndrome and experienced blissful relief.

"Ben Affleck, you have a beautiful cock," said the barfer, whose voice I immediately recognized as that movie actress—one of the teen stars of a generation-defining film 10 years ago. I finished peeing and looked at her. Underneath the unruly mane of badly dyed straw hair, the drying vomit on her bloated face and the running mascara, it was her: the former It girl. She seemed so out of place and sad in that graffiti- covered dive bar bathroom being tended to by a punk rock smack pixie.

Not in the bar for five minutes and I've already leveled up from Actress #1.

"I'm not really Ben Affleck."

Actress #2 (I'll call her "Nadia". That's not really her name, but neither is the exotic stage name she uses. Her real name is as boring and American as Kraft Singles) and her friend laughed.

"Stop talking," Nadia slurred, "I want to fuck Ben Affleck and you're going to be Ben Affleck—you're going to have a three-way with us. Right now."

I was confused, nervous and excited—a grossed out bumbling mess. I wasn't sure she could even properly consent to sex in her state, but I went for it—for the experience, for the sake of the story I'll be able to tell over drinks for the rest of my life.

The little one wanted nothing to do with me. The famous one smelled unwashed. Not just dirty, but dirty on top of dirty, as if she were doing research for a role as a homeless woman. She insisted on kissing. Her breath was a revolting mixture of vomit, whiskey, and clove cigarette. I had to remind myself in order to get hard, that for the first time in my life, I was about to starfuck a real celebrity, not just a scene chick who was naked on the Suicide Girls website. I mentally focused on what a disgusting scene I was participating in; the depravity turned me on. Nadia sat on the sink, hiked up her vintage miniskirt, pulled her underwear to one side, and guided me inside of her.

I asked about a condom and her friend mocked me, "Did you just crawl out of the 90s? No one wears condoms anymore." They laughed again. I reached for the friend's tiny breasts through the sides of her cut off Casualties T-shirt and she moved my hand away. Nadia sped things up to an impossible-to-maintain pace before pushing me off and dry heaving in the sink she sat on.

"Ben," Nadia said, "Let's get a drink."

"You," she snapped at the other girl, "you're boring. Leave." The Pixie gave us the middle finger and complied by exiting the bathroom first.

We moved to the bar. Actress #1 (not Nadia) had two cocktails in front of her. She saw me exit the bathroom with Nadia, downed both drinks, and mock saluted Nadia. Nadia was more famous and hotter, and even on such a crazy day, the natural order of the world was restored.

I ordered two Jack and Cokes and put a 20 down. Jackie, the Bettie Page lookalike tending bar, pushed my money back and said, "She doesn't pay for drinks." Everyone loves a celebrity, even a cracked-out shell of one.

As the drinks flowed Nadia seemed to become more coherent with each sip. She was funny: "Matt Damon looks like a leprechaun . . . he can act his ass off . . . best American actor working today. You . . . you're very good at playing you . . . but you've fucked J-Lo and that's far more impressive than an Oscar nomination."

"Who fucked J-Lo?" asked the greasy looking rock n' roll burnout drinking alone, staring and listening to our conversation.

"He did," said Nadia as she attempted to make an introduction between me and the guy butting in, "Roddy, this is Ben Affleck. Ben, this is Roddy, he plays bass in The Stasi. Say hi."

"Nadia, your brain is fried," Roddy said. "That guy's just some security guard who looks a little like Ben Affleck. I hope you didn't fuck him," he said with a put-on laugh.

"Fuck yourself, Roddy," Nadia said.

"Time for me to take you home," Roddy said.

Jackie put her hand over mine and quietly but sternly told me, "Don't let him take her home. He's bad for her. Do me this favor—get her home safe and you'll never pay for a drink in here again. Promise me!"

I made the promise. I could get her home safe. I had over 2,000 hours as an EMT for Delta Volunteer Ambulance in Bay Ridge. I wasn't a drug user—just a sometimes-drunk who could save a life if I really had to.

I stood over Roddy, still sitting on his barstool. I was half his age, half a foot taller and had fifty pounds on him. "Alright, tough guy," Roddy said, "You win. Have fun with her. I hope you get whatever STD she has this week."

Jackie mouthed "Thank you", as I ignored the old man and walked arm in arm, steadying Nadia for the four-block walk to her Clinton Street apartment.

We stopped at La Placinta, a bodega at Clinton and Rivington for a quart of coconut water, bananas, and a bottle of Aleve—a preventative measure that has saved me from hundreds of potential hangovers.

I could smell Nadia's apartment before she was able to coordinate herself to fit the right key in the lock. The odor of a supermarket dumpster in the summer filled the narrow hallway. She opened the door and it intensified and morphed, olfactory violations of new and terrible varieties. I held my breath and entered the biggest Manhattan apartment I had ever been in. It was also the filthiest; worse than any squat, crack house or shooting gallery I ever dragged my parents out of during the Dinkins years.

Piles of plastic bags and half-eaten takeout meals in Styrofoam containers were knee-high in some places. I had to kick Subway sandwich wrappers, empty cans of energy drinks and chicken bones away to clear a path to Nadia's bedroom.

I had her sit up and drink the entire coconut water. She cursed me with every sip. The banana was a battle too. I told her that a dose of potassium now would make her morning bearable, but she scratched at my hand with fingernails so dirty, they looked like she polished them with black varnish. Her fingers sickened me. There were obvious burns from a crack torch lighter that cooked the skin around her fingertips. The dirt under her nails was beyond anything I'd seen from even the most down and out indigent patient. She stomped on the banana with the last bit of fight left in her.

I told her the football-shaped Aleve were Xanax blues. She swallowed four and passed out. I covered her with a stained blanket and looked for a place to crash.

I found a couch buried under an avalanche of magazines and crumpled clothing. I tried to sleep but couldn't. A burst of energy came over me and I started cleaning like my mother used to on the days when she was flush with rocks. I went back to the bodega for trash bags and cleaning supplies and became a one-man cleaning crew.

Hours passed as I scraped and scoured surfaces, then filled seven bags with trash, glassine envelopes, blood-stained syringes, broken water pipes, soiled underwear, and hundreds of old school "We're pleased to serve you" blue, to-go coffee cups. I hardly made a dent.

From time to time, I'd check in on Nadia. She was dead to the world, but her chest rose and fell with each respiration—the most comforting sight in the world for the child of junkies.

"Who the fuck are you? How'd you get in here?" were her first words of the day as she shambled into the living room, appearing far less concerned than she sounded.

"I'm Luke. We met last night at Motor City. Jackie asked me to take you home. She was creeped out by some guy Roddy. You were pretty messed up"

"Aww, Jackie's a sweetheart. You too . . . unless you fucked me when I was passed out. Did you fuck me?"

"No, no," I said, "I tried to sleep on the couch, but I couldn't, so I started to clean up."

"Wait, we didn't fuck?"

"Well, kind of." I said, "in the bathroom of Motor—for like a few seconds. You don't remember? You thought I was Ben Affleck. You were in the bathroom with some chick, you suggested we have a threesome, but she wasn't into it."

"That's Sylvi," said Nadia, "She's a gold star dyke. She wouldn't be into anything with penis. You don't look anything like Ben Affleck. Thanks for getting me home, though. You look like a cop. Are you a cop?"

"I'm a volley."

"A what?"

"Oh, right. I'm a volunteer EMT. I brought my ambulance down to the trade center to help."

"Help what?"

"People," I said. "You know that the World Trade Center was attacked. The buildings were demolished. You know this right?"

"Fuck you, Ben Affleck. That didn't happen. I wasn't that high."

"Seems like you were."

She smiled and pushed stacks of unopened mail from her kitchen counter to the floor, giving her room to set up a couple of stained blue cardboard coffee cups with Nescafe and Splenda.

"No problem," I said, "seemed like Jackie wanted me to look out for you or at least keep you away from that guy."

"Yeah," she grunted. "He'd fuck me if I passed out. He always does."

She handed me a cup of lukewarm instant coffee.

"Don't think you're going to make a score going through my shit while pretending to clean," she said. "The only thing of value left in this whole apartment is a Golden Globe from 1995. I sold, shot, or snorted everything else, or somebody stole it. I keep that to remind myself—"

"I haven't seen it." I said, taking notice of the thin dried lines of blood spatter on the walls and ceiling.

I suggested that we get her cleaned up. I scrubbed her bathtub until it was only half as vile as when I found it. I used a kitchen sponge to wash the layers of grime off her body. It was long and sinewy, not what you'd expect to see from someone with a face so bloated. Some of the spots didn't wash off. The bruises on her legs looked like the ones on an overripe apple, and there were dark purple halos between her toes. I cleaned under her nails with toothpicks while she lathered her hair with dish soap. When the water turned dark gray, we'd drain the tub, rinse the dirt, and fill it again. It took three baths to get her clean, and finally her eyes came to life a little.

I wondered how much a sex tape would be worth. Would the squalor add value or would celebrity filth like this seem too off-putting for the viewer?

"Why are you doing this? Why are you being so kind to me?" she asked.

"Because" I said, "you need someone to."

"You're not going to start talking about Jesus now, are you? This isn't some kind of religious bullshit, is it?"

"Hell no."

"Did my mother or my agent hire you?"

"Neither" I said. "It just seemed like the right thing to do."

"So, do you go around helping lost junkies, or just lost famous junkies?"

"I just have some experience with this kind of thing. You remind me of my mother," I said. I remembered her lying on the floor, her dead eyes open wide. "That's why I hung around."

She started to cry, then threw her arms around me and laughed. "Gross! Your mother!?" She caught a glimpse of herself in the mirror.

"I can't die looking like this. I have to get hot again before I even consider ODing. Are you hungry?"

I walked to San Loco and bought an enormous bag of Guaco Tacos and hit up Video Stop for an entire season of *Law and Order* on DVD, which Nadia somehow managed to avoid even hearing about. I spent three days there. Between her naps, screaming fits, insane mood swings, crying episodes, vomiting, and alternating sweating and freezing we ate messy tacos and binge watched Jerry Orbach put away criminals and drop one-liners.

That's all I really remember besides abandoning my ambulance on the West Side Highway. They had me listed as one of the missing and presumed dead for almost a week. Turns out, you can't get fired you from an unpaid job.

We didn't fall in love or even fool around. We didn't leave her apartment and she didn't use the whole time. It was the most boring detox I've ever witnessed. On the third night she told me she was ready for rehab and her agent had arranged for an inpatient program.

I waited with her until the Town Car came to take her away. She was afraid of messing up, but not fiending hard enough to actually do it.

I carried her bags to the curb, and she kissed me on the forehead. I waved goodbye and when she was gone, I tapped the Golden Globe in my back pocket as a fire engine's siren screamed in the distance.

12

"As I open the lounge windows, I hear Nonna scream. My mouth is dry. Something terrible has happened."

HAIR
Anthea Pretorius

I walked up to my room on the path baked hard by the Karoo sun, the path I have walked—twice daily, in all kinds of weather—for the past thirty-two years.

"Ai! Ai! Ai!" I shout as I run on feet and legs that have forgotten they are tired. My son turns towards me. I throw my arms around his too-thin body.

"Shadrack!" My hands shake. With my apron I dry my tears. He smiles and I see the love in his eyes, but I also see that his smiling lips hold little joy. I open the door, pour water into the kettle and put it on the paraffin stove. We sit outside under the tree. Three years have passed since I last saw him and I have many questions.

His father, Jonas, was a farm worker. He was good with the sheep but drank too much and was often in trouble with Baas Piet. When he was drunk, he picked fights with the other workers, and beat Shadrack and me. I feared him.

One terrible month-end Jonas, his eyes red and his fist ready, started assaulting me using his fists and his feet. Shadrack, who was seventeen, tried to stop Jonas but his father threw him from the hut. I screamed for help. Two other workers, Themba and Petros, dragged Jonas outside. There was much shouting. Jonas grabbed a piece of wood and hit Themba, then shoved Petros backwards into the fire, where his shirt caught alight. The black pot overturned. Themba hit Jonas with a bottle until he fell down. Alinah, Themba's sister, ran to the farmhouse to call Baas Piet, who was furious.

We all had to get into the bakkie. Shadrack and I sat in the front and the three men were on the back. Petros died just as we drove through the farm gate on to the main road and Jonas stopped breathing soon after we reached the hospital. Jonas had broken my nose and fractured three of my ribs. My eyes were swollen shut. Shadrack had suffered broken fingers, a snapped collarbone, bruises and two fractured ribs. We spent three days in the hospital. It was a very bad time for us.

I am proud of Shadrack. He passed Grade 12 with two distinctions. Baas Piet advised Shadrack to look for a job in town but work opportunities were scarce, so he left for Cape Town. For seven months I had heard nothing from him. At night I lay awake worrying about him. When winter came Shadrack returned, but I could see that life in the city had not treated him well. He was dirty, tired and very hungry. His clothes were faded rags. He slept and ate, and slept again. Nonna gave us some of her son Hendrik's old clothes and a pair of shoes. Shadrack was ashamed but he accepted the clothes. Soon afterwards he left again. That was three years ago but today he has unexpectedly returned and I am overjoyed.

I give Shadrack the food I brought home. While he eats, I tell him that Nonna's sons and daughter are coming to the farm for the weekend and are bringing friends. I've cleaned the cottage down by the dam. Tomorrow I will bake cakes and fresh bread.

Shadrack nods. I ask him what kind of work he does and he tells me that he is a security guard. "Is the pay good?" I ask.

"Aikona!" he says shaking his head, "long hours for little pay."

I click my tongue to show my sympathy. He goes outside while I wash, then he comes inside again. From his bag he takes a pair of new takkies, socks, a blue jersey, two kopdoeke and Lux soap, Vaseline, candles, a black skirt and a white blouse. He also pulls out a small soft blanket wrapped in plastic. I clap my hands. My cheeks are wet as I thank him.

"I didn't know what you need, Ma Becca."

"Nothing, my son. I have you. I have work. I have a roof, a bed and food."

Shadrack clenches his fists. When he speaks, his voice is tense. "You have worked here for years and all you have is second-hand clothes, no money, too little food, no toilet, and no pension. It's a rubbish life. You have nothing!"

I bend my head low, afraid to look into the face of my son. Life is hard, I know, but to carry this weight inside is not good. I speak soft words to my son and later we sleep.

At five the next morning I am in the kitchen. At two o'clock two cakes stand on the dining-room table, the salads are in the fridge, the chops and steaks are in the steel dish and the teacups stand ready on the tray. Baas Piet is still in town. Nonna asks me if Jakes has put enough firewood in the boma down by the dam. I cannot find Jakes. He must be at the bottom kraal. I ask Shadrack to help me take wood down to the cottage. We walk behind the blue gum trees and load a wheelbarrow high with hardekool. Shadrack stacks the wood neatly and puts a few logs in the fireplace inside the cottage. Then he pushes the wheelbarrow back to the woodpile and walks back to my room.

"Hendrik will be delighted to see that you've baked your delicious chocolate cake, Rebecca. You know how much he likes it," Nonna says.

We hear the sound of cars and Nonna goes out to greet the visitors. I fill the kettle and make tea. When they come inside, everything is ready.

While they are enjoying their tea and cake, I sit in the scullery knitting another beanie for our church—beanies to keep the ears of poor children warm.

The young people drive down to the cottage. I wash the dishes. I take four vetkoek with mince, a banana and the last slice of chocolate cake for my son. Shadrack's face lights up and he eats. We talk until late. We hear music and laughter. We smell the meat on the braai.

"Ma Becca, I have to go back tomorrow."

There are still many things I wish to know of his life in the city, but the time for questions has run out. Much later I fall asleep.

Shadrack rises quietly, looks down at his mother's sleeping face and slips outside. His backpack is in the fork of the tree. He puts on socks and shoes. He has hidden R200 in the mealie meal tin. Ma Becca will find it later. He looks back lovingly at the dark hut, then he runs towards the dam, where he watches the inebriated youngsters. The girls complain that they are cold, so they all go indoors. Hendrik lights the fire in the grate. He doesn't know that beneath the wood are three CDs waiting for the heat. Shadrack sits patiently in the dark. When he thinks that enough time has passed, he stealthily approaches one of the windows. All the youngsters are sprawled in chairs and on the couches, sound asleep. The fumes have done their work. He puts on gloves, slips into the cottage and opens the sliding door and windows to air the room. From his backpack he removes zip-lock plastic bags and a hair clipper.

Shadrack props the girl with the long blond hair up with a cushion behind her back. He kneels, shaves her head with long, efficient strokes, catches the hair, places each strand carefully into a plastic bag and closes it securely. The brunette is next, then the boy with the ponytail. He leaves the hated Hendrik for last. After shaving off his hair, Shadrack also carelessly shaves a portion of Hendrik's carefully cultivated beard. He puts everything into the empty backpack, closes the windows and door, removes the gloves and unseen, he takes a shortcut to the national road a few kilometers away.

I wake up early, painfully aware of my son's absence. I cry in the dark. My body feels tired as I walk up the path to start the day's work. There is no movement at the cottage by the dam. I fry bacon, boerewors and eggs, and cook mealie meal porridge and slice the bread. I lay the table. I grind coffee beans and put them in the percolator.

On the steps at the back door, I sit and knit the last blue beanie from the wool Nonna bought. I hear her footsteps, so I put away my knitting and place the bag on the washing machine before walking into the kitchen.

"Good morning, Nonna."

"Morning, Rebecca," she says with a smile. "The children will probably be here soon. I am going to shower and dress."

An hour later no-one has appeared, so Baas Piet and Nonna drive down to the cottage. I make their bed and tidy the bathroom. As I open the lounge windows, I hear Nonna scream. My mouth is dry. Something terrible has happened. Nonna screams again and I shiver.

More than a hundred kilometers away, Shadrack is seated in an over-full taxi rocking its way towards KwaZulu-Natal, where he has been an apprentice to a sangoma for the past three years.

He smiles. *She will be thrilled with the powerful muti I am bringing!*

* * *

When Baas Piet and Nonna arrive, I peep through the curtains. Poenskop—*all of them!* I cannot believe my eyes. I run to the kitchen thinking *Shadrack! Is this the work of my son?* I cannot breathe. I must think. *No one saw him. No one knows he was here.* I hear the family enter the lounge. Nonna appears in the kitchen door. Her eyes are red.

"Nonna, what happened?"

"Their hair. It's their hair. It's gone!" Nonna is shaking. "Bring us fresh coffee, please. Make it strong." Nonna turns around and walks out. She is unsteady on her feet.

I place the hot coffee on the tray. Everyone is pale. Today there is no excited talking and laughter.

"I have a terrible headache," one of the girls says, "I can't face any food."

As I reach the kitchen the telephone rings. Baas Piet answers it in the passage.

Nonna comes back into the kitchen. "The police are on their way."

Then she sees the blue beanie next to my bag of wool on the washing machine.

"Rebecca, you should give the beanies to the children soon. The winter has started early this year . . ."

I take the stack of bright beanies I have knitted out of the bag and look at them. They are for the church, for my people. My hands shake. I turn around slowly. There is something bitter in my throat. I hold the beanies tight against my chest. I find I cannot look Nonna in the eye.

13

"She knew stealing was wrong, but she couldn't stop herself. Shoplifting was like roller blading through a minefield."

LAND MINES
Mark Jonathan Harris

Dana stands at a table of scarves in the men's department of Bloomingdales, feeling the softness of the cashmere, wondering if the price is too high for an apology. Does admitting you're sorry always have to cost more than you can afford? The pale gray Burberry check scarf is handsome, a perfect match for Jeremy's tan overcoat. Its expense makes it an even greater act of contrition. She glances around the store as she strokes the delicate Scottish wool. The nearest salesgirl is walking toward the dressing rooms with another customer. Dana's heart pounds, her stomach flutters, adrenaline courses through her. It's been years since she did this, but she quickly folds the scarf and stuffs it inside her large purse.

She started stealing at twelve, about three months after they moved to Los Angeles so her father could teach painting at Cal State Northridge. The San Fernando Valley wasn't a place she would have chosen to live. Then, her father and Robin never asked her. The ugly public school—a bunch of low buildings surrounded by cement and a steel fence—wasn't her choice either. Only shoplifting was.

At first, she took only what was small enough to fit inside her pocket—bubble gum, candy, lipstick, a pressed flower key ring. She did most of her shoplifting at the Rite Aid a few blocks from her new school. To avoid suspicion, she always bought something else. Buy a Coke, steal a compact. Pay for the chips, but not the M&Ms.

The first time her heart was racing so fast she felt she would faint right there at the register. When she finally caught her breath—a block past the drug store—and bit into the stolen Almond Joy, her stomach recoiled. She quickly ditched the candy in the street. Yet two days later she was at it again.

What she didn't eat she kept in a shoebox in her closet. Sometimes she'd take the box out at night and lay her treasures on her bed. Pathetic, most of them, cheesy made in China junk she'd never think of buying. They gave her pleasure nonetheless. Like post cards or souvenirs of places she'd visited. She remembered where and when she'd stolen each of them. Mementoes of her secret life, one that set her apart from all the other fifth grade rejects.

The teachers at Topeka Drive Elementary were younger and peppier than in her last school in Chicago, but the children were no friendlier. All that made school bearable was that she could walk there by herself. While her teachers droned on about math problems that bored her, or vocabulary words she never used, she planned which stores to steal from. The anticipation, the uncertainty, the risk of getting caught, was more exciting than any video game. The sweaty palms, the knot of fear in her stomach as she entered a store, the mix of relief and exhilaration when she emerged safely, thrilled her.

After a few months of petty drug store theft, she lengthened her route home to include the mall, moving upscale to brand names. Glittery Monet earrings, a pink and turquoise Tumi change purse, Ralph Lauren sunglasses. She never entered a store with a particular object in mind. She would just wander around and see what caught her eye. The items had to be small, something she could fit in the pockets of her father's navy pea coat—a coat he wore all the time in New York before her mother ditched him for a more successful artist. She'd rescued it from a pile of clothes Robin was donating to Goodwill when they moved from Chicago. Perhaps the coat was a mistake, called unwanted attention to her. The cuffs were frayed and the wide shoulders spilled over her slender frame. Other kids mocked her for it. "Where did you steal that? From some homeless bag lady?" Still, the jacket was warm and comforting on cool mornings and the pockets deep enough for all kinds of booty.

She knew stealing was wrong, but she couldn't stop herself. Shoplifting was like roller blading through a minefield. All her senses were heightened. She saw more, heard more; even her gum tasted sharper. Although she feared that at any moment there might be an explosion, the danger made her feel alive.

One rainy day, walking out of Nordstrom with a purloined Liz Claiborne scarf, she felt a hand on her shoulder. She turned to face a twenty-something blonde with too much lipstick and too smug a look. "Can I see your sales slip, please?"

She felt a heaviness, like wet cement, slowly fill her body. She'd finally hit a mine. She wondered if this was how soldiers felt when one exploded.

"A classic choice." The voice behind her at Bloomingdales is male.

Startled, Dana whirls to face a slender Black salesclerk she failed to notice before.

"But way too expensive." She tightens the grip on her purse to contain her panic and steps away from the table, her heart pounding against her ribs.

"You can't go wrong with Burberry."

"I could. You can't imagine how much." She laughs shakily at her narrow escape. "But thanks, I'll remember that." She laughs again, too loudly, as she rushes away from the puzzled clerk. She has to be unhinged to let another scarf tempt her into shoplifting. Is she trying to be caught again?

They made her wait in the office of Nordstrom's security chief, a short, mustached man in a pale blue shirt who looked as bored as the uniformed guard at her school. She sat in an uncomfortable plastic chair beneath a bank of television monitors bolted to the wall above her. The security chief sat across from her at his bare desk cleaning his fingernails with a paper clip.

He asked only which parent he should telephone. After that, silence.

He remained at his desk, eyes flicking back and forth between his nails and the monitors above her, ignoring her on purpose, she supposed. Let the kid squirm awhile, worry what will happen next. She had no clue what that would be. They didn't throw kids in jail for shoplifting, did they?

Her father took only a half hour to get there, less time than when he forgot to pick her up from her guitar lesson the week before. He was in his studio when they called and he arrived in jeans and a paint-spattered T-shirt underneath his windbreaker. He glanced at her in bewilderment as he entered the office, as if unsure she really was his daughter.

The security chief sat them both down across from his desk. "Your daughter's very young to be stealing," he said, handing her father the gold paisley silk scarf she'd swiped.

Harold ignored the evidence, reached for his wallet instead, and pulled out a credit card. "I'm happy to pay for it," he offered.

"That's not the point." The security chief pulled the scarf back. "Shoplifting's a serious offense."

"I realize that. I understand how serious this is . . ." Harold launched into a long and conciliatory apology, explaining that they had just moved to Northridge in August, that it was a difficult adjustment for the whole family, that Dana had never been in trouble like this before. They often shopped at this store, always paid their bills on time. He repeated his willingness to pay for the scarf.

The longer he talked, the deeper Dana plunged her hands into the pockets of his pea coat. Did all parents of shoplifters grovel like this? She wanted to scream at him to stop.

Perhaps his pleading embarrassed the security chief as well, because after a few minutes he agreed that there was no need to report this. "Just keep your daughter out of our store," he warned. "Because the next time we catch her, my first call is to the police."

They were both silent in the car. "I don't get it," Harold finally spoke. "You don't even wear scarves."

"I thought it was pretty."

"A lot of things are pretty, Dana, but stealing? What the hell were you thinking?"

The scarf was the kind her real mother wore. She'd thought of giving it to her if she ever visited L.A.

Harold kept staring at the road, waiting for an explanation. She had no answer that would please him.

"I know it's hard starting all over again," he finally said when they pulled into the driveway of the ugly ranch house they were renting. "But if you don't talk to us, Dana, we can't help. We want to understand . . ." He let the question dangle.

"I messed up, okay?" she muttered because she wanted to end the conversation.

Robin didn't want to talk about it either. She went into the bedroom with her father and shut the door. When they emerged an hour later, her stepmother had arranged an appointment for her with a shrink.

Dana's pulse throbs in her temples as she ducks into a gastropub. She sits in a booth and orders an Old Fashioned to collect herself. Although she rarely drinks more than wine, and certainly not at three in the afternoon, she needs to calm her agitation. It was truly mad to steal the scarf. She thinks of the shame and humiliation she just avoided; she imagines Jeremy's mortification if he had to retrieve her from the police station. Would he grovel like her father? Would he even come to get her? She'd hoped that moving in with him might bring them closer; it only magnified her faults. After 15 months living together, the qualities that had attracted him—her breezy free-spirits and disregard for convention—had become grave defects of character. His discovery yesterday of a stack of parking tickets in the glove compartment of her Honda reminded him again of all her flaws.

"Jesus! Don't you put money in the meters?"

"Sometimes the time runs out."

He added up the fines. "There are 200 bucks of tickets here."

"I know. I've been meaning to take care of them."

"You mean you haven't paid them yet?" Her negligence launched a tirade of indignation. How could she just ignore the tickets?

"You've made your point," she said after a minute. Yet he wouldn't or couldn't stop. The tickets were part of a larger pattern that somehow she failed to grasp: the unwashed dishes in the sink, the clutter on her dresser, the laundry piling up in her closet. And couldn't she even make the bed in the morning? He was still railing about her faults when they pulled into the parking garage of their North Hollywood apartment building. What the hell was wrong with her?

"Say something for Christ sakes," he shouted.

"So, dear, tell me about yourself." The psychiatrist was short and squat with graying hair and little makeup. Dr. Rosenthal leaned back in her leather chair and peered intently at her.

Dana shifted uneasily in her chair.

The doctor waited.

Dana's eyes wandered around the cluttered office. She took in the children's drawings on the wall, the wicker basket stuffed with toys, the wild-haired Barbies and helmeted G.I. Joes, the Victorian dollhouse with the tiny, uniformed maid standing at its front door, the large sand tray on a side table. Her gaze kept drifting back to the small but conspicuous stain on Dr. Rosenthal's cream silk blouse.

"You have a spot on your blouse," she said.

The doctor looked down at the offending blotch. "I'm sure the dry cleaners can get it out."

The stain looked like salad dressing or maybe grease, something fattening the shrink shouldn't have had for lunch. "What if they can't?"

Dr. Rosenthal looked at her a moment. "Are you asking about the blouse or about yourself?"

She felt her cheeks go hot.

"This isn't the dry cleaners, Dana. You're not here to be cleaned up or repaired or for me to remove whatever spots or defects you or your parents might think you have. My job is to help you understand your feelings so you can make the best choices for yourself. Do you understand?"

She stared at the stain again. She was sure the blouse was ruined. She glanced at her silly Cinderella watch with its cheap fabric strap to see how much longer she had to sit there. Though her father and stepmother could force her to see a shrink, they couldn't make her speak.

Dana sits in the darkened restaurant, replaying the morning's argument. "I don't know what you want me to say," she finally said. "That I'm a slob, irresponsible, that I let everything go to hell. Okay, you're right. I'm a terrible person."

Jeremy slammed the dashboard with his hand, as if he wanted to strike her instead. "I hate when you do that. It's not what I mean."

She felt a scream, trapped somewhere in her chest, struggling to break out, but she couldn't find words to release it.

"You're depressed, listless. In a terrible rut. You need to see someone—a therapist, a psychiatrist, somebody who can shake you out of it. It's obvious I can't."

Her father and Robin had thrown up their hands as well. She was so hapless, so deficient, that only a professional with advanced degrees could fix her.

"School okay today?" her father asked as he drove her to her third appointment with the shrink.

The truth, she knew, wasn't what he was asking for. Did he really want to hear how she spent the day trying to be invisible? It was a strategy she'd adopted in her last school in Chicago, one of four cities in which she'd lived because her father kept moving from one teaching job to another. Never speak in class unless the teacher calls on you. Avoid talking to the other girls. Eat alone rather than sit next to a weirdo or a loser. Better to be ignored than shunned, although it was always hard to tell why other kids weren't speaking to you.

To fend off more questions, Dana popped a piece of bubble gum in her mouth and turned on the radio.

"Would you please just pick a station and stick to it?" Harold stopped her hand as she switched from station to station.

She was happy to see his irritation surface. She didn't trust any of his and Robin's fake solicitude. They both had been acting as if they'd just read some book on how to be a good parent and were faithfully following its advice. Do not nag your child. Do not ask uncomfortable questions. Be patient, respectful. Give your child the space she needs. Or maybe they were just waiting for Dr. Rosenthal's miracle cure to kick in.

She clicked the radio off. "You ever go to a shrink?" she asked.

He hesitated a moment before answering. "As a matter of fact, I did."

"When?" She eased up on the gum.

"In college."

"You never told me before."

"I only went a few times."

"You get cured that fast?"

"I was having trouble sleeping at night, so I went to the health center for some sleeping pills. They wouldn't give me any unless I saw a therapist."

"Oh . . ." Her father's insomnia was disappointing. She had hoped for a fault or an affliction that they shared, a reason her mother had left both of them. She started to form another bubble with her tongue.

"Why do you ask about the shrink?" he said cautiously.

The bubble broke and she cleaned the gum off her face. "Just wondering."

"Well, I dropped out of school shortly afterwards and had no trouble sleeping after that."

"Yeah, but you can't drop out of grade school, can you?" she said and turned to the side window.

"If school's the problem, Dana . . ."

"Then what? We'll move again."

"I wish . . ." he started, then changed his mind.

"Yeah, if wishes were horses," she repeated the nursery rhyme her birth mother had often recited and flipped the radio on to end their conversation.

Harold remained silent until they pulled into the driveway of Dr. Rosenthal's office, which was attached to her hillside home. She quickly opened the door and started up the stone steps to the doctor's office.

"Have a good session," he called after her, as if he were dropping her off at her guitar lesson.

Dana orders a second Old Fashioned. Although the first slowed her heart rate, her mind is still racing. She isn't sure what she expects from the alcohol. Will there be revelation or amnesia at the bottom of the glass?

If she's so screwed up, so defective, why did Jeremy invite her to move in with him? And why is she always the one who must apologize? What about his flaws? The defects in *his* character? His self-righteousness, his constant faultfinding and disapproval. She wonders what Dr. R would say about him. Would the psychiatrist be surprised if she showed up on her doorstep again? What would she say about the stolen scarf inside her purse?

Each appointment, Dana expected her to bring up the shoplifting, but she never did. She suspected that the therapist was sneakier than she looked. She wanted you to believe she was a kindly Jewish grandmother who never heard a problem that couldn't be cured with chicken soup, while all the time she was just luring you to confess.

"I received the test results from your school today," Dr. R. announced at their fourth session. "You are a very bright girl, Dana, yet you're not doing very well in school."

"School's boring."

"They often are."

Dr. R. waited. She had the patience of a rock. At the rates her parents were paying, Dana imagined the shrink could wait happily for years.

"I don't give a shit about school."

"What do you give a shit about, dear?"

Dana laughed. It was funny to hear Dr. R. swear.

"Well?" the shrink smiled.

She looked around the office at the toys and objects Dr. R. had collected over the years. On the end table by the couch was a pretty, carved wooden bird, from Mexico she guessed. She wondered if it was valuable.

"What about your parents? Do you care what they think?" Dr. R. was uncharacteristically pushy.

She shrugged. "My father and Robin are already disappointed in me."

"And how do you know that?"

"I see the way they look." Her stomach tightened. "They want a different daughter."

"Different?"

"Yeah . . ." The tightness rose to her chest.

"And what do they want you to be?" the shrink prodded.

"What I'm not," Dana snapped. "Prettier . . . chattier . . . thinner. I don't know. *Different . . .*"

"That makes you angry."

"Duh," Dana mocked her.

"And now I'm making you angry."

"This is *stupid.*"

"Feelings are never stupid, Dana. They give us information about ourselves and about the world. But when we don't pay attention to them, we can become dumb. Even a girl as bright as you are."

"So I am dumb then." Her whole chest began to ache.

"About your feelings, yes."

"Well, my parents must be too, because they're paying you a lot of money for nothing."

"Go on," the doctor encouraged. "It's good to see your anger."

"Fuck you!" The force of it surprised Dana almost as much as the words. She sank back into the couch, wanting to vanish. She wouldn't let that happen again.

"And your birth mother, does she feel that way too?" Dr. R. persisted.

"I haven't seen her since New York. She just sends birthday cards."

"That must make you angry too."

Dana stared at the wooden bird on the table to avoid the shrink's gaze. She wondered what Dr. R. would do if she smashed the carving.

"It's not going to bring her back," Dana said.

"Neither will holding back your feelings."

The pressure in Dana's chest swelled like a balloon about to burst. The roaring in her ears drowned out everything the shrink was saying. She had tripped on another land mine and there was only one way to keep it from exploding. The moment the doctor opened the door to release her, Dana palmed the wooden bird on the table. As soon as she slipped it into her pocket, she was able to breathe again.

Her relief lasted only through dinner.

After dropping her at home, her father had returned to his studio to work. He often retreated there when he and Robin were fighting. Dana rarely heard them argue. When they were angry at each other, they just stayed away. Now she was alone with a sullen Robin.

She ate quickly, placed her dishes in the washer, and fled to her bedroom. She closed the door and took out her box of trophies from the closet. Spreading them across her bed, she saw how pitiful they were. She wondered now why she had stolen any of them. Only Dr. R.'s beautiful carving was worth keeping. The multicolored bird with its huge red eyes was the most striking object she'd ever stolen. The thought that Dr. R. would be bereft at its loss had made her strangely happy. But imagining Dr. R. now, rummaging through her cluttered office for the carving, Dana felt a queasiness in her stomach. The thought that the bird's loss might pain the doctor made her ashamed. It was one thing to steal from Nordstrom, another to swipe something valuable from someone who would miss it. A sour taste of the leftover lasagna Robin had warmed for dinner rose in her throat. She swallowed hard to keep from heaving.

Suddenly the door swung open and Robin stood at the entrance to her bedroom holding her backpack. Her stepmother's stunned look at the loot scattered across the bed revealed her dismay. Dana instinctively shoved the wooden bird under her pillow. "You're supposed to knock!" she yelled and rushed toward the door.

Robin backed away before Dana slammed it.

"I'm sorry," Robin apologized from the hallway. "I didn't mean to startle you. I thought you'd want your books."

Dana quickly propped a chair against the door to make sure Robin wouldn't reenter.

"You don't have to do that, Dana. I promise I'll knock next time. Really, I'm sorry . . ."

Dana flung herself on the bed. Robin could make all the promises she wanted, but Dana had seen the horror on her face. There was nothing she could do to erase it or change her stepmother's despairing view of her; she was as hopeless as her father's tattered pea coat, which Robin was so eager to toss out.

The nose-ringed, punk-haired waitress asks Dana if she wants another cocktail, as if she's a sorry lush who drinks by herself in the afternoon. She doesn't want another Old Fashioned; she doesn't want to return to the apartment either. The alcohol or the memory of her stepmother makes her stomach squish. Or maybe it's the Burberry in her purse that's roiling her gut, forcing her to her feet. She grabs her purse and rushes to the rest room. Standing over the toilet, she can only retch.

She splashes cold water on her face at the sink and takes deep breaths to calm herself. It sickens her that she's stolen the scarf. The gift would hardly make up for all Jeremy finds lacking in her. If caught, her arrest would only have confirmed his worst beliefs about her. A familiar heaviness comes over her, an ache and weariness that makes her want to sleep.

The moment she started up the steps to Dr. R's, she felt the pressure mounting in her chest again. Her stomach clenched and her palms were sweaty. But Dr. R. said nothing about the stolen bird.

What was she waiting for? She had to have noticed it was gone. Yet here she was asking about Chicago? Did Dana have friends there? Did she like her old school?

Dana barely heard her. The shrink swam in and out of focus.

"Are you all right, dear?" Dr. R. reached out to feel her forehead. Dana instinctively recoiled.

"You look so pale. Do you have a fever?"

"I . . . I stole your bird . . ." Dana blurted it out without expecting to.

"I thought you might have," Dr. R. said calmly. "It's a beautiful carving, isn't it?"

Tears stung Dana's eyes. "You're not angry?"

The doctor shook her head. "Did taking it make you feel better?"

"For a little while . . ."

"That's one of the troubles with stealing. The pleasure doesn't last very long. Then you have to steal again."

Dana had discovered that herself.

"There are other ways to tell people you're angry with them," the doctor continued.

"I'll bring it back."

"I'd appreciate that. I'm very fond of that bird. My husband bought it for me in Oaxaca."

Tears spilled down Dana's cheeks.

Dr. R. passed her the Kleenex box. "Maybe you were angry at me for what I said last week and wanted to hurt me, but look at how much you're hurting yourself. You don't have to punish yourself like this for feeling angry."

Dana's tears kept coming. "They all want someone different . . . My dad, my stepmom . . . My real mother left because she hated having me . . ."

The doctor leaned forward and handed her another tissue from the box. "I don't know your mother, Dana, but I do know this, and I know it from all my experience as a doctor: you're not the reason your mother left you. When a parent gives up her child, it's never the child's fault."

Dr. R leaned back in her chair and let Dana weep.

Dana pays the check and leaves the restaurant. The late afternoon light is already fading as it had years before when she slowly descended the stone steps from Dr. R.'s office to her father's waiting car.

Harold looked closely at her as she fastened her seat belt. "How was it today?" he asked.

She thought she'd left all her tears at Dr. R.'s. To halt them, she flipped on the radio as they pulled away.

Her father reached over and turned it off. "I'm sorry things have been so hard for you."

She didn't answer, just dabbed at her eyes with the frayed sleeves of his ragged pea coat. She turned the radio back on and saw him staring at the high-tech watch on her wrist with its bright red plastic band. "That's a new watch, isn't it?"

She avoided his eyes.

"Where did you get it?" he persisted.

"At Nordstrom," she confessed.

"Oh, Dana . . ." He reached over and gently touched her shoulder. "I wish you didn't do this."

"I know," she mumbled.

"Then why?"

She wanted him to pull to the curb, lean over, and hug her; the same wish she had the afternoon they caught her at Nordstrom. Instead of cringing in embarrassment, she'd wanted him to look past her petty thefts, put his arm around her, and say he loved her. But now, as then, he kept his eyes on the road and driving. If wishes were horses . . .

"I just don't understand," he said.

"I like stealing," she finally answered. "It's one thing I'm really good at."

Remembering her father's devastated look, she knows that wasn't true. If she'd been a better shoplifter, she would never have been caught. It's amazing that she escaped arrest today. No, stealing is just her clumsy way of expressing everything she can't cry about. She saw Dr. R. once more to return her wooden carving and then told her parents she didn't need to see the shrink again. She no longer had a desire to shoplift.

But now, years later, she's stealing again. This time she doesn't need Dr. R. to help her understand what she's feeling. She just needs the courage to acknowledge what she hadn't wanted to face.

On her way to her car, she passes a Goodwill store. What synchronicity to stumble on it. A thrift store was where she gave away her father's pea coat after her final session with Dr. R. The Goodwill store is open and she walks inside. It's a perfect place to dump the Burberry. Leaving Jeremy will be harder. But exiting the store, she already feels lighter.

Bay/Enterprise
LRT Station
103 Street North Entrance
To Trains
10230 JASPER AVENUE

CHRIS KOEHN

14

"Rusty never let an opportunity to fuck up go to waste."

FAIR TRADE
Andy Boyle

The weathered old man sat in a recliner, his gun pointed at both of us. Rusty had just gotten into the final locked cabinet to get the last ring when we got caught. I had told him we didn't even need that one, that it was just a ring from a Bowl game, but Rusty never let an opportunity to fuck up go to waste.

That's how we got here, wasn't it?

Rusty said the house would be empty. It wasn't.

Rusty said the man and his wife had left town the evening before. They hadn't.

Rusty said we'd be in and out in under three minutes. We fucking weren't.

Now we sat across from the old man on a burgundy sofa he directed us to after coming down the stairs, turning on the light, pistol in hand, catching us in the act. I didn't know anything about guns, but Rusty could've told you what kind the geezer was slinging. "The kind that kills you," he'd probably tell me.

The man studied us for a moment. He didn't look angry. More like he was disappointed—like a teacher who caught you cheating.

He cocked the gun. The barrel was massive, of the *make you have a closed casket* variety.

"Mind telling me what this is all about, fellas?" he asked.

I took a deep breath. It would be better to start at the beginning, I told him.

Rusty came back into my life on a Monday when we were both in our late 20s. It was summer and I was fifty bucks down in a game of Texas Hold 'Em poker in the back room of Bob's Tavern—this bar in Havelock owned by a man named, you guessed it, Bob. Bob never took a house rake, which made the game legal, and we were all expected to buy our fair share of beverages. The drinks paid for our chair rental, Bob would say.

I'd known Rusty since I was a kid, but he moved out of state freshman year of high school after his mom finally had enough of his dad's shit and shot the bastard. I lost track of him, the way you used to lose track of anyone before the internet followed our every move. I wasn't sure it was him at first sitting across from me. Same lanky frame, same straight Nordic hair that needed a wash, same sad attempt at sideburns. But he had the scar on his chin—the one I accidentally gave him. He didn't look my way once. I assumed maybe he'd forgotten about me, which would've been okay, in retrospect. Maybe even preferred.

Then I caught him bottom dealing.

I was going to say something, but I noticed he passed me pocket aces. Maybe he *did* recognize me. That hand won me four hundred bucks off an old-timer I worked with at the Kawasaki plant. Rusty had given the man kings, and with it, an extra dose of confidence. I didn't say anything when Rusty dealt me a full house half an hour later. When he gave me trip queens, I decided to fold those and cash out.

Out at the front bar, as I ordered a final beer before leaving, Rusty pulled up a seat next to me. He waited until Bob was out of earshot.

"Long time," he told me.

"How you been, Rusty?"

"I'd complain but, well, who'd listen?"

I nodded. "Appreciate your help back there. If it'd been anyone else sitting across from you, they would've seen your dealing."

Rusty thought about that. "But it wasn't anyone else sitting across from me, was it?"

Same old Rusty. I drained my beer and got up to leave. "Well, good seeing you." "Aren't you forgetting something?"

I looked around. "Don't think so."

Rusty swiveled the stool toward me, pointing to my pocket.

"My half. Which, if we're being honest, should be more like three quarters on account of you folding those goddamn trip queens."

I stared him down for a moment. He was still shorter than me by half a foot and had the same wiry energy from when we were kids. "Sorry, house rules. The winner keeps the winnings."

Rusty thought about that for a second, then nodded. He pulled out a pack of cigarettes and asked if I smoked. I didn't. He said to meet him outside anyway. He walked out the front door and I waited a minute before following him.

"You give me half," he said, leaning against a lamp post by the street. "And then the next score? You'll get at least a thousand."

"The next score?"

He threw his cigarette on the ground and crushed it with the heel of his boot. "We'll pull two large on the first job, easy."

"First job?"

"We'll probably make about forty grand apiece when it's all said and done."

"When it's all said and done?" I asked, shaking my head. "I don't even know you, man. Here." The money in my hand suddenly felt dirty, like it was going to get its grime and misdeeds all over me. I handed him everything I'd won that evening. Close to six hundred bucks. "I didn't really earn this anyway. You did."

Rusty pocketed the money and watched me coolly as I walked away. "If you change your mind," I heard him say behind me. "I'll be here Friday."

I hopped in my truck and drove to my quiet apartment in the shitty part of Lincoln near the state capitol building. On the door sat another note from the landlord. His patience was running thinner than the hair on his head. Either I paid rent by the end of next week, or I'd be sleeping in my truck.

As I unlocked my door, I very much wished I'd only given Rusty half.

I watched her from the playground, trying to stay low behind the steering wheel, hoping I couldn't be seen. Grace was only four, but you could tell I was her daddy. We had the same curly brown hair, the same ears. She had her mother's eyes and stubbornness. Grace ran around the playground, screaming with some of the other kids, joy on her face. I wanted to walk out and push her on the swing, maybe go get some ice cream. Do what a father is supposed to do.

Instead, I hid in my truck. Hoping her mother didn't see me and decide the police needed to be called.

It had been nearly six months since I'd seen my daughter outside of court-appointed visitations. Tomorrow I would get one of my two monthly scheduled visits with her, and each one killed my soul. I hated having a representative of the state there. I wanted to be the one to take her to the park, but I had to "earn" that right. I wanted to bring her a chocolate shake from DQ—her favorite when I was still with her mother—but no outside food was allowed. Instead, Grace and me sat in a square room, gray walls, no windows, with a handful of broken toys while a stranger with a clipboard sat and judged me.

Six months ago, while I was working at the plant, a suit showed up and served me with divorce papers. Completely blindsided me. It claimed I was an abusive husband, that I couldn't provide for my wife and daughter. All lies, seeing as my wife was leaving me for a rich banker in South Lincoln, a man she'd met during one of her many needed "girls' nights," a man who spent his money on anything trivial that made him look important, like a younger trophy wife. Not much I could do about it. My lawyer sucked shit because sucking shit was the best I could afford. It made me suck shit broke.

And now here I sat, watching my daughter from a hundred yards away. Like some kind of creep. I put the car in drive.

When my parents died, they left me enough money to pay for a half-decent wedding. Couldn't get a refund on that, sadly. The rest of my extended family was as broke as I was. Nobody I could turn to.

It was Friday, one of my days off. I was heading east without thinking, my subconscious pushing me toward a decision it had already made for me.

I pulled up to Bob's, walked straight into the back and found Rusty sitting at a table, a big stack of chips in front of him.

I motioned for him to follow me outside and he did.

"So," I finally said after Rusty lit a cigarette. "Tell me about this job."

The first few scores were simple enough. Easy, really. Rusty called them burger jobs, because you were *In 'N Out,* like that chain out in California. He had a contact who let him know about people who kept expensive Husker memorabilia out in the open in their homes. Signed hats. Championship rings. Footballs from important games. That sort of shit.

Easy to steal, easy to fence, easy everything. That's what Rusty said, at least.

My job was to sit outside and watch and text him if anything seemed sketchy. Rusty scoped the houses out on his own time, apparently, figuring out when people wouldn't be home. Sometimes we'd strike during the day, with him wearing a jumpsuit and carrying what looked like some kind of lawn equipment—usually a weed whacker. Then he'd get in through the back door, which, he told me, was unlocked nine times out of ten.

Sometimes we showed up at night. Rusty said those jobs were always more dangerous than ones in broad daylight. "People don't think burglars strike during the day," he'd told me once. "They almost expect them after the sun goes down."

I got the general impression that Rusty had long been enjoying a life of crime. But I never actually asked. Didn't want to know.

I'd only had to text him once, on our very first job, when a pickup pulled into the driveway. Turned out, they were just using it to turn the truck around and head the other way. Crisis averted.

I almost quit right then and there. I actually puked onto the street before Rusty got back to the car. If he noticed it, he never said anything about it.

But then he got in the car and we drove off and he told me, without any prompting, why he'd come to me for help. When we were kids, sure, we raised some hell, but the standard kind— Lighting stolen fireworks in trash cans. Toilet papering the house of someone who had talked shit. Nothing that would have even landed us in juvie.

"After my mom shot my dad," he told me, "you were the only one who came over to hang out."

"We were friends," I said.

"Still are, aren't we?"

I didn't answer as he drove to drop me off. Didn't need to.

The part of Rusty's plan that was genius? He replaced everything he stole with a replica. You can buy knockoff sports rings on eBay for thirty bucks. Got the same look and weight. The inscriptions are passable. Only they're not real gold, the gems are phony. Crazy what you can manufacture with ease these days. Guess we get to thank NAFTA for that.

If anyone ever noticed what was on their mantel wasn't the real deal, they never seemed to call the cops. And a week after the first score, he showed up at Bob's and slid me an envelope. Two grand in cash.

Made my rent, two student loan payments for my worthless journalism degree and three months' worth of child support the next day. I told myself this was all worth it because, really, nobody was getting hurt. I was paying off money I owed. It would provide for a better life for my daughter. And who was going to miss a signed football or two, anyway?

I'm the first bad man to ever justify his misdeeds as being for the greater good, I'm sure.

The key to this enterprise, Rusty told me one time, was to not get caught. He schooled me in the particulars of being on the other side of legality. You never deposited large sums of cash into your checking account, because that could trip off automated systems that alerted the authorities. You never drove your own car to the jobs—we'd always buy some cheap used piece of shit from junkyards, and then we'd turn around and sell it after the deal was done. We usually lost a few hundred bucks, but Rusty called that the cost of doing business. You used fake names whenever possible. And, I learned as we broke into more and more places, you had to continually lie to yourself that you were a good person.

My escapade into bad-guy-dom had an end point. Rusty had eight houses to hit, with the final one being a biggie. Rusty said it could, potentially, net us twenty grand. *Each.*

"If we pull a big score, people will know," I had told him, even though, truthfully, I didn't know what I was talking about. "And if people know, well, a bigger fish may decide they deserve a bit of the action."

Nebraska wasn't without its organized underbelly. Rusty'd told me stories about the connected Omaha family that ran shit around there.

They had a satellite organization in Lincoln, but that didn't amount to much. They mostly ran books, helped bribe low-level officials when necessary, and kept to the standard Nebraska state philosophy of *don't rock the boat.* The western part of the state was mostly run by biker gangs moving meth and other drugs. But eastern and central Nebraska belonged to the old school guys in Omaha, who kicked back up to even older school gentlemen in Kansas City. Rusty just called them The Kings.

And if we decided we wanted to move up in the world—say, started selling anything worth more than five or six grand a pop—we'd be required to tithe to The Kings, at 20 percent . . . or 40 percent . . . or whatever percent they decided.

Or face the consequences.

Six weeks go by and we're there. Last house. Last bit of recon before doing the final job next week. Rusty pulled the car to the curb in a tree-lined neighborhood. It was quiet. Upper-middle class. The kind of houses that had more bathrooms than bedrooms for some reason, in case everyone plus a few guests needed to piss all at once. Rusty normally did these scouting missions alone, but for this one he wanted me along.

He pointed to the modest home across the street. Something about it seemed familiar, so I asked who we were stealing from. I'd never asked that question until that night.

Rusty smiled when he told me. I thought I misheard him, so I asked him to say the name again.

He said those three syllables and I almost had a heart attack. I shook my head. Now I knew why I recognized the house—I'd seen a handful of press conferences on the lawn over the year.

"No way," I said. "We can't steal from *him.*"

"Why not?"

"Because he's, like, the closest thing we have to Nebraska royalty."

"So?"

"So, like, isn't there some kind of code?"

"What do you think we are, pirates?"

"No, but, like." Memories ran through my head of seeing the great man on television during my childhood. His wiry frame, full head of hair well into old age. His soft-spoken way of dealing with the media, with his athletes, with the fans. He was the embodiment of good sportsmanship and honor and everything else. If you thought *GO BIG RED* you saw his weathered face.

I shook my head. "This feels wrong. Like, it's a line we can't cross. Once we've crossed it . . ." I put up my hands in a *who knows?* gesture.

"Well, we need to do the job." He said it as if it'd already been decided.

"Why?"

"Because."

"Because why?"

He sat in the car uncomfortably for a second. I could tell something was bothering him.

"Fuck. Rusty. Look at me. What did you do?"

He wasn't meeting my eyes. "Don't get mad."

I was already mad. "What did you fucking do?"

Remember those consequences I mentioned?

Turns out, the guy Rusty'd been using as a fence had gotten a little too greedy. The man started to charge too much for our goods. One of his customers, a bit pissed at the price hike, called some old Omaha pals from a previous life to inquire about whether or not they could tell their guy to lower his rates.

These Omaha pals were *unaware* anyone was selling hot goods in Lincoln without their consent. They paid the fence a little visit, on orders from someone Rusty called Mr. Clean. After their little chat, the guy now gets to piss in a bag and pal around in a wheelchair for the next few months. Message received. Loud and clear.

A few days later, one tough-looking guy with a buzz cut showed up at a house Rusty was mowing the lawn at, one of his various odd jobs. They had a quick talk in the man's car, aided by the 44 the man kept in Rusty's mouth. The boys in Omaha—all The Kings' men, you might say, but you shouldn't—figured me and Rusty'd made about fifty grand in the last six months. So, for the inconvenience of not being aware of our presence, the man told Rusty, our newfound friends were owed half.

When Rusty told the man we'd maybe cleared ten grand total, he didn't give a shit. *You owe us, and until then, we own you.* Twenty-five large. Pay the fuck up. The other option, the man told him, was a fate worse than our fence, who had decided it was time to retire to Florida and move onto other concerns, such as relearning how to walk.

But there was a silver lining.

"Mr. Clean made an offer," Rusty said later at Bob's after our final house surveillance. "We grab the old man's championship rings. Just the ones from the 90s, he doesn't care about any of the bowl rings or conference rings. And then once Mr. Clean has them, we're done. We're square. Our debt is gone."

I pushed that thought away. "You believe him?"

Rusty shrugged. "He also said if we took anything in the future, they could fence it for us. For a 20 percent tax."

He was able to read my face, so he changed the tone of his voice.

"We only work for them once," he said slowly. "Then you can be done."

"I don't know," I told him. "I never thought it'd get this bad. I think I gotta say no to this one, Rusty."

His face looked pained. He hesitated before speaking.

"Fuck, what else?"

He swallowed. "He wants to see us."

Despite his name, Mr. Clean actually had a full fucking head of hair and a gray shaggy beard, nothing like the bald cleaning icon. When we arrived at the basement of the dingy former warehouse in Omaha's Old Market, he was waiting at a simple table in the back room. As he motioned for us to sit, he popped the top off a Tupperware container.

"Wife made me go on a diet," Mr. Clean said, taking a fork one of his cronies handed him. "Triglycerides and whatnot. Every meal is prepped." He took a bite and swallowed, grimacing. "Getting old is bullshit, gentlemen. I suggest you never do it."

Depending on how this meeting goes, I thought, *we may not get the chance.*

We couldn't hear the coffee shop above us where they charged five bucks for a cup of brown water that tasted just like what you'd get for a dollar at McDonald's. The walls down here were concrete. A single drain sat in the middle of the floor.

This was a place for potentially difficult conversations.

Mr. Clean gestured toward the chairs in front of him and we sat. The man ate about half of the contents of the Tupperware before looking up, pointing his fork toward us.

"So." Mr. Clean said between bites. "My wife's the big college sports fan. This job is really a present for her. You won't fuck this up, right?"

Rusty spoke first. This isn't how we'd agreed this would go down. "It'll get done."

Mr. Clean stopped eating. "Heard you fucked up a big job down in Texas."

Rusty didn't respond and I had no clue what they were talking about. A trickle ran up my back. Suddenly the idea of being broke and living in my truck didn't seem so bad.

Mr. Clean looked at me. "But you'll make sure he doesn't fuck up, right?"

This was my only chance. "Can I show you something?" I motioned toward my jacket. He nodded his assent as I slowly moved my hand to take out an envelope, surprisingly hefty for what was in it. I set it on the table.

Mr. Clean eyed it before squinting at me. "And what's this?"

"We owe you 25 grand," I said. "That's my half." I didn't tell him I'd gotten it all by maxing out every credit card I owned, at interest rates worse than someone like Mr. Clean would charge. But banks usually don't kill you if you fail to pay up.

Usually.

"I think Rusty can do the job on his own," I said. "I'll sit this one out."

"You'll sit this one out," Mr. Clean repeated. "Just like that, huh?"

My neck turned cool. I nodded. "Just like that."

Mr. Clean stared at me for a moment, then set his fork down. "I don't trust your friend to actually be able to do this job. You understand that?"

I nodded. "Yeah, but —"

"Good," he said, cutting me off. "And answer one more thing. You're not a fuck up, right?"

I was slow to respond. "Correct."

"So. You'll be the one who helps him," Mr. Clean said. "And that's that."

"But —"

Mr. Clean slammed his hand down on the table. He took a loud, deep breath through his nose, closing his eyes as he did so, which was somehow more terrifying than his outburst. When he breathed out, he finally looked up. "Meditation," he said. "My wife got me into it. Helps with my, ah, mood swings."

I was about to say something when Mr. Clean reached into his jacket pocket—a corduroy suit coat, with patches on the sleeves, like he was some kind of crime professor—and pulled out a photo. He slid it across the table like you'd hand someone a birthday card.

A playground. A little blonde girl sitting on a swing, the look of utter joy and love for the world in her eyes. A look I'd seen a thousand times, the only face in the world that mattered to me.

Grace.

My daughter.

Everything suddenly went red.

I thought if I was quick enough, I could reach across the table and get at the man's throat before his goons pulled me off him. Maybe crush his trachea. Take out an eye. Do some damage with the fork.

But before I could be an idiot, a beefy hand caught my shoulder from behind. A *click* of a gun echoed in the small room.

I took a breath. "We won't fuck up," I said, sliding the photo back to Mr. Clean.

"Good," he said, picking up the envelope full of cash. He peered inside of it, seemed to think about taking it, then slid it across the table back to me. "See that you don't."

I picked up the cash and Mr. Clean dismissed us with a hand. Before we left the room, I looked back at him and he threw a fist in the air, smiling as he said, "Go Big Red."

The old man studied us in his recliner. He had the same thin face, same thin gray hair, same discerning look I'd seen since I was a boy. I felt like I had gotten caught by God Himself doing something wrong. And now we would be smited.

"You did this," he said in his high, reedy voice after I explained our predicament, "because of your daughter?"

I nodded.

"How much are you getting for those?" the old man asked, pointing toward the rings Rusty had in his hand.

Rusty cleared his voice and said, "Nothing."

"How much *could* you get for them?"

Rusty thought about it for a moment. "Maybe twenty grand per national championship ring. Five or six per Bowl ring. All in all, I dunno, a hundred grand. Maybe."

The old man whistled. "That's about how much I made in a month back in the day. Pre-tax, of course. The pay's a little better now I hear." He smiled, as if we were in on some cosmic joke. "Tell me, why do they call him Mr. Clean?"

I swallowed a bit before answering. "Because," I said, remembering what Rusty told me on the long drive back from Omaha after our meeting, "when Mr. Clean gets mad at someone, it usually involves the use of heavy-duty cleaning supplies."

"Ah," the old man said. "Didn't know those types were jokers."

The wind picked up, shaking the downstairs sliding glass door. The sound echoed through the basement. The old man never took his eyes off us. It was like he was studying us, figuring out what play to call next.

Rusty's hands fidgeted. "We'll just leave these here and pretend like nothing ever happened," Rusty said. "We'll leave and you'll never see us again."

"You'll do no such thing," the old man said. He leaned back in his recliner, setting the gun down for the first time. "You know how many boys I turned into men over the years?" He paused, but we didn't say anything. "A few thousand. And do you know how many of them did stupid things like this? Quite a few."

He sighed and pointed a hand toward Rusty. "Those rings are

replicas. The real ones were stolen about a decade ago, to tell you the truth. When you get to be my age—and I hope you do, I really hope you do—you stop caring about such simple things like that."

"They're replicas?" I asked. "Then why keep them in the trophy case?"

The old man shrugged. "For one, they cost a pretty penny and look the real deal. And two, I have been known on occasion to have a touch of vanity. I really only cared about the national championship rings, if I'm being honest. But replicas don't matter." He leaned forward and looked me in the eye. "I suppose if you don't leave here with those, your daughter's going to be in trouble?"

I nodded. He then looked at Rusty. "And you. After you leave here, do you promise me you're done with this sort of foolishness?"

Rusty nodded and, by God, looked the sincerest I'd ever seen him look in his life. "I promise."

"Then I'd say a few thousand dollars' worth of replica rings and some certificates of authentication are a fair trade for the life of a little girl." The old man pointed to the basement door. "Close it behind you when you leave. The wife doesn't like the air getting out."

It took us a few minutes to realize what was happening. But once it hit, Rusty immediately stood and went toward the door. I followed but stopped when my hand reached the handle. I waited for Rusty to leave out a side gate in the backyard before I spoke.

"Sir?" I asked.

He turned to look at me. "Yes?"

"Do you know who took the rings?"

The old man studied me for a moment before speaking. "I don't know who took them, but I know who has them now." A big grin crossed his face. "Why do you ask?"

Everything Rusty taught me made the job easy. Didn't hurt that I already knew the floor plan of the guy who had the rings—I'd been inside during Grace's fourth birthday party, the home of my ex-wife's South Lincoln banker husband. Sometimes, you know, life has happy accidents. Also didn't hurt that I knew he liked to take the whole family out every Thursday night to Macaroni Grill. I was in and out of his house in two minutes. Rusty was right: They never lock the backdoor.

After Rusty gave the fancy replicas to Mr. Clean, he stopped showing up at Bob's. I heard he skipped town entirely, just a short time after someone tried to steal a national championship trophy from Memorial Stadium.

It took me awhile to find buyers for the Bowl rings I took with Rusty out of the picture, the ones the old man didn't care about. A few folks in Kansas, one pissed off Michigan fan, mostly people from out of state. All cash. Relatively untraceable. The dark web truly is a thing of beauty these days.

The rest of the money I used to pay down some of my debt, get a better apartment, and then hire a better lawyer. I've got joint custody of Grace now. It's a start. Even began getting some work freelancing for a few national magazines, mostly stories on the seedy underbelly of the Midwest. Finally using that journalism degree.

As for the old man, I left the national championship rings inside his mailbox, along with a note: *Thanks for the fair trade.*

I'd like to think it was.

RED LINE ALLEY

CHUCK KRAMER

15

"The world owed it to him. Because fuck the world."

THOUSANDS (OR, THE GUITAR HERO WHO REFUSED OPEN G)
Mike Zimmerman

When their first album came out, everything changed. February 1978. This wasn't no "Smoke on the Water," and man, I could fuckin' *play* it. I felt it. It was in my brain and went right down to my fingers. Mostly. I mean, I fucked it up when I played it. Sometimes I hit one out of ten notes, total shitshow. But it was *there.* It was so there.

Now the second album was out. A fuckin' year later! March 1979. That one's there, too. I mean, right there. I couldn't wrap my head around some of the fretwork and I fucked up these songs even more. But when it's there, man. That's enough. That's gotta be enough.

I introduced one of the new songs at the Redass—Burnrock's premiere dive—on Thursday night. The joint's actually the Redtail, named after hawks, I think. If you gonna play somewhere in Burnrock, Pennsylvania, you want the Redass. Our setlist hadn't changed in a while, we still played some Kiss too, but I brought up "Somebody Get Me a Doctor." Brand new stuff. And someone in the bar laughed. They weren't drunk enough. I didn't care. I knew enough. At the end of the night when I had a five in my hand I didn't have a few hours earlier, yeah, I knew enough.

Knew enough to know.

Stevie Shanks waited in a booth after our set. He stared me down as I put away my axe. I nodded at him. Davie Smith, Smitty, our bass player and singer, he disappeared like he always did. He liked playing but didn't much like us, and so didn't give a fuck. But I needed Eenie, our drummer. I caught the dumbass's eye while we packed up. Eenie's given name was Doug. High school kinda sucked for us. Eenie was always Dougie Downer or Depressing Doug. But now he was Eenie, drummer for Beefswelling. That only elevated a man so high. He tried using hair to cover up his shit. Long brown hair to cover his cheek acne. A shitty beard to cover his recessed chin. Eenie's arms were so skinny I wondered how he picked up his drumsticks. But he was Eenie, drummer for Beefswelling. And I was lead guitar.

Stevie Shanks was six-something tall and barrel-chested. Crew cut. Pock marks in his cheeks. Recessed eyes. He didn't look like a hood. He looked like a professional ballbuster, a cop, a drill sergeant, some fucking thing. But he was a hood. The number two hood in Burnrock. He first talked to me after a gig back before Thanksgiving '78. We didn't even know *Van Halen II* was even in the works back then, seemed like years. But Eenie and I had made some drops for Stevie Shanks a handful of times now. Pot and pills, I'm guessing, but I could never see inside the packages and didn't dare open one. Ten bucks here and there, easy money. That's why I never minded or felt afraid when I saw Stevie Shanks at the Redass watching us play. I felt like, I dunno, I was growing.

But as soon as Eenie and I slid into the booth opposite Stevie and he spoke to us, I knew this time was different.

"Y'know cocaine?"

Eenie would never say anything first, but I glanced at him just the same. I wasn't nervous, or maybe I was. "I heard of it," I said with a shrug. Of course I'd heard of it. But I didn't know shit.

"Business is growing. We need a couple extra hands. You in?"

"Hell yeah," Eenie said.

Stevie Shanks didn't like Eenie and ignored his answer. He waited for me.

"Yeah, we're in," I said.

He paused, then said, "Stakes are higher, kids. Know that."

"Sure, okay," we basically said.

He nodded. "You'll get instructions." He went to get up, paused. "You almost got that solo on 'You Really Got Me.'"

Why the fuck did I blush? "Yeah, it's a little all over the place."

"And what the fuck is that thing right before it?"

I felt myself shrink in my seat a bit. "Yeah, that's called 'Eruption.'

It's Van Halen."

Stevie looked like he would say something, but just went, "Uh huh." Yeah, I know I fucked up the solo. Sounded like cats dying."

Stevie Shanks left without another word and I couldn't tell if he gave a shit.

We followed the instructions. We each made a drop. Both went off without a problem. At least mine did, and Eenie said his did.

I guess, well . . . I didn't trust Eenie. That's hard for me to admit. We been hangin' since like the fourth grade. We're shit, we come from shit, and Burnrock treats its shit like shit.

And lemme . . . yeah, lemme just say it. I came from dirt. Lived in dirt, ate dirt. For real. Lived in a trailer for a while. A smelly farmhouse. A row home a bit. No grass, just dirt everywhere we lived. Sometimes lived with my mom, sometimes lived with people I didn't know. Moms ain't a guarantee of anything. School food was the best food, but I remember eating dirt when I was little. So that's that and maybe you get it.

But this guitar thing. It was the first time I ever heard anything positive from other people. I mean, shit, man, first time ever.

Eenie came from the same. That's why we hung. Eenie just wasn't that smart, but it was worse than that and it took me a long time to figure that out. But one night I figured it, and I didn't feel the same about Eenie after. See, I've gotten real rabid about this guitar thing. I can play like Ed Van Halen. Or I will one day. And that can take me places. Maybe. Maybe not with Beefswelling–that was Dave Smitty's name for the band and it made me laugh but what the fuck. I still have ideas about how my six-string will ride me outta this town. Maybe.

Yeah, maybe, okay, I know what you're sayin'. Maybe I don't got talent. But I got calluses. Calluses can get you there. But see, Eenie didn't know what a callus was. When I saw Eenie, I saw Depressing Doug. A bag-a-bones with zits who didn't wanna get better. At anything. But Beefswelling needed a drummer and I didn't know anyone else who would do this kind of thing for Stevie Shanks and his boss.

This had to be something. My first five-dollar bill, I found it outside the five-n-ten when I was eleven. Never saw one before. You dunno what a five-dollar bill means to me, like really *means* to me. I got my fuckin' diploma and I work in the basement of a sewing factory.

The cutting room was down in that dungeon, so I loaded and unloaded trucks, ran the conveyor up to the sidewalk loading dock. I pushed a spreading machine. I swept floors. I breathed in colorful dust. I picked purple boogers out of my nose twice a day. And I know what you're thinking, dude, you make three bucks an hour and can get fifty hours a week, you have a job and pay your rent, that's some good shit for a Burnrock 19-year-old right there. And you make an extra five bucks a week playing guitar like Ed Van Fucking Halen. A five-dollar bill. What's to bitch about? Well, I'm in the tens. Occasionally in the hundreds. And I wanna be in the thousands.

That's it. That's my bitch.

I bet that guitar gets me there, too. Or maybe something else.

People work on levels, get it? How else to describe it. Those millionaires, that's their level, right? Millions. Some people, doctors-lawyers, work in the hundred-thousand level. Most people, though, most people in March 1979 worked in the tens and hundreds. Three, five bucks an hour or maybe another twenty a week moonlighting. Me, man, I wanted to get past the tens and hundreds. I wanted to be solid in the thousands. That's legit.

Stevie Shanks looked me in the eye like I could get it.

A week after I made the coke drop, I walked out of the sewing factory, end of first shift, walked two blocks down Morejon Street and hung a left into an alley. My normal route to my shitty one-bedroom in the walkup on Paper Street. Then I would get high and pretend a girl was with me.

Stevie Shanks caught up to me before I made that left. And detoured me.

It was weird seeing him in daylight. He was three inches taller than me. He wore cowboy boots. Never noticed that before.

He said to come with him.

I asked what's up.

He said you'll see. But you have to come now.

So I did.

I felt like something big was coming. Something was about to change. Honest? I felt like I thought I'd feel when a record company A&R guy would give me a recording contract. I felt like I was worth something.

I was right.

Stevie Shanks drove me out into the woods in a beat-up Ford pickup. I dunno what year the truck was, but it rattled hard and he shifted gears with a steering column stick. He didn't say anything on the way. Until he did.

"How long you play that guitar?"

"Couple years."

"How come you play that shit?"

"What shit?"

"Anyone ever teach you open G?"

I shook my head.

"So you don't know open G?"

"Never heard of it."

"It opens up the world for a lot of guitarists. The blues masters."

"I got plenty to work on now."

"That showy shit."

"It's fuckin' amazing."

Stevie said nothing. Until he did.

"Savor every blowjob that guitar gets you, kid."

Stevie pulled up to an old tin Quonset hut back in the deep trees about ten miles outside of town. I think we were close to state game lands, but I wasn't a hunter. I saw another black pickup truck and a Duster parked in the trees.

I didn't ask Stevie anything. I just followed him into the Quonset hut. It wasn't huge—a curved tin can maybe thirty feet deep. Bare-bulb lights inside, some old lamps, and clubhouse stuff. Couple sofas, low tables with full ashtrays and open beer cans. I saw a dartboard on the back wall beyond a red felt pool table. One guy sat with his feet up on a coffee table smoking a cigar. Two others played pool. Some blues played from a tape deck over by the pool table. Didn't know who. There were dogs, too. Three that I saw, a German shepherd sacked out on the rug and two mutts roaming. One of them, a medium-sized white dog with light brown spots, greeted Stevie Shanks. He patted the mutt's head and it flinched a moment, but accepted his greeting. Then it slunk away.

"This the kid?" the guy smoking the cigar said.

"This the kid," Stevie replied.

The two guys shooting pool didn't pay us much mind, but the cigar smoker stood and approached. He was just as tall and broad as Stevie Shanks, but leaner. He wore a plain black t-shirt and an open flannel shirt, jeans, and thick black work boots. Steel-toed, I figured. His hair was cut close, but not crew-cut close. Thick black moustache. His face tight on his skull.

He offered his hand and said, "Rummel Mor."

Shit. This was Rummel Mor. Someone I'd only heard of. Stevie Shanks' boss. The boss of the whole thing. And I couldn't even tell you what the whole thing was. What the fuck did I know?

I shook his hand.

"Stevie says you been doin' good."

"I guess. I'm just doin'."

"One way to look at it." Rummel Mor took a couple steps back but did not sit or offer me a seat. "So I don't have a lotta time, kid—what's your name again?"

"Matt Miller."

Mor chuckled and blew out smoke. "Lotta fuckin' Millers in this town. And they all got first names with M. You related to Milt Miller?"

I shook my head no. I also shook my head no on Mike and Mark Miller. My mom raised me and never changed my last name. I didn't even know my dad's first name. Just the Miller.

"Whatever, what's another Miller," Mor said. "So I got this thing, Miller. It's just a thing, no big thing. But then it kind of is. Big to me, anyway."

I glanced at Stevie. Nothing from him. The other guys just clicked their pool balls.

"Stevie likes you, says you're doin' good, so that means I wanna like you, too. So I need you to do something for me."

My belly was boiling hot by then. I didn't say anything.

Rummel Mor smirked, nodded. "You can do something for me?"

"Sure, I guess," I replied.

"Well maybe you can, maybe you can't."

I didn't know what that meant.

Mor let out a short whistle over his shoulder and said, "Meanie!"

Nothing happened.

Mor sighed and said to the pool players, "Bring her over. Christ."

The pool players—big, clean-cut guys just like Rummel Mor and Stevie—put their sticks down and moved around the pool table. Then I could see what they were doing. The white and brown-spotted mutt that greeted Stevie must have been Meanie. And Meanie didn't wanna come. One of the pool players got hold of her scruff and dragged her whining across the carpet and transferred that scruff to the boss's hand.

Meanie's ass dragged and her tail roped under her belly. Her shanks trembled. Rummel Mor petted her gently and said some gentle things. Then he let go of her scruff and told Meanie to stay. Her ears drooped and her head lowered, but she stayed.

Rummel Mor looked at me. "That's Meanie."

I nodded.

He took a step in my direction and puffed on his cigar.

"Kick her," he said.

I must have looked stupid. And then sounded stupid when I said, "What."

Mor blew out a big cloud. "I said, 'kick her.'"

I looked around the room. All eyes on me. Not amused eyes, not fucking-with-me eyes. Just waiting.

Meanie let out a whine. Rummel Mor again told her to stay. She did. Wide-eyed and looking like she wanted to turn to water and disappear.

"Well?" Mor asked me.

I involuntarily shifted my right foot. Keds high tops that were second-hand, a size too large and might just fly off my foot.

Meanie. Any other day I'd think her name was funny, I could introduce her to Eenie.

I noticed one of the pool players turn away, pick up his stick, and resume playing. I felt Stevie behind me shifting his weight.

Now I felt like turning to water and disappearing.

How do you . . . Christ, how do you kick a dog?

Rummel Mor could read me pretty good because he said, "You gotta *kick*," and his black steel-toe boot caught her ribs. Meanie wailed and went down and then bolted to the rear of the hut, yelping the whole way. Once she reached somewhere, she went silent.

Rummel Mor leaned into me and shrugged with smoke.

"That's what it takes to win the Super Bowl."

I couldn't say anything.

"Don't sweat it, High Life. This isn't pass or fail." He puffed more clouds and sat back down on the sofa. "It's a baseline."

I wasn't sure what happened and I wasn't sure I wanted to know. The sounds Meanie made stayed in my brain and I didn't hear from Stevie Shanks. But I guess I shouldn't have worried. The next Thursday night, Stevie Shanks met me again after the Redass gig. We took a walk. Eenie was not invited.

We walked away from the Redass down Shale Street. Stevie didn't mention the dog. To anyone looking we were just two guys talking shit. But if you got in close and could hear Stevie, you'd know we talked about the most serious shit. He told me things. I heard him. I had to. No choice. All the happiness left me, all the humor, the joy of playing those mangled solos, the dreams of playing big stages . . . for the first time someone told me something that forced it all into the background. I suppose some would just call that shaking hands with the real world for the first time. I was on a path to the thousands. For real.

Stevie made it all sound good. People been watching. Word's been passed. Time for me to step up. I agreed I would. And that I could, because some of what he told me made me angry. He asked my opinion about something. I made a suggestion. He said yes to it. That's how it went. Me and Eenie had to meet Stevie Shanks down the railroad bed by the river Friday night after last call. I knew the spot. It was dark and the river deep there.

"Just one step closer to the big time, kid," Stevie said.

* * *

I was gonna be great. I just knew it. This is how: You get to be the best guitarist in Burnrock. Then the best in Anthracite County. Then the best in eastern PA. Then you go to Philly. After that, hey, I'm beefswellin'. Dave Smitty callin' me asking for backstage passes.

What a dream. What a plan. So real. Sometimes on Thursday nights I could see Marlin Sharpless, the droopy fuckin' owner of the Redass, behind the bar scowling at my guitar playing, and I could see the figuring going on in his brain: Is two hours of this Beef band bringing in more money than two hours of the jukebox? I guess he couldn't figure it out. We sucked. But we kept on playing. Live music alive.

I dreamed of playing Martz Hall down Pottsville. They got bands in there. Could fit five hundred people easy. I got word that Van Halen was coming to the Spectrum in Philly on May 19th. I would be there even if I had to steal a car. Front fuckin' row so I could watch Ed. So I could be that shit.

Yeah, I would be that shit. Someday.

Eenie and I drank at the Redass Friday night and then headed out. Edging in on two in the morning, streets quiet. We walked down the hill towards the river and the railroad tracks that paralleled it. The tracks ran on an elevated bed to protect them from river rise, so we hop-stepped down the steep bank to the riverside under some scrub trees. In a city like Burnrock, spots just like this one ran all along the river and were used for all manner of activities, usually involving beer, weed, and rubbers. The cans, quart bottles, and trash bumped your feet. The river churned quietly a dozen feet away.

Rummel Mor, Stevie Shanks, and the two other guys I saw playing pool that day were already there. Tall muscular shadows. Later in life someone would play me some Springsteen and I'd hear certain lyrics and almost puke in my mouth wondering: *how did he know?*

Rummel Mor spoke first. "We'll make this real quick, boys. Real simple."

One of the pool players handed Rummel a paper packet. He held it up, silhouetted in the tree branch glares.

"Know what this is?" he asked.

I didn't say anything, but it looked exactly like the package I carried for the coke drop. Eenie said nope, but something in his tone.

It was a proud nope. A weak nope.

"Yeah, well, you do know," Rummel said. He pointed to one end of the packet. I could see even in the gloom that it was wrong. Sloppy-taped. Like someone had been at it. "The person who bought this brought it back to me. This half-key was twenty-eight grams light. That's exactly one fucking ounce. And that kind of amount ain't random."

Rummel tossed the pack back to the nearest pool player.

"I ain't Boscov's. I don't take returns and exchanges." Now he got right in Eenie's face, spine stiff, hands folded behind his back, his glare four inches higher than Eenie's. I thought Eenie might fall over backwards. "I go to the Super Bowl. Not every year. Every day. Do you understand that?"

I saw Eenie's Adam's apple bob. His face twitch. I never heard a man scream at someone without screaming.

"You made your drop like a pro," Mor said. "After taking an ounce for yourself."

Eenie said zip. I knew Eenie did it. Because it was an Eenie thing to do. He was always cocky when no one was around. If no one was around, Eenie would justify the ounce. He deserved it. The world owed it to him. Because fuck the world. But right then, people *were* around.

"Now maybe you want the coke for yourself so you can feel special at your bar gigs, give coke to the girls. Or maybe you're selling it." I could see Mor's eyebrows rise then. "Which means you are now my competition."

"I ain't shit," Eenie muttered, then corrected, "I ain't done shit."

"Get on your knees, Doug," Rummel Mor said, voice neutral but full of command.

"What the fuck is this," Eenie muttered. "I dint do nothin'."

"Kid, get on your knees or I'll cut your fucking fingers off," Mor said.

Eenie did it. He kneeled in the dirt.

The four men lined up in front of Eenie. I suspected they were military somehow and now I knew. Four men in a line facing us, same distance apart, same muscles, same neutral stances.

"You want out of this, Doug?"

"I dunno what I did," he mumbled. "I dunno, just don't."

"Doug, you want to be square, yes or no."

"Yes," Eenie replied, his voice robotic. I could see parts of him shaking.

"Suck our cocks, Doug," Rummel Mor said.

Eenie gaped at Mor. That shook him out of his shakes. Eenie said, "What?"

"Suck our cocks, Doug," Mor repeated, same tone. "Go down the line. Get square with us."

I didn't know nothin' right then, but now I know Rummel Mor, for all his military certainty, would sometimes run things like he was inside. This was inside shit.

"Fuck, man," Eenie whispered.

"Start with me, Doug," Mor said.

It took a bit, but Eenie finally shuffled on his knees over to Mor.

"You're taking too long," Mor said.

Eenie reached up. Hesitated. Then reached further. His hands on the buckle of Mor's black leather belt. Getting ready to undo it.

"Miller," Mor said, looking past Eenie right at me.

Eenie unflapped Mor's belt.

"Miller," Mor repeated. "Christ, High Life, I don't want my dick sucked."

Eenie froze with his fingers on Mor's jeans. "Wait, what?"

I did it. Stepped forward and slid a doubled-up guitar string around Eenie's neck and yanked it tight. Eenie was so skinny, such a narrow, sinewy neck. He spasmed, had no clue, then did, and did a fish flopper. That's what Stevie said it would be like. A fish flopper. But he never mentioned the mewling. Or the blood. I think I said something when I felt the warm blood kick back onto my hands and forearms. Oh shit, Eenie. Oh shit.

I have strong fingers, hands, forearms. Guitarist fingers, factory forearms.

I used an old A string.

Eenie bled and mewled and we both fell into the dirt and garbage and I felt the life go out of him, the fade at the end of a song.

In the end, Stevie Shanks had to pull me off him. He took the guitar string away. Told me to wash my hands in the river and come back up to the street.

The river was cold and quiet and took the blood off just fine.

Up on the street, the two pool players tossed Eenie into the pickup bed and covered him with a tarp and bricks.

"Don't you throw him in the river?" I asked.

"You use the river when you want them found," Stevie said.

They sent me on my way but not before Rummel Mor walked me away from the pickup truck and the others.

"Okay, kid. Okay. You did this, and this is this. But you work with me you gotta remember something. I go to the Super Bowl every day. So you gotta show up. Know what that means?"

"I think so."

"Know so."

"Okay."

He leaned in, grabbed the back of my neck. Christ he was strong. "Right now, you did this thing, you think you're there. But you ain't fucking there. Cuz it's like this. Anybody can kill a dog. But can you kick one? Every day?"

I didn't answer.

Rummel Mor laughed and released my neck, hard. "We gotta work on that bleedin' heart of yours," he said. "You gotta learn how to kick dogs, High Life. But you did good. Gimme your hand."

I did. He made like a hard, clamping handshake but it wasn't a handshake because his hand was full of folded bills. And then *my* hand was full.

"You playin' the Redass next Thursday?" he asked. "That guitar hero stuff?"

I blinked, not realizing Beefswelling was out a drummer because I couldn't believe what was in my hand but I managed to say, "Yeah, s'posed to."

He nodded. Not at me. Just at the night in general. "Hear you play okay, hittin' some notes. You know any Howlin' Wolf? Stones?"

"Not really no."

"Maybe we'll come see."

I nodded.

They left and I walked back up the hill into town and buildings. In my fingers I still felt Eenie's pulse coming up through guitar string. His fade out. I added in my head. Knew him twelve years. I put my back to a brick wall and breathed. Stevie laid it out the previous night on Shale Street: It wasn't about what Eenie did—it was about me. If I didn't do that to Eenie, Rummel woulda killed us both. The damn dog thing wasn't enough, Rummel needed to know. So I did it. Do or die's a worthless saying until you have to do or die.

Eenie opened his mouth to all of them. I couldn't believe that. Christ. I pulled out the wad of cash. One second your hand's dripping blood, next one it's full of money. How about that.

I counted the folded bills and I can't say a new feeling washed over me. More like it boiled up a little higher each time I counted a bill.

Rummel'd given me $1,050.

I was in the club. Even got fifty extra bucks.

Let me tell you . . . man, yeah, let me tell you. Fifty extra bucks when you're sittin' on a thou is some serious change. At that moment, I could go anywhere and do anything. I was so excited I did nothing.

Soon after, though, I scored those Van Halen tickets. Twentieth row. Good enough.

Soon after that, I made it through "You Really got Me" without fucking up. Dave Smith found us a drummer, too. And I know I'm dumb, but Smitty had been in on it from the start. Thursday night at the Redass is the best night to score your medicine. That's why Stevie Shanks had always been there. That's why Marlin Sharpless let us play when we sucked so hard—he got a cut. The whole thing, Thursday night Beefswelling at the Redass, was about sales. And three other bands played four other bars throughout Anthracite County. This was Rummel Mor's road to the Super Bowl, live bands and lady's nights. Stevie Shanks wants me to learn some shit called "Hellhound on My Trail," but then I'd have to fuck with tuning my guitar to that G shit.

Nope. I'm Ed Van Halen, folks, and I don't have to do a fuckin' thing I don't want to.

BROOKLYN BRIDGE

JAY BECHTOL

16

""He waited to see if his mother would shout for him to come back, if his father would drop his spatula and come out and apologize.

"When neither happened, Paco walked towards the car."

TAQUERITO
Hector Acosta

Paco stood in front of the grill, his apron a battlefield of stains. He kept his eyes on the row of tortillas placed on the flattop, taking them off the grill the moment they swelled up like corn balloons. He knew if he hesitated, they would become full of ugly, black, charred marks, which always reminded him of the liver spots on his grandfather's face.

"Don't burn any of those," Paco's dad said, standing by the skewer station at the end of the trailer. His muscular, brown arms glistened as they sliced through the pineapple sitting on the counter. The blade cut through the fruit's prickly skin, revealing the glistening, yellow meat his dad would use to bookend the trompo tower he was building. "¿Me escuchas? We don't have money to waste on mistakes."

"Hay, cálmate, Javier," his mother said, a pen tucked behind her ear. "Paco is doing just fine." Turning back to the customer waiting outside the order window, she said, "What can I get you?" in a light, breezy tone.

Sometimes, Paco wondered what his parents were like when they first met. Before they had him and moved to the States, before bills and jobs etched wrinkles on both of their faces. Before the fighting began, loud shouting matches and hushed, tensed arguments which almost always ended with the sounds of slamming doors.

The trailer was supposed to change things. Paco still remembered the day his father hauled the red, thirteen by eight stainless steel trailer home. Red, his father had said, "¡para que nos vean desde la calle!" With the trailer, his mother would no longer have to come home with knees raw from loosening the grout from bathroom tiles of the houses she cleaned. His father could quit his job working the grill in someone else's kitchen, putting up with long hours and abuse from chefs who had less experience but were hired to *elevate the simple Mexican food.*

A deal was worked out with a nearby gas station, allowing the trailer to be parked at their lot for a small monthly fee. At first, the newness of the food truck and his dad's expertise at the grill brought in a stream of customers wanting to try their tacos and aguas frescas. His parents manned the trailer by themselves during the week, but on the weekends Paco was expected to help out.

"Hey, do you have those any Birria tacos," the guy at the order window asked.

"I'm sorry," Paco's mom said, a tight smile on her face, "but no. We have some really good trompo ones though," she said, pointing to the rotating spit of red meat Paco's dad was manning. "They're the best in the city."

"Trompo? I don't think any of the YouTube clips I saw mentioned trompo," the guy muttered, more to himself than to Paco's mom. He already had his phone out and was flipping through its screen.

"We really wanted to try some Birria tacos," the guy said, motioning to a group of four others who stood a little bit away from the trailer. His fingers drummed on the small counter where bowls of onion, cilantro, and plastic silverware were kept. Looking down at his phone, he said, "Oh wait, Twitter says Burrito Boys over at the food park has them." Without even a goodbye, he turned from the window and walked back to his group.

"Pinche gabacho," Paco's father said, watching the guy leave. "Just wasting our time."

"I'm telling you, we need to update the menu," Paco's mom said with a sigh.

"The menu is fine." Javier cutting another pineapple, the sound of the knife hitting the board echoing in the trailer. "The moment we get birria tacos, there will be something new they all want to try. No, Maria Elena, we're sticking with what's worked."

"Pero eso ya no funciona," Maria said. "Business is down."

His parents had been having this same argument ever since the food park opened a few months ago. The park was only a couple of miles away and had a cast of rotating food trucks, which attracted customers with fare like veal grilled cheese sandwiches, Nashville chicken bibimbamp, and seven-layer gyro fries. The park had even begun to syphon away their regulars.

"Things are going to pick back up!" Javier shouted, slamming the knife into the cutting board hard enough for the entire counter to shake. "We just have to keep at it. ¿Verdad, Paco?"

Thankfully, before Paco had to answer, a couple came to the window to pick up an order. They were older than Paco, though if he had to guess, not by much. The guy was shorter than the girl, with a stocky build and faded tattoos wrapped around his arms, which he had around the waist of the girl. She had long black hair, purple tinted lips, and curves which a pair of tight jeans highlighted.

"Anything else I can get you?" Paco's mom asked, dropping a small cup of their home-made salsa into a bag.

"Can you throw some extra salsa in there?" the girl asked in Spanish. "I really like it."

"Of course," Paco's mother responded, Paco imaging her calculating how much the extra bags would eat into tonight's profits. She dropped two more cups of salsa into the bag and took the money from the guy, which she placed inside the cashbox she kept under the counter. Lately, she'd been keeping a careful eye on it, the result of a recent spree of food truck robberies.

Starting up the grill and lining up a new row of tortillas, Paco watched the couple walk toward their car, his eyes drifting down to the girl's ass as it swayed back and forth with her steps.

"¡Paco, las tortillas!"

The row of tortillas in front of him crackled and shrank as a light blue fire danced on their edges. Smoke filled the trailer, smothering Paco's face. He backed away from the grill, his elbow bumping into a tray full of trompo meat lying on the counter behind him. Through the smoke, Paco watched in horror as bright, red ribbons of glistening pork went flying, the meat making a sickening sound when it hit the floor, like a belt striking flesh.

"Maldita sea." Paco's dad shoved him aside, throwing handfuls of salt unto the grill. "All you had to do was listen to my instructions," he said.

"Lo siento," Paco said, his face hot from the smoke and embarrassment.

"He didn't mean to," his mother added, standing by Paco.

"He never does," his father said.

"Javier . . ." his mother said.

"Javier, nada, Maria," his dad said, turning his attention to Paco. "When are you going to step up?" he asked, picking up another tortilla off the floor. "You're sixteen, but half the time act like you're twelve."

"I'm trying, but it's not like I asked to be here," Paco said, the words sizzling on his tongue like meat on the grill.

"¿Lo escuchas, Maria?" Paco's dad asked. "When I was your age, I worked before and after school every day, all the money I earned going to my mother to help with the bills. Besides, what's so important that you can't be here, huh Paco? Not like we ever saw you going out with friends. All you did before was stay in your room playing Nintendo."

"Fuck you."

The words carried pent up frustration and embarrassment and were out of his mouth before he realized he said them. His mother gasped, her fingers digging into his arm while his father's face twisted, a redness exploding across his cheeks as his eyes grew wide. His right arm went up, and Paco shrank back. But the hand never came down. Instead, his father turned his back on him and said, "Vete. No te necesitamos."

We don't need you.

"Javier . . ." his mother said.

"Whatever," Paco said hating the trembling in his voice. Untying his apron, he shoved past his mother and reached for the trailer door.

"¿A dónde vas?" his mother asked.

Ignoring her, Paco stepped into the Houston night. He was halfway across the parking lot, with no idea where he was going, when the realization of what he'd done started to sink in. He needed to go back and apologize.

"Hey, you need a ride?"

Paco stopped and looked around, finding the guy who had just picked up his order standing next to a light blue, two-door car.

"Do you want a ride?" the guy asked again.

Paco glanced back to the trailer. His mother stood by the doorway, watching him. Paco could see his father working the grill, the smoke from it creating a veil which turned his father's face into a vague, unrecognizable image. He waited to see if his mother would shout for him to come back, if his father would drop his spatula and come out and apologize.

When neither happened, Paco walked towards the car.

"Super messed up what happened to you," the guy who'd offered Paco a ride and introduced himself as Toño—short for Antonio—said, pulling out a slim, remote control out of the side of the sofa and frowning when he saw it was missing the batteries. "Me and Letty heard the whole thing," he said, his hands slipping into the crevices of the sofa once more.

Handing Paco a beer, Letty took a seat next to Toño. "How are you doing?"

Taking the beer, Paco said, "Okay, I guess." The three of them were in the living room of Toño's third floor apartment, the food Paco's dad made on a small coffee table between them. Toño and Letty sat on an old, beat-up couch, Paco sitting on a recliner which had stuffing coming out of the right armrest like thick, white fungus.

"We figured you wouldn't want to go home," Letty said. "At least not right away."

This was true. He'd been dreading being at home by himself, waiting to hear the sound of his dad's truck pulling into the driveway and knowing they would want to talk about what happened. Or worse, hear them come in and go straight to their room, leaving him to wonder when they would dole out whatever punishment was coming. No, better to jump at the offer to 'chill at my house for a while' that Toño had proposed while blowing through a yellow light.

Shifting on the recliner, Paco felt the phone in his pocket vibrate. It had been going off ever since he got into Toño's car earlier that night—his parents trying to reach him, Paco figured. Drinking from his beer bottle, his third of the night, he ignored the call. The first beer he'd drank mostly out of a sense of politeness, but by now, he was starting to appreciate the taste, as well as the fogginess it gave his thoughts.

Sliding the batteries into the controller, Toño turned on the television and said, "Ni te preocupes. Honestly? Your dad's lucky Letty was there to stop me from stepping in. Guy was being an asshole to you for no reason."

"I messed up some tortillas," Paco said quietly, unsure where the need to defend his dad's actions came from.

Toño waved Paco's word away. "Big deal. I pulled so much dumb shit back when I was your age, and you think I ever let my dad talk to me the way yours did?" Reaching for one of the tacos on the coffee table, he unwrapped it and took a large bite, bits of meat falling onto his shirt. "Best thing I ever did was move out. Meant he couldn't do the whole 'under my roof' thing anymore. Sometimes that's what it takes, doing something big so that it gets their attention. Reminds them you're not a little kid anymore."

Next to him, Letty rolled her eyes. "If you're going to give Paco advice, at least swallow first."

"I'm just telling him what I wish someone would have told me when I was his age."

"Baby, you're like two years older than him." To Paco, Letty asked, "You're what, eighteen, right?"

Paco nodded. "Yeah, close."

"See? I bet he knows all this already."

"But you still think this is good advice, don't you?" Toño asked.

Paco lifted the beer to his lips and was surprised to find most of its contents already gone. "Yeah," he said. And it *was* good advice. Or at least, it sounded good. In fact, he almost wanted to confront his dad right then and there. Tell him that okay, maybe he made a mistake, but at least he was there, wasn't he? Didn't giving up his weekends count for anything?

"God damn, he might be an asshole, but your dad makes a hell of a taco," Toño said. "How are you all messing this up? You guys should be rolling in customers."

"Toño!" Letty slapped him in the arm.

"It's okay," Paco said and shifted in his seat. "We were doing pretty well at the beginning. But then that food truck park opened up, and people started going there. And my dad is kinda stubborn about updating the menu."

"Fucking food park. Letty and I know all about that park!" Toño said excitedly. "See, Letty here broke it down for me when we first met, laid the truth kinda like I'm doing with you. She told me all about how they take advantage of us. Like when they move into neighborhoods and the rent goes up—what did you call that, Letty? Gentesomething right?"

"Gentrification," Letty said.

"Gentrification! Yeah. Fucked up stuff. And then that thing where they take our stuff, but not really our stuff stuff."

"He means appropriation," Letty said and asked Paco, "Do you know what that is?"

Paco nodded, his mouth dry and his head heavy with confusion and alcohol. "Like when white people wear dreads."

Letty laughed. "Yeah, like that."

"And the food trucks," Toño said, "Tell him about the food trucks." Toño reminded Paco of one of his uncles, the one who after years of struggling with a gambling addiction, found religion. He now spent every family gathering trying to convince all the other uncles and aunts to come with him to service, and he spoke in the same rapid, hushed tone Toño now used.

Letty leaned and kissed Toño on the lips, her hand caressing his cheek. The show of affection stirred something ugly and hard in Paco's stomach, and he tried his best to ignore it. Turning to Paco, she said, "They take all our recipes and combine them with whatever they think is trending or will be trending. And how many of those food trucks, the ones at the park who charge five dollars per tacos, are run by people who look like us, huh?"

"Zero," Toño answered for her.

Paco's phone buzzed in his pocket again. This time he reached into his pocket and viewed the message.

Donde estas. Llámame.

"I bet that's your parents asking where you are," Toño said.

Paco nodded.

"We can take you back if you want," Letty said.

"If you want nothing to change, we can," Toño said. "Is that what you want, Paco? To go back and be all 'Lo siento papi, I'm super sorry'? I'm sure that'll get him to respect you." Balling up the tinfoil which had been covering the taco, he tossed it to the nearby wastebasket. "Look at you, even now you're just sitting on your ass and letting me lecture you. Is that how you're going to go through all your life? Huh?" Toño's voice had an edge Paco hadn't heard before. "Be their little taquerito?"

Paco picked at the stuffing coming out of the armrest. "Screw you," he said.

"What?" Toño said and leaned forward, his hand on his left ear. "I couldn't hear what you said *taquerito.*"

"Fuck you!" The words exploded out of his mouth, like they did back in the trailer. This time though, they weren't the only thing Paco flung, the beer bottle following the words and sailing across the living room. The bottle missed Toño by a wide margin, shattering against the wall behind him. Letty jumped at the sound of the bottle breaking, but Toño didn't even flinch.

"Told you he had it in him," Letty said after a second of silence from all three. She walked over to Paco and crouched so her eyes met his. "We're going let you in on a secret, Paco," she said, her words as soft as the fingers which moved up and down his leg. "Because we think we can help each other."

Paco could smell her perfume, the way it wrapped itself around the scent of spilled beer and the spiced meat from the tacos. It made him dizzy, and he tried to keep his focus on Letty's gaze, fighting the urge to gaze down her shirt. "Secret?"

"Oh shit, babe, look" Toño said. He pointed at the television. The anchorwoman on screen was talking about the food truck robberies. The robbers, she said, were described as a Latino couple, and the police were asking for the public's help in identifying them. "They're talking about us," Toño said, as Paco turned to look back at Letty, who smiled, her fingers still moving up and down his leg.

"You ready, Paco?" Letty asked from the front passenger seat of Toño's car, adjusting the face mask to make sure it covered the entire bottom half of her face. She'd tied up her hair in a ponytail and wore a cap which she kept tucked low to her forehead.

"No turning back now, buddy," Toño said from the driver's seat. He too wore a face mask over the bottom half of his face, in addition to a pair of large sunglasses and a black hood he pulled over his head.

Paco sat in the backseat of the car, with the cap and sunglasses Toño gave him still in his lap. His stomach cramped up, and if he'd eaten anything, he was pretty sure it would be all over the seats by now.

His knees bounced up and down and there was an odd numbness to his face, kind of like when he'd gone to the dentist and they'd given him some anesthetics. He glanced out to the darkening sky and thought of what Toño and Letty had told him, back in their living room.

"We gotta take back what's ours," Toño had said. "Why should they be the ones making money off our food?"

"You get it, don't you?" Letty had asked. She'd moved back to the sofa, but the smell of her perfume and the memories of her fingers walking up and down his leg had remained with him.

"I guess," Paco had said. "I don't know if they deserve to get hurt though—"

"No one gets hurt," Letty interrupted Paco.

"Most hand over the cash as soon as we tell them '*this is a robbery*,'" Toño added, making a gun motion with his hands.

"But what about food trucks that are ran by people like us," Paco asked, speaking slowly, trying to parse out his thoughts. "Or you know, not like us, but like, people making food from their countries and stuff?"

"We scope out the trucks first, and only go for the ones ran by appropriators," Toño said. "And you wouldn't even have to do anything. Remember what I told you? They don't put up a fight. A bunch of the trucks we hit already close down or moved from their spots. Think what would happen if the whole park closed down. I bet you guys would get more business."

"Don't you want to help your family," Letty had chimed in. "Show your dad you're not just some good for nothing huevon?"

Back in Toño's car, Paco checked his phone and said, "Give me a second." Two more text messages from his mom imploring for him to call her. Turning off the phone, he slid it back into his pocket and put on both the cap and face mask. Reaching behind him, he pulled up the hoodie Toño had gotten out of his closet and loaned him. It was a size too big, hanging loosely off his body, but he figured it would make it harder for people to identify him.

His heart pressed against his chest, the world darkening around him as he put on the sunglasses. He didn't open his mouth of out fear he'd find words to back out of this, and instead just nodded at Toño, who watched him from the rearview mirror.

"Okay. Vamos," Toño said, his words muffled by the face mask.

They'd timed their arrival to the park to coincide with its closing, staying in their car and watching as the crowd thinned out and the trucks closed shop. By the time they started walking towards the trucks, the parking lot was empty.

Paco's breath came short and ragged as he tried to keep up with Letty and Toño's pace, beads of sweat already forming on his forehead and pooling around the collar of the hoodie. The humid weather threatened to swallow him, the face mask continuously shifting and sliding down as he walked. The sound of crickets and the gravel under his feet accompanied Paco as he walked a couple feet behind Letty and Toño. The couple seemed to be having none of the issues he had, their walk determined and their focus on the trucks straight ahead.

There were four of trucks, each of them about ten feet from the other. Around them were a couple of wooden benches and seats, which, much to Paco's relief, were empty. Out of the four trucks, two were closed down, their metal awnings covering the service windows and all their lights turned off. The other two trucks still had their headlights on, and those were the ones Toño pointed at.

You and I will take those two," he told Paco. "Letty will go around and check out the others and see if anyone's around." Stopping, he turned and waited for Paco to catch up to then. "You got that?"

"*¿Me escuchas?*" The echo of his dad's voice almost drowned out Toño's, and Paco was briefly transported back to flipping tortillas in front of the grill.

"Paco," Toño hissed, shoving him in the shoulder. "I asked if you got that?"

Readjusting his mask, Paco blinked away the illusion and nodded. "Yeah," he muttered, wondering if they could hear how hard his heart was beating. "I got it."

"Just like we talked about," Letty said, reaching into her backpack and pulling out a small, silver handgun. Toño already had one in his hand, a black pistol that Paco still couldn't believe was real and not just a toy.

"It's just for show," Toño had said when he caught Paco looking at it. Just like he'd said in the living room. "Think of it like a cheat code to a videogame. It helps them not feel bad about giving the money right away." he'd said back then.

Unzipping the backpack on his shoulder, Paco pulled out his own gun. Unlike Letty and Toño's, his was just a toy, something he was infinitely thankful for. He was pretty sure if they'd handed him a real gun, he would have pissed his pants and asked to be taken home. As it was, holding the toy gun felt surreal. When he briefly handled the gun in the Toño's living room, the plastic gun had almost no weight to it, but now, it felt like the heaviest thing he'd ever held in his hands.

The three moved towards the trucks, Letty separating from Toño and Paco as they drew closer to the first truck, a green colored one with music playing out of its speakers.

"Hey Tommy, come help me lift the cooler, will you?" came a voice from inside the truck.

"Hold up, I'm almost done with the tanks," said a second voice.

Touching Paco's shoulder, Toño motioned to himself and then the truck where the voices were coming from. He then motioned to Paco and pointed to the truck on the left, a black one with BETTY'S BBQ stenciled in red on the side of the truck.

"We kicked ass by the way. Ran out of the curry pizza right away."

"I told you we would!"

Taking a deep breath, Paco headed towards the barbecue truck, just as Toño went around the first truck, gripping his gun in both hands. He could hear movement from the inside of the truck he was approaching, and after confirming no one was outside, moved to the side of the truck, keeping himself pressed to the cold, aluminum paneling. *No one is going to get hurt,* he told himself over and over again. Counting to three, he stepped around the side. "No one, no one move," he said, trying to make his voice deep and unrecognizable. Instead it came out stuttering, so low that the man and woman cleaning the truck didn't even hear him.

"No one move!" He tried again, and this time they heard him, the man and woman looking up at him. The woman, who looked the same age as his mom, gasped and dropped the rag she'd been using to clean the stove when she spotted Paco's gun, while the man, heavy set, with a bushy beard and shaved head stepped forward.

"Sorry man," the man said, his voice jovial as his eyes focused on Paco's gun. "We're closed."

This isn't right, Paco thought, seeing the way the woman's eyes brimmed with fear, how the man's shirt was stained with grease and sweat, the same way his own father's shirts often ended up like at the end of the day. He wanted to say *I'm sorry*, tell them this was a dumb prank. But what came out of his mouth was "Give me your money."

"What?" the man said.

"Your money, give it to me. No—no, no one has to get hurt." The words spilled out of Paco's mouth in a rush, his eyes frantically looking around the inside of the truck for a cashbox like his parent's kept.

"Give it to him, Bill," the woman said.

"And if I don't? You gonna shoot me? Huh?" Bill took another step forward.

"I'm not playing!" Paco shouted. "Just give me the fucking money." It took everything Paco had not to take a step back or run away.

"I don't think you gonna do nothing. You can't even keep your hands from shaking." He turned to the woman and said, "Call the cops, Laura."

"I wouldn't do that," Toño said, appearing next to Paco, his gun aimed at Bill. "And you, stop moving or I promise you I will fucking blow your brains out."

Bill stopped moving, his attention on Toño. Recognizing the dangerous tone in his words, his shoulders slumped, and he said, "Alright man, chill."

"I'll chill when you do as my buddy asks and hand over the cash. Come on. Throw it over. The cellphones and the keys to the truck too."

Narrowing his eyes, Bill sucked in a breath and through gritted teeth said, "You're not taking my truck."

"We just gotta lock you in for a bit."

"Fuck you."

"Give him the money, Bill" Laura shouted, and Paco wanted to join, yell too, his eyes darting back and forth between Toño and Bill. *No one is going to get hurt*, he told himself.

"You either listen to your wife here, or I'll shoot her," Toño said, turning his focus and gun to Laura.

"You son of a bitch," Bill muttered.

"Go check on our partner," Toño muttered to Paco, keeping his eyes on Bill as the man reached under the counter.

Nodding, Paco took off in the direction of the two last trucks. He was almost to the first one, a blue colored one with a large panda wearing a sombrero painted on its side and the name PHO-JITAS across its side when he heard the gunshots. The sounds had come from behind him.

Standing in the middle of the field, he turned from one direction to the other, unsure of where to go. Another shot rang out, and this time he was sure it'd come from Bill's truck. *No one is going to get hurt.*

"What was that?" Letty shouted, running towards him. She shifted a bulging backpack on her shoulder as she reached him. "What was that?" she asked again.

Without a word, Paco turned and pointed to the direction of the barbecue truck, just as Toño stepped into view. To Paco, he looked so small and frail, like a stick figure planted on the soil. Even from where they stood, Paco could see he was holding his side. He took a couple of steps forward, swayed, and then slumped against the truck.

Paco managed to take two steps towards him before he felt Letty's hand on his shoulder. "We have to leave, now." Her voice lacked any of the warmth from before. It was cold and emotionless. "I tied the two I found, but we don't know about the one in that truck."

"We can't just leave him!" Paco said, whirling to face Letty.

"There will be other trucks. We have to leave now though. Toño had the keys, so we can't take his car."

Paco stared at her. "It was all bullshit, wasn't it?" he said quietly. "All the talk about gentrification and appropriation and taking back what's ours. You don't believe in any of it."

"It doesn't matter what I believe, we have to—you know what, I'm leaving, you can stay here if you want." Letty stepped around him and started towards the edge of the park, where the clearing gave way to thick shrubs and trees. Her perfume filtered through his mask, strands of her hair whipping into his face as she ran past him. Without thinking, Paco reached for her backpack and grabbed the loose strap, pulling hard.

The motion brought them down to the ground, Letty managing a surprised yelp as she landed atop Paco, her elbow digging into his side and knocking the wind out of him. "Let go!" she shouted, pulling at the backpack, her leg kicking at Paco.

Grabbing the strap with both hands, Paco held on and tried to bring the backpack to his chest even as the heel of her foot struck him. Pain exploded all over his face, his vision blurring and a ringing sound pressing against his ears. Tears mingled with blood and dripped down his chin. But he still held on to the strap.

"You fucking, god damn, kid," Letty muttered, reaching towards the backpack's zipper. Just as it seemed as if she was going to reach it, she froze.

Paco did too, both of them hearing the sound of approaching sirens. Glancing towards the parking lot, Paco could just make out the red and blue glow which grew wider and wider, enveloping the surrounding area.

"Fuck!" Letty shouted and let go of the backpack. "Fuck!" She shouted again and picked herself up from the ground. She looked downed to Paco, her mask having slipped from her face during the struggle. Her mouth opened, as if to say something, but instead she just turned and ran in the opposite direction of the sirens.

Breathing hard, Paco pulled himself up to a seating position and placed the backpack between his legs. Pulling out his phone from his pocket, he waited for it to power on. He glanced at Toño, who now laid face down on the ground, just a few feet away from the tire of the barbecue truck. Shaking, Paco looked at his phone. He didn't have much battery life left, and he hoped it would last. He had a lot to explain. Dialing the phone number, he put the phone to his ear and tried to ignore the shouts and sounds of footsteps coming his way.

"¿Hola, papá? Paco said, his voice cracking when the line picked up. "I need to tell you something."

CLOSED
CLOSED
CHRIS KOEHN

17

"'You know you aren't going to amount to shit, right? Some people are just born wrong. Like Jets fans.'"

LAST STOP AT THE D&L
Linda B. Adams

e needed gas. The thought made him laugh because Helen always said he had too much. But the laugh caught in his throat. There was nothing funny about anything right now.

The gas gauge throbbed red at him. Ten minutes ago the tank symbol had flashed at him. Now it was on solid. No longer 'get gas soon or you'll be in trouble.' Now it was an accusatory 'you're screwed.'

"How am I supposed to get gas where there isn't any? Huh?" He didn't realize he'd spoken aloud. He'd been in the car so long he forgot there were other people in the world. He'd almost forgotten about Helen. But she was like a road map that always led back to the same place. Every road standing out blue like veins against parchment. It was hard to forget someone you'd carted around like luggage that had become worn and tattered but was still serviceable.

Helen, though, was long past serviceable, her body going to rot in the trunk. Which was useless anyway because the whole damn car was about to be useless. He was in the long dust of the long road that stretched through west Texas. The last Airstream he'd seen, tucked against the side of a mountain like a spent bullet, had been too many miles back to remember. This was the land of dirt, dust, and mountains. You could lose track of the fact that you were in America because there was nothing to help you remember where you were. Nothing to pass the time or the miles.

The fuel gauge blinked once and his beloved 1966 Mercury Comet Caliente decelerated. He pounded the steering wheel with his fists as if that might help. He thought about just letting the car die right there in the middle of the road, but then thought better of it. With the car's last sputtering breath, he managed to pull over to the side. The world may have moved on into something unrecognizable, but that didn't mean he could just stop giving a shit. He hadn't been raised that way.

Besides, there was the trunk to consider. The car would attract less attention parked on the side rather than in the middle of the road. He spurted laughter at that. Because, really, whose attention was he going to attract?

He'd never planned on this. Hadn't believed what people had said was true. This was *America*, even small towns in the middle of nowhere had at least one gas station. So he hadn't bothered to bring full—or empty—gas cans with him. Had pressed all the luck he'd ever had. Which, admittedly, had never been much and was now even less.

He put the car in park, which was little more than a formality; the car was deader than a tits-up fish, as his grandfather used to say. By the time he'd realized those words didn't even make sense, he'd adopted the phrase himself. The road was as flat as a cookie sheet. The car wasn't going to move. Neither was he unless he got out and walked. But to where?

"Might as well be on goddamn Mars," he said, punching his fist against the dash.

He sat as the heat grew like a furnace with no air conditioning to counteract it. The black interior claimed the heat of the day. It was like being in a cauldron. He thought of Helen—a thousand years ago now— in her short shorts and legs that went on close to forever. About how she'd yelped when she got into the car, swearing that she'd left the skin of her thighs on the seat. Back then he'd known how to sooth her. Back then he'd known a lot of things.

Now all he knew was he had a dead car and a dead body. "Neither of which I want," he said and laughed. He didn't like the sound that came out. He thought he heard a tinge of madness in there and that wasn't good at all. He needed his wits about him.

You think you're not already mad, Merton? You have your wife in the trunk.

"Shut up, Ma." He hadn't needed her bullshit when she'd been alive; he sure didn't appreciate it now that she'd been worm food for almost thirty years.

But I'm not wrong, Merton. You know that.

"Shut *up*." He gritted his teeth. Spittle flew and landed on his hand. He stared at it as if it were something foreign.

Careful, Mert. You'll get dehydrated. And then what? Huh? You never did think things through.

"Oh, Helen." The fact that her voice had joined his mother's in his head wasn't lost on him. Nor was the fact that her death had done nothing to make his feelings about her go away. If anything, he was angrier. Her death had just made her stink. And with no AC, the car was going to smell like the roadkill out on FM 439 before the vultures showed up.

He ran his options through his head. There weren't many. He could stay in the car and wait for help to happen along while he roasted like a chicken in a convection oven. In that unlikely event, he'd have to explain the body in the trunk. And there was no way to do that without going to jail. Besides, not only had he not bothered to pack some gas cans, he hadn't bothered with water, either. He could get out and walk, see if he could find a station ahead. There sure wasn't one behind.

If there were other options, he couldn't see them. "You wanna help me out now, Ma? No, of course not."

He hung his head, felt the sweat drip down his brow, his hair crusting to his scalp. He was in a stifling car having a conversation with his dead mother, weighing options he didn't have. The world was dead. Had been since The Great War of 2025. No planes. No cell phones. No grid. Hell, most people didn't have cars and couldn't afford the gas if they did. He supposed he could consider himself lucky that he'd been able to keep the Mercury running.

"Everything's dead," he said. He felt a twinge of remorse for killing Helen. But that twinge was more for the Helen she'd been when she'd burned her skin on the car's seats than the woman she'd become.

He sat there, sweating, watching the heat haze over the asphalt, shimmering in the air like old ghosts. He considered rolling down the window, but it was pointless. He couldn't sit in the car for the rest of his life. Of which there might not be much if he didn't get moving.

You'll die out there, Merton.

"I'll die in here," he said and opened the door. The heat outside was a palpable thing, like getting too close to a campfire. A drop of sweat landed in his eye and stung.

He patted the trunk of the car. "You're on your own now, Helen."

The hot metal burned his hand. But it wasn't true, really, was it? Because he'd have to come back to the car. The damn thing was registered to him. Stupid. But the car had been his only ticket. Just because it had finally been punched didn't make it a bad choice to begin with. It had been his *only* choice. He shook the sweat from his eyes and started walking. The heat haze was always in front of him, blurring the world on the horizon.

He looked at the mountains that ringed the road and lurked in front of him like giant anthills. A jackrabbit scurried out from nowhere and startled him. The rabbit stared at him, blending in with the world around it, its eyes solid black.

"What's up, rabbit?" He liked the sound of his own laughter even less than he had when he'd still been in the car.

He wasn't hungry, but he knew he would be. Wondered if he should capture the rabbit, wring its neck, and skin it. Build a fire and cook its meat, eat what he could and stuff his pockets with the rest. It was a good idea and he knew it. Except he had no idea how to go about doing any of those things.

The sun was pulling the moisture from him, stealing what it could. He wondered how long it would be before there was none left. How much longer Helen's body in the trunk would matter. If he was dead, what difference would it make if they traced the car back to him? And who, exactly, would 'they' be, anyway?

He pulled hot air into his lungs, pushed it back out even hotter. He felt the skin of his face redden and begin to sting, then ache. He watched the air shimmer in front of him and remembered sitting next to the barbecue in the backyard with his grandfather. If other people in the family had a sense of decorum, his grandfather was lacking in any sensibility. He said what he thought.

And that day in front of the barbecue, he'd told Merton just what he thought of him.

He'd taken a puff of one of his ever-present Swisher Sweets, pushed the cherry-scented smoke out in a limp ring. Then he'd turned to Merton. "You know you aren't going to amount to shit, right? Some people are just born wrong. Like Jets fans." He took another puff of the sweet smoke which smelled to Merton like shoe polish dressed up with maraschino cherries.

"I'm ten," Merton had said as if that were an excuse.

"And that's why we gotta have this talk, Merty. Because it's true and you know it. Your ma knows it, too, although she won't be kind enough to tell you. Maybe grandparents get some kind of special pass. Or maybe it's a curse. How I see it is no one else is going to have the balls to tell you you're a fuck-up."

"Ma says that's a bad word."

His grandfather had laughed hard enough to cough at that one. "Your ma'll tell you all kinds of things but she won't tell you the truth. Which I just did. The question now is what you're going to do about it."

"I'm ten," Merton offered again. It hadn't been much of a defense the first time and didn't work this go around either.

"Your father was ten when he shot off his own damn foot. What's that tell you?"

He got up to turn the brisket, then closed the grill cover and sat back down. "Yeah, you'll likely get married, maybe even have a kid or two. Hell, even a fool with corn flakes for brains can accomplish that much. But you ain't gonna *do* anything."

"How do *you* know?"

"Easy. You got no imagination. Things are what they are with you. You got nothing else."

"I don't see—"

"Course you don't. Which is the problem." He took another puff on the cigar, saw that it had gone out and put it in the ashtray.

As Merton walked in the desolation, he wondered if his grandfather had been right. If imagination might have saved him from the situation he was in. Then he let out a parched laugh. "No. No way. 'Cause you can't imagine a full gas can out of thin air. Can't pull a damn gas station out of nowhere."

But then he wondered if he could. Because what was that he was seeing in the distance, through the haze? He had no idea how long he'd walked. Only that the sun had a different position in its arc, quite a different one. It wouldn't be dark for a while, but the day had begun to dream of the darkness.

The haze made his eyes water, the thickness of the heat pulled air from his lungs. He could feel his scalp burning through his scrim of hair. He rubbed his eyes, blinked. Still saw something square jutting out from the dirt and scrabble. He stopped himself from running because that would steal whatever energy he had left. If it was really there, it would be there no matter how fast he moved.

"You can't make up shit, Merty. That there is a building." He thought it was his grandfather speaking from the burnt embers of his mind, but it was his own voice that emanated from his lips.

As he limped closer he could see that it *was* a building. And not just any building. Hell, it was a gas station. The pavement around the gas island was cracked and overgrown with weeds. Something that looked like it wanted to be a tree had started to wrap itself around one of the island's supports. Dead metal that had once housed a pay phone clung to torn siding. Merton didn't know if the lone pump still worked.

A weathered sign hung from a telephone pole. D & L STORE. Below that: PIZZA, WINGS, SUBS, DELI, BEER, ATM, GAS, AMEX, MC, VISA DEBIT CARDS. Underneath BEER was TX LOTTO. That, at least, made sense. There'd been no lotto anywhere since shortly after The Great War began. Who the hell cared about money when the world was falling apart? Overnight the world had become one in which food and water were the main currencies. And scarce ones, at that.

The place had to be closed. Pieces of the siding were torn off and hanging like dead vinyl skin. And weeds threatened to hide the gas pump. Merton shook his head, wondering how in blazes *anything* could grow in this wasteland. Some of the weeds had choked, leaving only bits of green clinging to withered stems. The thing that wanted to be a tree looked hardy enough. But who ran a general store like that, in such disrepair?

Still, hope sprang eternal in his heart. Maybe there was some old water in a dead cooler. Maybe even a beer. Because that, at least, wasn't crossed off the sign. He felt moisture wanting to come to his mouth at the very thought. But there was too little left.

Open or not, gas or not, the place was shelter, at least.

"Well, I'll be dipped in wax. Somnabitch if you ain't real. I was wondering. Figured you were one of those mirages. Ain't much else around here, that's for sure. You broke down?"

Merton looked around to see where the words were coming from, afraid that they had emanated from his head, that his grandfather had been wrong. And maybe he had been, because Merton was sure good at imagining voices.

A man stood in the doorway, his black jeans gone grey with dust, frayed at the bottoms. His boots were scuffed brown. Merton thought of the skin of armadillos. The man wore a black T-shirt with CBGBs embossed on the chest in white. He raised his hand in a wave, reached up and tipped his cowboy hat. "Ain't a man out walkin' in these parts without a reason. What's yours, partner?"

"Run outta gas." The words came out in a croak. He refused to consider that the door had been closed. He'd been sure of it. And he hadn't seen it open.

The man smiled, put the hat back on. Merton was close enough now, but the brim's shadow made it impossible to see the man's face. "Well, that's a hell of a run of luck. 'Course, I reckon your luck's changed. This is the last gas station for a hundred miles."

"That so?" Merton swallowed, feeling his throat hitch with the runnel of saliva that trickled down it.

The man nodded. "For sure."

Merton tried to clear his throat. "Listen, man, you got some water?"

The man slapped his hand against his forehead, managing to avoid dislodging the hat. "But of course! A man needs water as much as a car needs gas. And that's the truth. No way it ain't. Am I right?"

Merton nodded.

"Well, come in out of the heat and let's get your whistle wetted. This heat ain't good for nothin' but dead armadillos. You'd better believe it."

Merton's blood felt cold. As if it had stopped flowing for a fraction of time. He blinked against the sun and the feeling was gone. He followed the man inside. He'd been ready to lick the sweat from his own skin. His thirst had become an entity, a force; he decided he'd probably follow the man into hell for a glass of water. A small laugh escaped him as he considered that he was *already* in hell. Or at least some version of it.

A counter stood at the far corner of the store, next to the deli. Three stools stood vigil in front of it, the red Naugahyde seats torn and spewing stuffing. Merton thought he saw the head of a boar in the deli case, bloody and fresh and covered in flies. He blinked and it was gone. The case was empty except for some dusty plastic leaves that decorated the inside of the glass along the edges.

The man smiled. "Sorry 'bout that. Closed the deli near on twelve years ago. Coulda kept it open with roadkill, but we ain't gone that desperate, right?" He laughed. "Ever had armadillo? Hell, partner, not *everything* tastes like chicken." He laughed harder and hitched up his jeans.

Merton looked at him. "About that water?"

"Well, I'll be dipped in wax. World all gone to hell and my manners with it." He walked over to a cooler, glowing with fluorescent lighting, pulled a bottle of water out. "On the house, partner. Least I can do for a fellow traveler."

Merton took it, stopped himself at the last minute from grabbing it out of the man's hand. He twisted the top and drank. It tasted of rust, but he didn't care. Didn't care either when some of it dribbled down his chin. He pulled the bottle away from his mouth and twisted the cap on, fighting the urge to pour the rest over his head.

"Desert sucks the life right out of a man. That's what I always said. Still sayin' it, eh?" He laughed again. "You hungry?" He pointed to a rack full of chips and nuts.

Merton walked over to the rack and pulled a bag of corn chips. His body wanted salt almost as much as it wanted water.

He tore open the bag and turned around to face the man. "So, any chance I could get gas?" The question made him feel rude, like all he could do was take, take, take, ignoring the man's hospitality. But wasn't that what you did at stores? Get what you needed and be about your business?

"You ain't gonna make it to El Paso, Merton Matheson."

"Excuse me?" The corn chip dried up in his mouth like salted dust.

"El Paso. Your destination." The man spoke slowly, as if he were talking to someone who was just beginning to grasp the language.

"How did you—"

The man took off his hat and set it on the counter, pulled out one of the worn stools and sat. He held up his right hand, cutting Merton off. "No. See, that won't do. Travelers do not ask the questions." He shook his head. "Nope. They don't."

"Then what—"

The man raised his hand again, then tapped his temple. "A little slow, ain't ya?"

"Well, no, I just—"

The man snorted. "Yeah, you just got your wife's body in the trunk. No harm, no foul, right?"

Merton looked at the deli case and saw that it wasn't a boar's head at all, but Helen's. Her hair was snarled, her eyes wide, her mouth etched in a silent scream. He blinked and the case was empty again.

The man spun around in the stool, full circle. When he was back facing Merton again, he said, "You know this place isn't here for everyone, right? I mean, you got to know that much at least. A man who kills his wife and stuffs her body in the trunk of a car couldn't have fallen off the turnip wagon yesterday." He looked up at the ceiling and snorted a laugh. "Then again, been a long time since we seen either a turnip or a wagon, right?" He laughed hard and slapped his knee.

"What is this place?"

"You. Don't. Follow. The. Rules. You don't get to ask questions, see?"

"But—"

"Shut up already. Yap, yap, yap. Like a goddamn yippy dog. Fuckin' ankle biter. Reckon you always said that about your wife, but I call bullshit on that. Here to tell you, right here and now, that *she* shoulda stuffed *your* body in the trunk. Done us all a favor."

"But she—"

The man snapped his thumb and fingers together in the imitation of flapping jaws. "Jumped up Christmas, but you don't know when to shut it. This ain't about her. It's about *you*. See, you went about things all wrong."

Merton started to open his mouth and closed it. Tightened his fist around the bag of corn chips until he heard a satisfying crunch.

"You know why, Merton?" The man tapped his temple again. "Nothing upstairs, that's why. If you had enough up there to light a neon sign it would be screaming vacancy."

"Listen, where do you get off telling me how to run my own life?" Merton dropped the bag on the floor.

The man laughed and leaned back on the counter. "I'm not telling you anything about how to run your life. Seems to me you already done that. Poorly, but done it just the same."

"What do you know about it?"

"Enough to know that you're here." The man leaned forward. "Now, listen. I'm not unreasonable." He waved his right hand in the air, dismissing. "People might tell you so. But that's not calling it fair. Not at all. Nope, I'm a reasonable man. Just ask me." He laughed again and slapped his knee. The crack was loud in the empty store. Because Merton saw now that it was empty. Dust covered the floor, the counter, the deli case, the stools. Cobwebs hung from every corner of the ceiling. The cooler from which the man had pulled the bottle of water was no longer lit. Something unrecognizable had congealed on the bottom of it. Had, in fact, formed a dried pool in front of it.

Then it became obvious to Merton. He was in hell and this man was the Devil. "You're him, aren't you?"

"And who might that be, partner?"

"The Devil."

The man laughed until tears streamed down his face and he could no longer hold himself up on the stool. "The Devil? Ain't that rich? Tell you one thing, you got a sense of humor, Merton Matheson. Give you that much. The Devil!"

Merton walked over to the man, stood in front of him. He crushed the package of chips beneath his feet as he went. "Then what was that crack about not being unreasonable? Huh? What was that?"

The man stopped laughing abruptly, as if someone had shut off a faucet. "I ain't he and I ain't here to bargain with you, Merton Matheson. I don't give one hoot about what you've read or what you think you know. You ain't Faustus, either, so don't go pulling that shit and groveling."

"Then what? I'm out of gas. I kept that car running. Since 1966! And it's not my fault my wife's dead. It's not!"

The man sat back down on the stool and motioned for Merton to take a seat on the empty one beside him. "Okay. I'll give you the car. Yeah, I'll give you that much. Although you did too many upgrades for my taste, nice touch keeping it that original Jamaican Yellow. And I know it can't be at all easy maintaining such a vehicle in this new world we've made. So, kudos, Matheson. Kudos. But if it ain't your fault your wife's dead, then whose is it?"

Merton looked down at the floor. "I'm not telling you anything. I don't even know who you are. What is this place, anyway?"

"Well, that much oughtta be clear even to a dimwit such as yourself. It's a general store. You miss the hand-lettered sign out front?"

Merton looked at him, eyes narrowed. "The only thing I'm missing is whatever point you're trying to make."

The man pointed to the cooler. "Take a look. Tell me what you see."

Merton felt a snake uncoil in his belly. He didn't want to turn around. Because whatever was in that cooler—*really* in that cooler—was something he didn't want to see.

The man got off the stool and nudged him in the shoulder. "So what's it gonna be, partner? The lady or the tiger?" He burst into laughter and bent double.

Merton turned around because there was no choice. Just as there'd been no choice with Helen. He'd had to kill her. He didn't want to, but he'd done it just the same.

The cooler was full of pictures. Except that wasn't exactly right. It was full of *memories*. Scattered and out of order, but the stuff that makes up a life. *His* life. He and Bobby Farrell swimming in the Lampasas River underneath Maxdale Bridge when they were eleven. His grandfather turning brisket over on the grill. His mother reading a book while he ran his toy trains over the carpet. He and his stepfather working on a 1950 Plymouth P-19 Fastback. And there he was, running on the track team at Morrigan's Keep High. The cooler was full of his life, like moving pictures trapped behind glass and metal. Then, with Helen on their wedding day.

"What is this?" he whispered.

The man put his hand on Merton's shoulder. "It's your life. Whatdya think?"

He looked at Helen, who was radiant. "I think I don't want to see any more."

The man clapped him on the shoulder. "Why? You already lived it. Might as well have a look."

Merton turned around. "I don't want to have a look. I'm done with this place. Whatever it is, I'm done with it." He walked toward the door.

The man grabbed him by the shoulders and yanked him back. "Nope. Sorry. Doesn't work like that. You gotta look. Those are the rules."

Merton shook free. "I don't think there are any rules, mister. I don't think there are any at all."

He made it close to the door before the man stepped in front of him. "You killed her. You think that wasn't breaking the rules?"

Merton felt his eyes begin to water. "You think I wanted to? Is that what you think?"

"Well, it sure wasn't an accident, now was it?" The man crossed his arms and leaned against the door.

"Of course it wasn't. She asked me to. She said when the cancer got bad enough that I had to. Because she didn't want to be in pain. She didn't want to go out like that. If you knew anything—anything at all—you'd know she shouldn't have gone out at all. She was the best thing in my world. And she wanted to be buried in El Paso with her parents. Except you can't exactly arrange a funeral for a woman who's not supposed to be dead, now can you?" Merton smacked the side of his head. "Oh, that's right. There *are* no funerals now. The wheels of the world have moved past traditions, haven't they? We live in a world where a man can kill his wife because he has to."

The man's eyes widened until all Merton could see on his face was horror. "No. That's not the way it was."

"I loved her! I did what she asked." Merton pushed the man aside and walked out.

Dust blew and the sun opened its oven door on his skin. He turned around and the place was gone. There was no general store. There was nothing but more dirt and the useless scrub that was the only thing stupid or brave enough to grow in these dead lands.

Merton walked back in the direction of the car. He wouldn't survive this. He knew that now. But he could survive what was left with Helen. He knew when he opened the trunk she'd look just as beautiful as she had on their wedding day.

He looked up at the unforgiving sun and smiled.

CONTRIBUTORS' BIOGRAPHIES

EDITORS

ROGER NOKES (Editor-in-Chief; @McCaffery_write) writes fiction under the pseudonym Stanton McCaffrey. His short stories have been featured in *Guilty, Mystery Tribune, Vautrin, Shotgun Honey, Yellow Mama, Out of the Gutter, Between Worlds,* and *Heater.* He has published two novels: *Into The Ocean,* and *Neighborhood of Dead Ends.*

ALBERT TUCHER (Contributing Editor; @AlbertTucher) is the creator of prostitute Diana Andrews, who has appeared in more than 100 hardboiled stories in venues including *The Best American Mystery Stories 2010.* Her first longer case, the novella *The Same Mistake Twice,* was published in 2013. In 2017 Albert Tucher launched a second series set on the Big Island of Hawaii, in which *Blood Like Rain* is the latest entry. He's currently serving as president of the Mystery Writers of America NY Chapter, lives in New Jersey, and loves NJ Turnpike jokes.

JAY BUTKOWSKI (Managing Editor; @jtbutkowski) is a writer of crime fiction and an eater of tacos who lives in New Jersey. His short stories have appeared in various online and print publications, including *Shotgun Honey, Yellow Mama, All Due Respect* and *Vautrin.* He is the Managing Editor and one of the co-founders of **Rock and a Hard Place Press**, an independent publisher of noir chronicling "bad decisions and desperate people" in short and longer format fiction, as well as in the flagship ***Rock and a Hard Place Magazine***. He's also a father of twins, a doting fiancé, and a middling pancake chef.

PAUL J. GARTH (Associate Editor; @PauljGarth) is an editor for **Rock and a Hard Place Press**. His short fiction has been published in *Thuglit, Tough, Needle: A Magazine of Noir, Plots with Guns, Crime Factory*, **Rock and a Hard Place Magazine**, and several other anthologies and web magazines. His novella, *The Low White Plain*, part of the "A Grifter's Song" series, was release in June 2022. He lives and writes in Nebraska, where he lives with his family.

LIBBY CUDMORE (Associate Editor; @LibbyCudmore) is the author of hipster mystery *The Big Rewind* (William Morrow, 2016) and "The Wade Agency" series in *Ellery Queen Mystery Magazine*. Her work has been published in *Tough, The Big Click, Hardboiled* and others, as well as the anthologies *Hanzai Japan, Welcome Home, Mixed Up* and *A Beast Without A Name: Stories Inspired By The Music of Steely Dan*. She co-edited *Lawyers, Guns and Money: Crime Music Inspired by the Music of Warren Zevon* with Art Taylor. She is the hostess of the weekly #RecordSaturday live-tweet event on her Twitter account and the co-host of three podcasts: *The OST Party*, focusing on movie soundtracks; *The Shattered Shield*, where she discusses the FX cop drama *The Shield*; and *Misbehavin: A Righteous Gemstones Podcast*.

R.D. SULLIVAN (Associate Editor; @_TheRussian) is a writer of fiction, comedy, and letters to the editor. She lives in Northern California with her family and three solidly mediocre dogs, where she runs, in no particular order, a corporate office, a winery, a subcontracting business, and herself ragged. Her own writing has been featured at *Fireside Fiction Magazine, Shotgun Honey*, and *Tough*, as well as in the *Killing Malmon* and *Murder-A-Go-Go's* anthologies. You can track her down over at govneh.com.

CONTRIBUTING WRITERS
(In order of appearance of work)

MIKE McHONE's (@mike_mchone) work has appeared in *Ellery Queen*, *Sherlock Holmes Mystery Magazine*, *Mystery Weekly Magazine*, *Mystery Tribune*, *Guilty Crime Magazine*, *Punk Noir*, the *AV Club*, the *Detroit News*, and is forthcoming in *Alfred Hitchcock's Mystery Magazine*. In 2021 his short story "Lesson of the Lamp" appeared in **Under the Thumb: Stories of Police Oppression**, edited by S.A. Cosby. Although he lives in Detroit, anyone can pay him a visit at www.mikemchone.com

JENNIFER STARK's (@JenEgan72) writing has appeared in *Bull: Men's Fiction*. She is currently at work on a novel about 18th century criminals forced to immigrate to Louisiana. She holds an MFA in creative writing from Southern Illinois University.

AISLINN KELLY-LYTH (@LawAislinn) is a London-based lawyer who took up creating writing during the pandemic. Her short story "Refuge" was Highly Commended in the Costa Short Story Awards 2020, and her piece "Keeping Distance" was published in *Idler*.

STEPHEN J. GOLDS (@SteveGone58) was born in North London, U.K, but has lived in Japan for most of his adult life. He writes primarily in the noir and dirty realism genres and is the co-editor of *Punk Noir Magazine*. He enjoys spending time with his daughters, reading books, traveling the world, boxing, and listening to old Soul LPs. His books are *Say Goodbye When I'm Gone, I'll Pray When I'm Dying, Always the Dead, Poems for Ghosts in Empty Tenement Windows I Thought I Saw Once* and the story and poetry collection *Love Like Bleeding Out With an Empty Gun in Your Hand*.

MARC WATKINS (@Marc__Watkins) lives in Oxford, Mississippi. His words have appeared in the Pushcart Prize, *Litmag*, *StoryQuarterly*, *Boulevard*, *Slice Magazine*, and *Third Coast*. His crime writing was featured in France with *13e Note Editions* and he has written about rural crime for *Criminal Element* and *Transfuge*. His website: https://marcwatkins.org/about/

Born and raised in the Bronx, JASON ALLISON (@Jasonallison) was a homicide detective for the New York City Police Department. His fiction has been featured in the lit-noir journal **Rock and a Hard Place** and shortlisted for the Al Blanchard award. He has consulted for numerous authors and presented to members of the Mystery Writers of America and attendees of ThrillerFest. He can be reached at jason-allison.com.

SCOTT VON DOVIAK (@vondoviak) is a Derringer Award-nominated writer whose short fiction has appeared in the *Saturday Evening Post*, *Mystery Tribune*, and *Shotgun Honey*, among others. His novel *Charlesgate Confidential* (Hard Case Crime) was named one of the top 10 crime novels of 2018 by Tom Nolan of *The Wall Street Journal*. He is the author of three nonfiction books on film and television, including *Hick Flicks: The Rise and Fall of Redneck Cinema*. He lives in Austin, TX.

B. W. CARTER spends his days administering child welfare programs from the confines of a tiny monochrome cubicle. He spends his nights in a slightly larger, slightly more colorful cubicle, waterboarding word counts with demented glee. He's been published at *Mystery Tribune*, *The Yard: Crime Blog*, *Flash Fiction Magazine*, *Tales to Terrify*, and *The Drabble*, among others.

ROBERT P. OTTONE (@robertottone) is the author of the horror collection *Her Infernal Name & Other Nightmares* (an honorable mention in *The Best Horror of the Year Volume 13*) as well as the young adult dystopian-cosmic horror trilogy *The Rise*. His short stories have appeared in various anthologies as well as online. He's also the publisher and owner of Spooky House Press. Robert is an English as a New Language teacher, as well as a teacher of English Language Arts. He can be found online at SpookyHousePress.com. He delights in the creepy and views bagels solely as a cream cheese delivery device.

JOHN BOVIO (@john_bovio) is a writer, artist, and chef. His work has appeared in various publications and galleries around the world. He lives in Oakland, California.

EDDIE McNAMARA (@EddieMcNamara) is the author of the forthcoming novel *Graveyard Stompers* (Gutter Books, early 2023). He wrote *Toss Your Own Salad: The Meatless Cookbook* (St. Martin's). His work has appeared in *Penthouse, Vice, Thuglit, Shotgun Honey, All Due Respect, Switchblade, J. Journal,* and a bunch of other places.

ANTHEA PRETORIUS holds a Master's degree in Publishing. At the University of Pretoria, she produces a range of brochures, marketing materials and other information products. She is the Editor of the *JuniorTukkie* Magazine and the *JT Newsletters.* Her first poetry collection, *Haiku from the Tip of Africa,* was published by Naledi in 2019. *Stanzas* has published three of Anthea's poems: "Did you see?" appeared in *Stanzas* in 2018; "Please wash me, Mama," appeared in *Edition 20 of Stanzas* in July 2020. "The Light in Cucumber," will appear in the forthcoming 2022 edition. Her creative writing appears in various anthologies and magazines. Two of her poems were published in the 2017 AVBOB National Poetry Competition. This was followed by a South African television series entitled, *I Wish I'd Said* (*Ek Wou Nog Sê*), which was broadcast on DSTV VIA Channel 147 from 28 August to 30 October 2018.

MARK JONATHAN HARRIS is a Los Angeles writer/filmmaker who has written both adult and children's fiction and produced numerous documentary films, including three which have won Oscars. One of his latest films is *Foster* which he wrote and directed and was nominated for Best Feature Documentary Screenplay by the Writers Guild of America. He also teaches filmmaking at the School of Cinematic Arts at the University of Southern California, where he is a Distinguished Professor.

ANDY BOYLE (@andymboyle) is a Chicago-based journalist whose work has appeared in *Esquire, NBC News,* the *Boston Globe,* the *Chicago Tribune,* the *Chicago Sun-Times* and more. Raised and educated in Nebraska, his work was cited in the 2012 Pulitzer Prize for Breaking News. He's also the author of two non-fiction books through Penguin Random House.

MIKE ZIMMERMAN (@zimwrites) sold his first short story to *Gorezone* magazine in 1989. He is a 2022 National Magazine Award finalist and author of the crime novels *A Mosquito Over Sunset* and *Where the Sun Don't Shine*. His story "Metabolize to Freedom" appeared in **Rock and a Hard Place, Issue 7**. Find him at www.zimwrites.com.

HECTOR ACOSTA (@Hexican) is an Edgar-nominated author whose short stories have appeared in *Shotgun Honey, Tough* and the *Best American Mystery and Suspense* anthology. He's written *Hardway*, a wrestling inspired novella and lives in Texas with his wife, pets and more plastic robots than a man his age should have.

LINDA B. ADAMS (@lindabwriter) is a member of the Horror Writers Association and holds a B.S. and an M.A. in English. She has written numerous short stories and is at work on her sixth novel. She used to live in Texas, where many of her stories are set. She currently lives in Northern New York, where she works in an academic library when she's not putting fictional characters in difficult and unsettling situations..

CONTRIBUTING VISUAL ARTISTS
(In order of appearance of work)

BRUCE HARRIS writes crime and mystery stories. His work has appeared in *Mystery Magazine,* **Rock and a Hard Place**, and *Guilty Crime Story Magazine* among others. His baseball murder mystery, *Death in the Dugout,* is published by Demain Publishing and available on Amazon. He also writes extensively about Sherlock Holmes. His latest book, *It's Not Always 1895 – A Sherlock Holmes Chronology* is available on Amazon.

CHUCK KRAMER (@chuckkramer6167) has freelanced as a photographer for *Windy City Times* and *Nightspots Magazine* since 2005. His pictures have also appeared in *InChicago* and *Show* magazines and he's shot book covers, album covers, and author portraits for many Chicago artists. The Dominguez Art Gallery in Pilsen presented his fine art photos of poets reading at the weekly Weeds Open Mic in 2016. In March 2019 his show "Faces: Out and Proud" was featured at Chicago's Center on Halsted. In the fall of 2019, "Vistas and Visages" was at the Bezazian Library in Uptown and his photo "Reflections" appeared in the Microcosmic show in Highland Park, IL. His study of New Orleans street musicians appeared in *Knack* magazine in 2019. Other photos were recently published in the *Chicago Quarterly Review* and the online e-zine *The Muses Gallery.*

KAREN BOISSONNEAULT-GAUTHIER (@KBG_Tweets) is an Indigenous artist/photographer creating cover images for *Synkroniciti, Pine Cone Review, Feeel Magazine, Dyst,* Arachne Press, *Wild Musette, Gigantic Sequins, The Unmooring, Vine Leaves Literary Journal, Gateway Review, Doubleback Review,* and many more. Walking her Siberian Husky named Kiowa under an aurora borealis is forever a dream. Visit www.kcbgphoto.com for all her endeavors.

ALLISON RENNER (@AllisonRWrites; she/her) is a writer, editor, and photographer living in Memphis, Tennessee. Her fiction has appeared in or is forthcoming from *Misery Tourism*, the *Daily Drunk*, *Six Sentences*, *Rejection Letters*, *Atlas and Alice*, and others. She can be found online at allisonrennerwrites.com.

CHRIS KOEHN (@chriskoehn) is a former journalist hiding out in an old church just north of the Canada/Montana Border. His writing and photography has appeared in Canadian newspapers and many curious corners of the web.

JAY BECHTOL (@BechtolJay) likes to write, so he does. He occasionally takes pictures, too. Examples of both can be found at www.jaybechtol.com